Lightning Strikes Again

by

Caitlyn Callery

Lightning Strikes Again

Cover Art by *Tina Lynn Stout*

The Wild Rose Press, Inc.
PO Box 708
Adams Basin, NY 14410-0708
Visit us at www.thewildrosepress.com

Publishing History
First Edition, 2025
Trade Paperback Print ISBN 978-1-5092-6376-9
Digital ISBN 978-1-5092-6377-6

Published in the United States of America

Dedication

To the memory of my wonderful cousin,
Carol Agnew,
who spent her whole life fighting
for what she believed was right.

She was everything I would like to be.

Other Books by Caitlyn Callery

Viscount in Hiding
A Betrothal Agreement
The Smuggler's Daughter
The Earl Pretender
Seek Her Like Gold
A Deal with Her Father
Acting the Nabob

Chapter One

Tunbridge Wells, Kent. Thursday, 6th May 1926.

Daisy Redmond stood with the other clippies who worked for the RedCar Bus Company. Just like the others, she looked ready to start work at a moment's notice, dressed as she was in her uniform, satchel slung over her shoulder to collect the fares.

Nobody would board a bus today, though. Behind where the clippies stood, the Tunbridge Wells ticket office was closed to the public, its doors unlocked only so the strikers could go inside to drink the well-stewed tea the office staff had made, or to use the meagre facilities.

Beside the four RedCar clippies stood three AutoCar Company clippies, their black uniforms and brown satchels a contrast to the navy-blue suits and red satchels worn by Daisy and her colleagues. Usually, professional rivalry kept the two sets of workers apart, but for now, that rivalry was forgotten in the struggle against the unfairness of greedy company owners and a government that allowed workers to be exploited by them.

"Three days," muttered Henrietta, one of the AutoCar women. "Three bloomin' days, standing here, not getting paid. What a waste of time."

Silently, Daisy agreed with her. She could ill afford to lose the wages. Not only that, but if she couldn't work, there were many other things she'd rather do than stand here, getting sore feet from the hard pavement and an aching back from being too long in one position. However, she was careful not to show those thoughts. The strike had to be supported.

Jerry, the shop steward, turned to Henrietta, his glare disapproving beneath the white peaked cap that matched his white driver's coat with its dark red collar. A large badge pinned to his chest denoted his unique works number.

"Did you say something, Henny?" he asked, mildly. Daisy had never heard Jerry speak in anything but a mild tone, even on the hustings, when he addressed the workforce *en masse*. Somehow, his quiet, even voice carried through a crowd, farther than a firebrand's shout would have done.

"No," sighed Henrietta. "I'm going for a cuppa. Want one, Jerry?"

Jerry smiled, said that would be lovely, thank you, and turned back to his picketing duty.

A man walked by, his suit and tie proclaiming him an office worker. He wore a trilby hat and carried a rolled-up umbrella, though the day was warm and dry, and the sky was blue.

"When are you lot going back to work?" he asked, bitterly. "I've had to walk three days running now."

"We'll go back when the miners get justice," said Jerry, for the umpteenth time today.

"We're not doing this for our health," added Charlie Taylor, another RedCar driver. He drew himself up to his full height, his chest pushed out aggressively. His fingers clenched into fists, and he bared his teeth in a vicious semblance of a smile.

Daisy tensed and sent a silent plea toward Charlie. *Don't start anything. We don't need trouble.* She'd promised her family there'd be no trouble.

"Move along, sir," said one of the special constables who flanked the picket line. He stepped between Charlie and the man, and Daisy sighed, relieved.

"This is a lawful strike," continued the constable. "Union members are entitled to take part in it."

"I'm entitled to ride a bus to work," argued the man.

"No, you're not," muttered Charlie. He flexed his fingers. Daisy held her breath.

"Yes, sir," said the constable, wearily. "Move along now."

The man glared at the picketers, then at the constable before he shook his head and walked away, muttering under his breath and swinging his umbrella in a manner that conveyed his irritation with them all.

Daisy relaxed.

"When this is over," said Charlie to the AutoCar driver standing beside him, "you can have that passenger. I won't stop for him."

The other driver laughed. "At this rate, your bus'll be empty. He must be the tenth passenger you've barred today."

The driver was right. Charlie had passed judgment on several people, all of whom had voiced dissatisfaction with the way the strike had affected their lives. With each person who said enough was enough, the strikers had made their point, and shouldn't they get back to work now, Charlie's temper frayed a little more. Daisy thought it was a miracle he hadn't hit someone yet.

She did understand his frustration, though. The first two days of the strike had gone so well, they'd been lulled into a complacent optimism that all would be fine. The unions would win, they'd thought. The mine owners would be forced to rescind their demands that miners work longer hours for less pay, and justice would be served. In those first two days, there had been a jollity about the strike, a carnival air. The public had supported them, everyone had been willing to forego a few days' pay, and spirits had been high. Even the special constables, who'd been sent in by the government to "deal with the strikers," had not behaved as their masters expected. Drawn mostly from the ranks of the working class themselves, the constables had sympathized with the strikers.

Today, day three, there was a definite change in the atmosphere. The government, enraged by the unpopularity of their position, had doubled down and started to fight dirty. For one thing, the Chancellor, Winston Churchill, had used emergency powers to requisition all the paper leaving the mills. Without paper, the union-supporting journal, *The British Worker,* was reduced to just four pages, giving them no room to put the union arguments, nor to fight back against the propaganda in the establishment newspapers, which had grown in size.

Daisy hadn't thought it would make much difference. People already knew what the strikers were fighting for. However, when coupled with the inconvenience the strike caused, the government arguments seemed to be enough to sway public opinion.

On top of which, an army of what Charlie called "chinless wonders" had volunteered to do the struck jobs. Many of those people did not usually work for a living at all and, for them, breaking the strike was a lark, something to do for a few days because they were bored. They didn't much care who was right and who was wrong.

In response, attitudes had hardened on the picket line, and now Daisy could smell trouble brewing. All it needed was for someone to say the wrong thing, or for the wrong person to pass by when the special constables were otherwise occupied. When that happened—and it would—it would create the spark, and somebody would get hurt.

And here, unless she was very much mistaken, came the match to strike that spark.

A delivery van chugged toward them, the name "Pearson" boldly painted on it. That was insult added to injury, for not only were unionized delivery drivers supposed to have joined the strike, but Pearson's was a huge company owned by one of the most reviled men in the entire county of Kent, if not the whole of the southeast.

Walter Pearson was known to be hard-nosed. Ruthless, even. He usually got what he wanted, and he didn't care who was hurt by it. Daisy could attest to that, for Walter Pearson, and his family, had left her to struggle and starve, and had never given her a second's thought afterward.

"Scab!" shouted Charlie as the smartly painted van drew level. "Stop him, lads!"

Jerry called for calm. He shouted for the pickets to come back, but his words fell on deaf ears. Their blood was up, and a Pearson's van was just too tempting a target.

The driver braked sharply to avoid hitting the strikers, who now streamed into the road. The men surrounded the van, banging on its sides, rocking it violently. Jerry implored them to stop, while Henrietta led half the clippies in shrieks of encouragement. The hopelessly outnumbered constables glanced at each other, uncertain what to do.

"Scab!" yelled Charlie, again. He wrenched open the van door and pulled the hapless driver from the cab. In the split second between being pulled out and being surrounded by the mob, Daisy saw who he was.

She gasped, horrified, as Frank Pearson was swallowed in the tide of angry humanity.

Frank Pearson. One of Walter's sons, and a man Daisy hadn't set eyes on for nearly twelve years.

The reluctant, heartless, father of her son.

****

Frank knew he was in trouble when the strikers stepped off the pavement and swarmed into the road. There was no way round them, and he wasn't prepared to plow through, so he had no choice but to brake. The van stalled, leaving him a sitting duck as angry men surrounded it, banging on the paneled sides and rocking it on its axis. Thankfully, he'd made his delivery and was returning to the depot, so there was no cargo for the strikers to destroy.

It was going to take every ounce of persuasion he could muster to get out of this in one piece. Even with the special constables he could see huddled on the pavement, things looked bleak. The officers, outnumbered ten to one, didn't look keen to come to his rescue. Which meant Frank was, to all intents and purposes, on his own.

The van door was pulled open and hands reached in. He didn't resist. He was more likely to be hurt if he tried to stop them. Seconds later, he stood on the road, surrounded by the mob. Two men held his arms while others pressed in on him, cutting off all avenues of escape.

He knew some of the strikers. He'd attended the primary school in Fieldhurst alongside Matt Fuller, and Charlie Taylor had once worked for Frank's father at his flagship store, here in Tunbridge Wells.

Frank groaned inwardly, as he remembered the day Charlie had been fired. At the time, Frank had been on Walter's payroll, being groomed to take over some aspect of the business, in the unlikely event that Walter ever relinquished control. He'd watched Charlie being escorted from the premises by two of Walter's bully boys, yelling that he would get even. Frank prayed this was not the day he tried to deliver on that promise.

Not that attacking Frank would be "getting even" with Walter, who'd probably cheer these men on. But Charlie was not to know that.

"Scab!" barked Charlie. He'd shouted it several times now. Frank suspected it had more to do with raising the temperature for his fellow strikers than a need to insult Frank. Which was not good. He hoped Mother had a stock of arnica, because he had a feeling he was going to need it.

Possible salvation pushed from the back of the jeering mob, although he didn't dare hope for too much. Jerry Balcombe, the shop steward, was a reasonable man, but he might well be overruled, his instructions lost in the anger and frustration of his cohort. His voice was all but drowned by the overall din and, though he shoved at the men, he struggled to get close to Frank.

Men yelled, "Get him, lads!" and, "Land him one,

Charlie." Encouraged, and more than happy to oblige, Charlie Taylor bunched his fingers into a fist and drew his arm back. Held in place, unable to move, or even to try to defend himself, Frank tensed, ready for the blow.

Charlie's fist came forward. Frank closed his eyes.

The blow did not come.

A groan of disappointment went through the crowd. Frank cracked open an eye and saw Charlie's fist, held fast in Jerry's cupped hand.

The sounds of the mob died. It was suddenly so quiet, Frank heard the breeze ruffling his hair. He smelled the diesel of his stalled engine, the hot rubber of his pneumatic tires, the coal tar soap and hair wax used by the men surrounding him. He saw the angry muscle jump in Charlie's cheek as he glared at Jerry.

A second went by. Two.

"Let go of him," Jerry instructed the men who held Frank's arms. His voice was quiet and low, and filled with authority.

There was a slight hesitation before the men did as they were told. Free now, Frank still stood between them. He made no attempt to move, though every nerve and sinew screamed at him to get away while he could. Instinct told him that trying to do that would be a mistake. So he stood still, as tense as ever, ready for the next attack, hoping it wouldn't come.

"He's a strike breaker," insisted Charlie.

"That doesn't mean you can beat him up," said Jerry.

Some of the men muttered, unhappily. A few openly backed Charlie. Others quietened, unwilling to go against their shop steward.

Frank took the chance to put his case. "I'm not a

strike breaker." He spoke clearly, as loudly as he could without shouting.

The men turned to him, their faces a mixture of interest and disbelief.

"Our company is not part of the strike," he told them.

"Don't give me that," sneered Charlie. Other men murmured. Whether they agreed with Charlie or not, Frank couldn't tell, though he had a fair idea they did.

"We aren't unionized," he continued, hoping he could give them all his facts before they turned on him again. "We're too small. I'm the only driver on staff. Not only that, I don't even get paid. I do this…" he gestured with his thumb at the van behind him, "…voluntarily. Volunteers can't really go on strike, can they?"

Mentally, he crossed his fingers that the men would listen, and believe him. The constables were making their way closer to him now. He prayed they'd reach him before Charlie overcame Jerry's control of the situation and everyone went for him again.

Charlie was certainly gunning for a fight. He glared at Frank, his eyes glowing with unholy fire. His cheeks were puce with rage, and angry spittle glistened on his lips. "Do you think we came down with the last shower of rain?" he demanded. "You're one of Walter Pearson's boys."

Others murmured agreement. Frank could not argue. It was, after all, the truth.

Charlie faced his audience. "He's working for his dad," he said. Each syllable sounded like a curse.

Two burly men blocked the constables so they couldn't come any nearer. Not that they tried particularly hard.

"We aren't here to cause trouble," Jerry reminded his men, but Frank could see he was fighting a losing battle. These men were in the mood for action. It hadn't helped that Frank's father had been mentioned. Walter Pearson was not a beloved employer. He'd never set out to be.

"I'm not working for Walter Pearson," Frank called out. The men turned to him again. Some were uncertain, others skeptical. "It is true," Frank went on, willing them to listen, "I am his son. I can't deny that, even if I wished to." And boy, at the moment, did he wish to. More fervently than he'd ever wished to deny it before, which was saying something. "But I don't work for him."

"That van's got 'Pearson' written on it," shouted one of the men. Others cried agreement.

"H. Pearson," answered Frank. "I'm working for my brother, Harry Pearson. He has his own business. It's nothing to do with Walter."

The men quietened again. Some looked more carefully at the sign on the van. The tension in the air loosened a little. The burly men stepped aside and the constables pushed nearer. Jerry now stood at Frank's side, giving him his silent support. Charlie glared at them both, clearly annoyed at being denied the chance to beat Frank to a pulp.

"For what it's worth," added Frank, deciding he might as well lay down all his cards, "I think your cause is a just one. If I did work for Walter—or for any unionized company, for that matter—I give you my word, I would not break the strike."

Those words did the trick. The men's anger deflated like the air from a child's balloon. As if by silent consensus, they stopped menacing him, turned, and headed back toward their picket line. Charlie Taylor and Matt Fuller lingered for a few seconds more before they, too, seemed to realize the futility of this fight. They followed the others, leaving Frank to stand on the road beside Jerry, who looked as relieved as Frank felt.

"Thank you," said Frank, on a heavy sigh. He'd never meant it more.

"I didn't do anything," answered Jerry. "You talked yourself out of that trouble. And I can't guarantee you won't get stopped at other picket lines around the town. Feelings are running high, and they're going to get higher."

"I'll be careful. I only have to get the van back to Harry's depot and I'm done for the day." Frank retrieved the crank handle from the cab of his van and restarted the engine, then glanced one last time at the pickets milling about on the pavement.

Which was when he saw her.

The clippie was one of several standing in the ticket office doorway. Some of them chatted to the men, others talked among themselves. They wore the uniforms of both the bus companies that served Tunbridge Wells: some in black tunics and skirts, with brown money satchels, while the others wore navy blue, their satchels red. The AutoCar clippies wore peaked caps, balanced at a jaunty angle on the heads. The RedCar clippies, of which she was one, wore red, floppy-brimmed hats, a cross between a bowler and a cloche. Her hair was either fashionably short or tied up and bundled under her hat. Either way, he couldn't see it, although he was willing to bet it was a rich chestnut color, silky-soft and shining. Further, he would wager that her eyes were a dark, dark brown, so deep a man could dive into them and never surface again. Her skin was a smooth, blemishless cream, her nose pert, her full lips a deep, red wine color that owed nothing to lip rouge. She wasn't tall, about five foot three, which was a height Frank had once thought perfect.

"Daisy?" He called out before he thought about it, and immediately wished he hadn't. If it wasn't her, he would look a fool—more of a fool than he'd already shown himself to be by driving a delivery van past a picket line.

He hadn't been thinking then, either. Eager to get back to the depot, he'd ignored the fact of the strike and taken a shortcut through the town center. He'd had no thought for how his actions would seem to others, and hadn't considered any consequences that might occur.

Just as he hadn't thought through the consequences of calling out to her now. Consequences for her, as well as for himself.

He was a Pearson. He didn't need Charlie Taylor to spell out what that meant to these people. Her colleagues, people she had to work with. It was possible that she didn't want them to know she knew him. She might hate them to discover that she'd once been everything to him.

Then again, that had been a long time ago. Twelve years, to be exact.

Twelve years. During which hardly a day had gone by when he hadn't thought of her.

In the early days, when she'd first left him, he'd been confused at her betrayal. Then he'd become resentful and annoyed. Finally, he resigned himself to it and told himself he didn't care that she'd gone. He was glad for his lucky escape. She clearly didn't want him. She'd changed her mind, moved away…

Except, she hadn't. For here she was, in the middle of Tunbridge Wells, just as beautiful as she'd been on that morning when they'd parted, him for the army and expected glory, her to stand on the sidelines, waving her handkerchief at him, knitting socks, and…whatever else women did while they pined for their would-be heroes.

That was a laugh, he thought bitterly. Whatever Daisy Redmond had done back then, it hadn't included pining for him. She hadn't even thought enough of him to write, explaining that she wouldn't wait for his return.

She'd promised him letters by the dozen. She hadn't sent even one. For her, it seemed, Frank was out of sight and out of mind.

And now, here she was, standing on a picket line, taking part in a nationwide strike.

He knew she'd heard him call her. Above the hubbub of the picket line and the sounds of the street, the shoppers with their children and their laden baskets, the iron ring of horse hooves pulling heavy carts, the roar of an occasional private motor car, she'd heard him, because when he shouted, she half turned, and their eyes met.

It was definitely Daisy.

Her eyes widened and her face paled at the sight of him, and she rushed into the ticket office. Charlie Taylor moved into Frank's line of vision, as if to protect her from the venomous stare of the strike-breaking son of a hated employer. Charlie's eyes narrowed, and his lips pursed. Menace seemed to heat the air around him.

Jerry appeared at Frank's window, making him jump. "Move on, Mr. Pearson," he warned. His eyes added, *while you still can.*

Frank firmed his chin, defiantly hiding whatever he

was feeling. He wasn't sure he even knew what that was. All he did know was that there was a hollowness in his stomach and a lump where his heart should be, a thickness in his throat, and a sour taste on his tongue.

He put the van into first gear and drove off along Mount Pleasant Road.

Chapter Two

Daisy stood in the foyer of the ticket office. It was dark; the pickets outside not only barred the door to any member of the public foolish enough to think the place was open to serve them, they also blocked the daylight which normally came through the plate glass window. At the best of times, that light didn't illuminate the place well, and the electric lamps were usually on during working hours. Today, of course, nobody was working, so the lamps were off, by order of the management. They had allowed use of the small gas stove at the back of the office, though, and Doris, one of the ladies who usually manned the ticket desk, was boiling kettles of water.

She smiled over her shoulder at Daisy. "Cup of tea?" she sang, then frowned when she registered Daisy's agitated state. "You all right, my love?" She crossed the room, neatly stepping around the over-large customer service desk.

"I'm fine." Even to herself, Daisy didn't sound convincing.

It was Frank Pearson's fault. How could it be, after all these years, the mere sound of his voice was enough to put her so off-kilter? And what right did he have, anyway? Calling to her across the crowded pavement, making sure all and sundry knew he knew her! Now they would wonder how she, Daisy Redmond, low-paid and overworked clippie, came to be on first name terms with the son of one of the wealthiest men in Kent.

There was nothing wrong with telling them she used to work for Walter, of course. Nothing wrong with admitting her father had been his chauffeur for almost twenty-five years, and that, as a favor to Dad, Walter had found her a position in one of his shops. Nobody would fault her for that. Lots of people had worked for Walter Pearson over the years.

She didn't think her colleagues would be quite as understanding, though, should they learn she grew up in one of Pearson's tied cottages, and had run wild on his land with his own children. At that age, there had been no "them and us." They had played and run, squabbled and argued, laughed and cried together, and nobody had ever given a thought about who lived in the big house and who didn't. It hadn't mattered then.

"You sure you're all right?" Doris asked again. "Don't tell me you're fine, because you don't look fine." Her soft Kentish burr was soothing and warm, and instantly made Daisy feel better.

"It was just…"

Just what? What could Daisy say to explain her current state? *I saw a face from the past? A man I once thought hung the moon in the sky? A man who made me think he would love me forever, then abandoned me without a second thought?*

"It all gets too much, doesn't it?" said Doris, with a click of her tongue. "It's one thing to support the strike, but some of those men take it too far." She steered Daisy to a seat behind the desk. "All that 'passion for the cause.' Pity they don't use that passion up in other ways, eh?" She gave Daisy a saucy wink and busied herself with the newly boiled kettle. "So now, what have they done to get you all upset?"

"Nothing." Doris raised an eyebrow. "Honestly," Daisy insisted. "They haven't upset me." It was the truth. Daisy's discomfort had nothing to do with the strikers. Well, not directly.

If one was pedantic, she supposed, one could say that if Charlie and his mates hadn't spread across the road, Frank would have driven by. Daisy wouldn't have seen him, and he wouldn't have seen her. Then he wouldn't have called out to her, would he?

She hadn't known it was him until he stopped. Not that it mattered. She'd have been just as terrified for any man they'd pulled out of the cab, whoever he turned out to be. The strikers were angry. They saw the driver as a traitor to their cause, and they wanted to hurt him for that. There was nothing Daisy could have done to stop them. She couldn't have made herself heard above the shouts and jeers, and the screeched encouragement from Henrietta and her friends, if she'd tried.

Nor would they have taken any notice of her if they had heard her. Jerry was the shop steward, and even he'd had trouble getting them to listen. The men, whipped up and spoiling for a fight, had been intent on inflicting damage on the strikebreaker. They'd wanted to "rearrange his handsome features," as her father might have put it.

For Frank Pearson was handsome. There was no denying that. With his thick hair, so dark it was almost black, and his twinkling blue eyes, Frank Pearson was born to turn female heads.

It vexed her a little that he hadn't changed at all in the last twelve years. With the straight blade of his nose, high cheekbones, and that full mouth with its lush lips that curved readily into a cheeky grin, he was just as she'd seen him in a thousand dreams.

Not dreams. Nightmares. Any dream about Frank Pearson would have to be a nightmare, after the way he had treated her.

He'd been too cowardly to do his own dirty work, of course. The cruel message had been delivered by his father. And yes, she realized that, at the time, Frank had been up to his ears in mud in a trench in northern France, so he wasn't in a position to come and tell her how he felt, face to face. But he could have written. He could have been kinder.

And now he thought he could call to her across the street, and all would be well? He believed he could wave and smile, and she'd be pleased to see him? He had a bloody nerve!

The office door opened and Charlie stepped inside. He still wore his belligerent expression, as if he needed to fight, as if nothing else would be right with him until he did so.

"What's going on, Daisy?" He glared at her. He always wore a deliberate air of menace, drawing it around himself like a cape, and he used it now in trying to intimidate her.

Daisy refused to be intimidated. "I'm having a cuppa with Doris," she said, defiantly misunderstanding his meaning. "Why?"

"I meant outside. How d'you know Frank Pearson?"

"My dad was his dad's chauffeur before the war," she said, with a shrug she hoped seemed nonchalant. "I know all of them."

"Leave her alone, Charlie Taylor," said Doris, handing the freshly poured cup of tea to Daisy. "She's come in here to get away from you and your rabble-rousing for ten minutes. You want to pick a fight, you go back out there, because I'll not have it in here. Do you hear me?"

"I only asked," he answered, petulantly.

"I only told you. Go on. Sling your 'ook." Doris shooed him with her hands, much as she would have scattered chickens in a farmyard. Charlie scowled, but he left the office and went back to the picket line. Doris winked at Daisy. "Brings out the worst in some people, this sort of thing," she said. "I'll be glad when it's all over."

"Me, too," thought Daisy.

****

Instead of heading down Mount Pleasant Road and out toward Ramslye, Frank turned into Monson Street, one of the main shopping thoroughfares of the town. There, he parked at the curb and sat, with his engine idling.

He had just seen Daisy Redmond. He shuddered. Talk about ghosts from the past.

She hadn't changed much. Oh, she hadn't been exactly the same as the last time he'd seen her, of course. Twelve years had transformed her from a long-limbed, slender girl of eighteen into a beautiful woman, her figure a little fuller, her curves slightly more pronounced. But it was definitely her.

He'd been told she no longer lived in this area, that she'd met a man who'd swept her off her feet and taken her to a new life in a different part of the country. That she hadn't wanted to remain here, surrounded by memories and regrets. Not after her father was killed in the trenches.

Frank's mother had told him of Albert Redmond's fate when he wrote to her, asking her to make sure Daisy was all right. He'd expected letters from "his girl" and received none, and that had worried him.

"I'm sorry," Mother wrote back. *"I thought she would have told you. Fact is, Daisy was very angry. She blamed us for her father's loss, and didn't want anything more to do with the Pearsons. Then she met this man, and took the opportunity to leave the area with him."*

Mother didn't know the man's name, nor where he had taken Daisy. She thought it was Buckinghamshire, or Bedfordshire, but she couldn't be certain. Not that the actual place mattered. Gone was gone, wherever Daisy had ended up.

That she had blamed Walter Pearson for her father's death was understandable. Frank had blamed Walter, too. Albert Redmond had been almost fifty years old, too old to be called up, and already in poor health. He certainly wasn't fit enough to be sent into the thick of the fighting. Yet Walter had accepted him into the "Pearson's Pals," the regiment he'd formed from the men who worked for him. It was Walter's way of contributing to the war effort, sending his "boys" to do their duty. Although, Frank had noted cynically, most of the "boys" accepted into the regiment were low-paid, unskilled workers whose jobs could be easily taken by women, who were then paid even less than the men had been. Frank curled his lip. True to form, his father had "done his bit" at minimal cost and inconvenience to himself.

Frank had been incensed to learn that Albert had been permitted to join the "Pals Regiment," but his mother had defended Walter's decision.

"Your father urged him to reconsider," she'd written. *"Albert would not hear of it. He wanted to play his part. If he hadn't been admitted to the regiment your father formed, he would have gone to the recruiting office and signed up to something else."*

Which was probably true. In 1914, just about every man in the country had felt that feverish urge to join the ranks and do his duty. Frank had been infected by it himself. Along with thousands of others, he'd hurried to the recruiting office, eager to give himself over, terrified the war would be finished before he could play his part. Albert, it seemed, had been no different.

All the same, it took a long time for Frank's anger at Walter to fade.

He'd also been angry at Daisy. She might have blamed Walter for the loss of her father, but she'd had no call to treat Frank as she had. Frank was nothing like his father. She knew that. Just as she knew Frank intended to come back to her when the Germans were routed. The least she might have done, if she'd changed her mind about their future, was to write to him, and let him know, in her own words. Instead, he'd had to hear it from his mother, then been left to wallow in the mud and water of the trenches, dodging bullets, and wondering why the woman he loved had so easily forgotten him.

It surprised him to realize he was still angry with Daisy now, twelve years later. The betrayal had been great at the time, but it was long ago, when he'd been a different person.

"I was a boy," he murmured. The Frank of that time had been eighteen years old, fresh-faced and idealistic. He'd believed in love and dreams, and a bright future on the horizon. He'd been a fool. But not as big a fool as he would be if he gave her his time now.

So what if she was back in the area? It didn't matter to him that she was here, living and working in Tunbridge Wells, just a stone's throw from his home in Fieldhurst. Why should it?

She was a clippie on the buses. Did that mean she didn't have a husband? Even now, after all the changes to working practices brought about by the war, many companies preferred not to employ married women. He had no idea whether the bus companies followed that policy or not but if they did, the fact that she worked there indicated she was single. Had the great love she'd left Frank for turned out to be a flash in the pan? Or had she been widowed, like so many women had been? If so, why had she returned to Tunbridge Wells after her husband's death? Especially if the area held so many bad memories for her. It made no sense to him.

"Doesn't have to make sense to you, does it?" he muttered. "She's nothing to do with you. Forget her, and get back to what you're supposed to be doing."

He put the van in gear, and drove back onto Mount Pleasant Road, down the hill and out of the town to Ramslye, where Harry had his depot. The more distance he put between himself and Daisy Redmond, the better.

H&R Pearson Transportation was housed on a farm, in a disused barn which had been converted into a warehouse. There was room on the ground floor for three vans, although the one Frank drove was the only one the company currently owned. To one side of the vehicle bays was Harry's office, its walls made of plywood, painted white. Next to it, another office had recently been constructed for Harry's partner and fiancée, Regina, or Reggie, as she was known. In the far corner, there was a lift to take goods up to the first floor, where rooms and cupboards stored everything from furniture to foodstuffs.

Next door to this main building, Harry had converted the farm's stables into a mechanical repair workshop. Usually, if Harry wasn't in his office, he could be found in the workshop, tinkering with something, and loving every minute of it.

Today, there was no sign of him, or Reggie, which was unusual. One or the other of them was usually on the premises during the working day. Today, they'd both disappeared, and the place was securely closed. Frank had to unlock the warehouse door before he could drive inside.

He parked in the vehicle bay and did his usual post-run checks to ensure the van was ready for tomorrow. Then he looked around for a clue to his brother's whereabouts.

"Harry?" he called. "Reggie?" The air rang with his shout, but nothing else sounded in the barn. A quick look into the repair workshop showed him that was empty, too. He returned to the vehicle bay and saw the note pinned to the wall. In Harry's bold writing, it said,

Frank,

Have to go for an appointment. Won't be back today. I had hoped to meet with you but you weren't back in time. Can you see me, as soon as possible, please?

Harry.

Frank wondered what Harry wanted. If he'd been a paid employee, he might have worried he was about to take a cut in wages. With most transportation workers having joined the strike, the trains had stopped, so goods were not coming into the stations. That, in turn, meant there was nothing for drivers like Frank to collect and deliver to their customers. There were still a few local deliveries to be made, goods from farmers to local shops and such, but they weren't anywhere near as busy as usual. A paid employee might have been temporarily laid off by a firm that couldn't afford to keep them on for the duration.

But Harry didn't pay Frank. Frank had never wanted him to, and had refused the offer of wages when he began working here. His employment had only come about because Harry had been attacked by a gang of thieves, who'd left him with injuries that made it difficult for him to work. Frank, who had recently quit his job at Walter's office, had stepped in to help while Harry recovered, and had never left. So why would Harry need to see him now?

"You'll find out soon enough," he mumbled. He locked the depot, then made his way to the side of the barn where he had parked his two-seater Bentley.

He intended to go home. He drove down the long farm road, meaning to turn right at the bottom and head toward Fieldhurst. Except, when he got to the junction, he turned left, and drove back into Tunbridge Wells.

He just needed to see her more clearly, that was all. He'd only caught a glimpse of the woman as he drove away. Tensions were high and the air was rife with danger, so who knew? Maybe he'd not seen what he thought he saw. A second look, in more detail, would probably reveal a woman who was nothing like Daisy at all. After all, he hadn't seen her since 1914.

Driving past the Pantiles, he relived, for the thousandth time, that fateful evening.

Chapter Three

Fieldhurst, Sussex. 13th August 1914.

After a wet and windy start, August had turned hot and humid. The air was heavy with the threat of a coming storm, and the light held a strange quality, both clearer than normal and yet dimmer, too. Everyone was languid; it was far too warm to be anything else.

Yet underneath, there was a tension, a feeling that time was running out, that the life they'd enjoyed for so long was slipping away, and there was nothing they could do to bring it back.

At eighteen years old, Frank had never been interested in things one read about in newspapers. They meant nothing to him, had no bearing on his existence. He didn't listen to the political talk of his father and older brothers, and he was bored by the men who came to dinner just so they could join Walter in putting the world to rights.

Those men knew exactly where the government was erring when it came to Irish Home Rule, and Suffragettes. They were agreed on how the country should react to the far-away tensions between the USA and Mexico, or to the ambitions of the German Kaiser, and the recent assassination of an Austrian archduke. They drank Walter's Scotch and guffawed at his crass jokes, and reassured each other that the country was going to hell in a handbasket.

Frank couldn't have cared less about any of it. His interests that summer were fixed on the cricket, the beautiful film star Mary Pickford, and the sudden change in his lifelong friendship with the chauffeur's daughter, Daisy Redmond.

They'd played together, he and Daisy. They ran wild, racing each other across the Pearson grounds, her skinny legs pumping madly as she kept up with Frank's longer stride. And when they weren't racing, they fished in the river, or swung like monkeys in the trees, or joined other children in games of cricket and Sussex Softball.

But then, things changed. Frank's voice deepened, and he sprouted a few thin strands of hair on his chest. Daisy acquired curves, and a certain knowing way of looking at him, as if she held all the secrets of the universe, tucked inside her. Her pretty dark eyes became more doe-like, the lashes surrounding them darker and longer than they'd ever been before. Her skin was softer, clearer. Her lips were full and pink and bow-shaped, and each time he saw her, he had an almost overwhelming desire to kiss them, to discover if they tasted as sweet as he imagined they would.

Not that he planned to act on that desire. Frank knew better than that. If he did anything so stupid, there would be consequences he wasn't keen to pay. For one thing, Daisy was still tomboy enough to knock him down and black his eye, and Frank didn't fancy explaining to his brothers how a girl had done that to him.

Brothers who would likely black his other eye for being so disrespectful to someone they looked on as an extra kid sister. And after they'd finished with him, he had no doubt her father would come down on him like a ton of bricks.

All in all, a kiss from Daisy would come with far too high a price. So, all summer, he watched her and wished, and did nothing.

Then war was declared, and everything was suddenly different again. For the first time, events outside Frank's own life were important to him. Like everyone else, he became an overnight expert in what was happening across the Channel and what needed to be done about it. He was caught up in the tide of anger and anti-German sentiment, and filled with the desire to do something, to play his part.

He joined up on the afternoon of the 13th August, then went to tell his father what he'd done. It was unbearably warm, the temperature in the mid-eighties, the sun like a baker's oven. The earth was hot and hard beneath his booted feet as he trudged up the drive to the house. All the windows were open wide, but when he went inside he realized it didn't help: the rooms were stifling, the heat overpowering.

Walter sat at his desk in his study. The hot day had unbent him enough that he'd taken off his jacket, and he sat in his shirt sleeves, something that would have been unthinkable, even in these temperatures, if he'd been in his office at his flagship store, surrounded by people who relied on him for their wages. Even here, at home, he rarely relaxed to this extent. Until today, Frank had never seen his father in anything but perfect array. It was disconcerting, to say the least. It drained Frank of his certainty and confidence, as if everything he'd ever known and understood was, somehow, gone.

"What is it?" Walter asked as Frank stepped, tentatively, into the room. In his entire life, he had never before come here voluntarily. He'd only entered when he received a summons from Walter, which was usually issued so he could receive a dressing down for some childish misdemeanor. More often than not, if the offense was bad enough to warrant a summons, it meant Frank was about to get a good hiding.

He swallowed. The memories of those other forays into this room made the bile churn in his stomach, while his heart beat so fast, he thought it might burst. He wished he'd not come, wanted to turn and run, to disappear into the army tomorrow without telling his father.

Alas, he knew he could not.

"I'm a busy man, Francis," Walter said, testily. Walter was the only person who ever called him by his baptismal name. "If you have nothing to say, then…"

"I've joined the army." Frank didn't mean to blurt it out like that, but he had to say it, and he had to do it quickly, before courage deserted him.

The irony was not lost on him. He'd just signed up to fight young, fit men who would be trying to kill him. Yet here he was, quaking in his boots, frightened of the wrath of a middle-aged man who spent his life at an office desk.

Walter's reaction was much as Frank had expected. He forbade it. When Frank told him it was too late for that, he threatened to march his wayward son back to the recruiting office, where he would tell them Frank had made a stupid mistake, and then make him hand back his precious king's shilling.

"Even you can't do that, Father," said Frank. He was amazed at how calm he sounded. It was as if, once he'd defied Walter in a way that couldn't be undone, the larger-than-life figure who'd stood over the family for years like the Colossus at Rhodes over the harbor, was suddenly diminished, his power and influence gone, fear of him no longer a factor.

Walter stood and threw his pen onto the desktop. Blobs of ink spattered across the polished wood and leather surface. He didn't seem to notice. "This is ridiculous," he seethed. "You cannot go to fight. It isn't for the likes of you. You're a future captain of industry, not…you aren't for the front line!"

He paced across the room to the walnut drinks cabinet, and poured himself a double Scotch, which he did not water down. He knocked it back in one swallow, poured a second, then turned to Frank, the son he, no doubt, presently regretted having sired. "You can't go," he said.

"They need soldiers," Frank pointed out.

"I dare say they do. But not you. They'll have to excuse you."

Frank refrained from pointing out that if every man whose parents objected had been excused, there would be nobody left in the army at all.

"If it comes to it, I'm sure Pearson's can play its part." Walter frowned as he thought. "I do see they need soldiers to shove at the enemy. Fine. I have plenty of able-bodied men working for me. They can form a regiment. I'm sure we can do without them for a few months, and that'll be more than enough to say we did our duty, wouldn't you think?"

The idea that it was all right to send those young men to fight and die, when it was not acceptable for Frank to do the same, sat heavy on him. He tamped down his revulsion and explained, once again, that it was too late. He had signed up, and he would be reporting for training in the morning, whether Walter liked it or not.

Having done his duty by telling his father to his face, Frank walked out of the study, his ears ringing with Walter's yelled demands that he come back, and how dare he be so willful.

From the study, Frank went out to the summerhouse, where he sat, contemplating his future. Built a few years ago, when such things were all the rage, it was made of wrought iron, painted a glossy white, with large panes of glass on all sides. The lead roof tapered up to a point on which stood a weather vane. Inside, it was as comfortable as any of the rooms in the main house, with rugs on the wooden floor and lacy curtains at the windows. There was a pine table, and a matching set of dining chairs, and a credenza, on which two ice buckets stood sentinel, one at each end. On the other side of the room was a long and comfortable sofa, covered in blue velveteen, with white antimacassars draped carefully across its headrests. It was the height of garden luxury.

He stayed in there for hours, drinking in the English summer, committing it to memory for when he was in France, in the thick of it all. He wasn't absolutely sure what to expect over there, but he thought it would probably be noisy, chaotic, and dangerous. It would help to have an image in his head of what he was fighting for, what he would return to when the job was done.

Through the open windows of the dining room, he heard his family sit down for dinner. He made no effort to join them. He wasn't dressed for it, and he had no appetite for another verbal drubbing from Walter, nor for the anxious way his mother would, undoubtedly, look upon him. The peace and tranquility of the garden would be a much better image of home to take with him.

After eating, the family split in the traditional way, with the adult sons staying to drink port and discuss important issues with Walter, while Frank's sisters went with their mother into the drawing room to sip tea and…do whatever ladies did when the men were not around. He heard the chink of glasses, loud guffaws and good-natured bantering. He fancied he smelled their tobacco, mixing with the heady perfume of Mother's roses and the cloying, sickly sweetness of honeysuckle.

Eventually, the men joined the ladies, and Frank was left alone. The sun set, a big red ball in a baby-blue sky, a few wisps of high white cloud tinged with oranges and violets. Gradually, the sky darkened, turning to grey, then navy, and finally, a deep, rich black, lit only by the lemony tint of the almost-full moon. Electricity crackled in the hot, heavy air. It wouldn't surprise Frank if there was a thunderstorm before the night was out. A fox barked, short and sharp. A badger lumbered across the garden. Frank watched it, a dark and determined shadow on the silver lawn. The night grew still. Too still, as if the world held its collective breath. He hardly dared breathe himself.

It was almost midnight when Daisy came. "Thought I might find you here," she said, softly, as she stepped into the summerhouse. Her dark skirt skimmed her slender hips, its high waist and narrow line making her legs seem long and giving her an illusion of height, something she actually lacked. If she was more than five foot three inches tall, Frank would eat his hat.

Her blouse was made of light grey cotton. Demure and elegant, it looked cool in the heat of the night. She held a shawl in one hand; he doubted she would need it.

Her hair seemed almost black in the moonlight, though he knew it to be the color of chestnuts, a deep, red brown, shot through with gold. Growing up, she'd worn it in long ringlets that cascaded over her shoulders in a gloriously thick mass. Back then, Frank had delighted in pulling it, or tying it in knots, just to make her scold him. Now, she'd piled it into a loose bun on top of her head, well out of the reach of a mischievous lad's fingers.

Not that Frank wanted to pull her hair any more.

"Why'd you think I'd be here?" he asked, in answer to what she'd said.

Daisy sat on the sofa and stretched her legs in front of her, then leaned back in a relaxed slouch that would have horrified his parents. His mother would have thought the pose unbecoming in a lady, his father would have expected more formality and respect.

"I saw Ray on the front drive," she said. "He said you didn't come to dinner." Ray was one of Frank's older brothers, and he'd obviously been on his way out for what was left of the night. Like Frank, Ray wouldn't have stood on ceremony with Daisy.

"I wasn't hungry." It wasn't a lie. Frank's appetite had deserted him this evening. Whether that was because he was nervous of what waited for him tomorrow, or because he was angry at Walter's reaction to his news, he couldn't say. Perhaps it was a mixture of both.

"Ray said it 'ticked off the old man' when you didn't appear." She mimicked Ray's irreverent drawl to perfection.

Frank grinned. "Doesn't take much."

Daisy sat up, her back ramrod straight now, hands resting demurely in her lap. Her new pose changed her in an instant from hoyden to lady. Or it would have done if she hadn't studied Frank so candidly.

"Ray says you joined the army."

Frank looked at her, and their gazes held for several seconds. The air crackled and sparked. Frank couldn't be sure if it was the threatened storm or the presence of Daisy, but the hairs on the back of his neck stood to attention, as if someone had run a careless finger over them. He repressed the urge to shiver.

He was the one who looked away. He stared across the garden, misshapen now by night's shadows, creating silhouettes that looked nothing like their daytime counterparts. A breeze stirred the tops of the trees, though it didn't touch the lower branches. In the distance, the sky lightened, just for an instant. Seconds passed before he heard the low growl of thunder. Nearer, two cats yowled at each other.

"I did," he confirmed what his brother had said.

Daisy nodded, emphatically. "Good for you." He raised an eyebrow, surprised at her reaction, and she grinned. "I take it that's not what your father said?"

Frank shrugged and tried to look nonchalant, although inside, his feelings churned and roiled. Would it really have hurt Walter to be proud of him for doing his duty?

"I'm proud of you," said Daisy.

It startled him. Had she read his thoughts? Or had he spoken aloud? "You are?"

"Yes, I am. That Kaiser Bill needs a good hiding, and you're just the man for the job. I'm proud that you're willing to do it." She chuckled. "Little Harry is green with envy, apparently. Ray says he's torn between calling you his hero, and sulking because he can't go himself."

Frank smiled and shook his head. His youngest brother, Harry, was twelve years old. He wasn't old enough to join the fray, and wouldn't be for years to come. By the time he was old enough to enlist, this war would be well and truly over: popular opinion said it would be finished by this Christmas. That was one of the reasons Frank had been so quick to sign up. He wanted to play his part, and didn't intend to miss his chance because he'd delayed.

Another rumble of thunder sounded in the distance. Frank could smell the singeing lightning on the air now, though he had not seen its strike. The heat was wet and heavy, oppressively bearing down, making each movement an effort, each breath a labor.

"I…" Daisy suddenly seemed shy. She swallowed, and looked down at her hands, still folded in her lap. In the dim light, he couldn't see her blushing, but he knew she did so.

"I was wondering…" She brushed her fingers over her cheek, pushing a strand of hair that had escaped her bun away from her face and hooking it behind her ear. "Would you…?" She swallowed again. Her chin came up, and she stared straight at him, as if she was determined to get past her nervousness and say what she wanted to say. "Could I have a photograph of you? In your uniform, I mean."

Frank stared at her, uncertain he'd heard her correctly. Daisy wanted a photograph? Of him? "Why?"

Now it was her turn to try and look nonchalant. Like him, she failed. "You'll…look smart," she said. "In your uniform. I'd like a keepsake. I can look at it when you're away, and think of you. And when you're back, it'll be a reminder of this time."

She licked her lips. The innocent movement went straight to Frank's groin. He tensed, and wondered, not for the first time, at his reaction to her. It wasn't the way he should react. Not to Daisy. She was a girl he'd grown up with, not some floozie he'd met in a bar.

Discomfited, he paced to the door and stood, hands shoved into the hip pockets of his trousers, while he stared out over the night garden. Every nerve was taut, every muscle primed and ready. He willed his body to behave, to remember who she was.

His body did not cooperate. His thighs tensed until they were painful. An ache in his lower belly threatened to overwhelm him. He didn't dare present his profile to her; he was certain she'd be able to see his arousal, even in the dark.

The fox barked again, making him jump.

"I've never known anybody who's going off to war before," she continued.

"Not sure you know anybody now." His voice was strained. He swallowed, trying to bring himself back under control. "I've got twelve weeks of basic training before I go to France. With my luck, it'll all be over, bar the shouting, by the time I get there."

"You stepped up. That's what counts."

She stood. He heard her heels click on the wooden floor of the summerhouse. Her hand rested on his back, warm against his spine. The electricity sizzled through him. From the storm? He didn't know.

"You're a hero, Frank Pearson."

He swallowed again, harder this time. "No. I'm not." The words were strangled.

"To me, you are." Daisy's voice was no more than a whisper. She moved from behind him and stood at his side, her head upon his shoulder, one arm across his back in a caring possession of him. His body tightened even more, and there was a swooping sensation in his stomach, something like the feeling he'd had once when he stood on a cliff edge and looked down at the waves crashing on the rocks below. His mouth dried and his throat constricted. He tried to cough, to clear it. It took two attempts.

"I'm going to miss you," she went on in that same sultry whisper.

His skin tingled. Goosebumps rose. The tiny hairs on his arms bristled.

"I'll count the days till you're back." Her voice caught. "You make sure you come back."

He couldn't speak. Couldn't answer her. So he put his arm around her. He told himself he meant it to be reassuring, a comfort so she wouldn't worry, but she put both her arms around his waist, and clung to him, desperately. Her heat seeped through his shirt, his skin, deep into his core. Comforting *him*. She looked up at him. Their eyes met, and he saw the shimmer of her unshed tears, the longing, the concern, the love within her.

Slowly, he lowered his head until his face was no more than a couple of inches from hers.

Daisy's lips parted, the merest amount. Her skin shone in the moonlight, and her eyes glistened. The rose fragrance of her soap scented the air, mixing with the clean, tangy lemon of her shampoo, and an indefinable sweetness that was Daisy's alone.

The fox barked. In the distance, a dog answered. The breeze strengthened. It rustled the leaves on the rhododendron bush six feet from the summerhouse door.

The distant sky strobed, then darkened again.

Frank's lips touched Daisy's. A barely-there contact, like the first sip of a cool drink on the hottest day. She tasted of mint, and tea, and wondrousness.

He sipped at her again, felt the soft fullness of her mouth, the satin smoothness of her cheek, the tiniest tremble betraying her nerves.

"Are you all right?" he whispered.

She didn't answer. Not with words. Instead, she held his head in her hands, pulled him closer, and kissed him back. There was an inexpertness about her move, an innocent clumsiness that was more seductive than the most coordinated act of a trained courtesan.

Frank could no longer think. He certainly couldn't reason. The only thing he knew was, he could not have pulled away from her now if his life depended upon it. His arms went around her, holding her closer, and he felt her heart beat against his chest, its rhythm as fast and erratic as his own.

Light flashed across his closed eyelids. He didn't know if it was real or in his head. He didn't care. The world was lost. All that was left was him and Daisy and this kiss.

He pressed the tip of his tongue against the seam of her lips. She opened to let him in. There was the gentle scrape of her teeth, the warmth of her mouth, the seductive dance of her tongue moving against his. His breathing shallowed and his thighs hardened until his muscles shook. He caressed the nape of her neck, his fingers pushing into her hair, so gloriously soft, so silky cool. He tugged at her topknot. The pins holding it in place fell to the floor in a shower of soft pings and taps, and her hair fell, heavy and free, a riotous mass of deep brown curls across her shoulders, and down her back. It was so long. So, so long. He fancied she could sit on it.

An image came to him, of her sitting on top of him, that beautiful hair falling around them like a curtain, shutting them away, shielding them. His trousers tightened even more, and he groaned.

Daisy sighed softly into his mouth, and pushed him closer to the edge.

Frank wanted to touch her. To feel every inch of her, to explore her skin, her secret places. He needed to learn her body, the weight of it, the texture of it, the way it would tremble beneath his fingertips, the warmth of her curves, and her planes.

Her.

He didn't move. He didn't dare. For what if he did something wrong? Something she didn't like? What if he didn't please her, if he was somehow…lacking?

What if she laughed at him?

He'd only ever been with one other woman. A year ago, the parlor maid had led him with her come-hither eyes and her knowing smile, and Frank, a boy wanting to become a man, was all too eager to follow. There'd been frantic kisses, and hot, clumsy fumbling. He'd all but embarrassed himself in his haste. He'd certainly left her unsatisfied, a fact she'd made known, in no uncertain terms. She'd listed his inadequacies, mocked his eagerness, and disparaged his manhood, contemptuous of his attempts to please her. The woman had all but destroyed him.

He could not make the same mistakes with Daisy. He'd sooner pull back, do without her, than disappoint her. Yet, at the same time, everything within him screamed at him to go on, to race forward and take all she offered, before the need for her swamped him. It took all he had, pushed him to the limit of his endurance, but he forced himself to ignore this raging need, to move slowly, to take his time and savor every moment.

So he strung out his kisses, making each one last a lifetime. He moved his hands across her, caressing her, inch by agonizing half-inch, torturing himself as much as he did her. He played with the ends of her hair and stroked the back of her head, the nape of her neck, her cheek, her jaw, her throat. At fever's pitch, he moved lower, his fingers skimming her blouse, until his hand rested beneath her breast, holding it, weighing it against his palm before moving on, down, down, down.

She was so tiny. So dainty. His hands spanned her waist. Her hips were narrow, almost boyish. His fingers moved back up, caressing her, making her shudder, until he reached her breasts again. They were pert and slender, fitting easily, completely, into his palms. Through the soft cotton of her blouse, he played with her nipple, nipping it between the tips of his forefinger and his thumb. It stood to attention, begging for more. Frank wanted to crow in triumph.

The lightning flashed again. It was closer now, more insistent. Still, though, seconds passed before the thunder growled. *Not here yet. But soon.*

One by one, he undid the buttons on her blouse until it gaped open, displaying a shift so fine it was as if it wasn't there, a filmy layer that did nothing to hide those perfect breasts, yet covered them too much. He wanted to tear it from her, to free her to his gaze, his touch. To him.

Carefully, reverently, Frank pushed the material away. Her skin was a smooth, soft cream in the thin light, crowned by the raised darkness of her nipples. He played with her again, tweaking and rolling those delectable peaks between his fingers, squeezing, stroking, pinching, before bending to take them in his mouth, first one, then the other.

Daisy groaned and clung tighter to him. He picked her up and held her to him, her body pressed to his, soft breasts to firm chest. Her skirt fell to the floor and her legs fastened around his waist, pushing the warmth of her core against the hardest part of himself, making him ache and burn and throb. He didn't know anymore if he kissed her or she kissed him. Her fingers tugged his hair, scraping his scalp, her moans filling the night as he moved to the sofa.

He lowered them both down, then sat back, gazing wondrously at her. She lay, her eyes glittering, top teeth worrying her lower lip, hair fanned out over the velveteen, her body his.

"Beautiful," he whispered.

The lightning flashed. Once. Twice. It filled the summerhouse with its blue light and burned the air. Thunder rattled the windows.

Daisy smiled as she reached up, undid his shirt buttons and pushed her hands inside. Her fingers brushed his bare skin. A muscle jumped and he breathed in sharply. She stroked his stomach, his chest, his nipples. His fingers circled her ankle, then moved up, caressed her calf. He forced himself to take this slowly, to make it last, when he wanted to charge forward.

Inch by agonizing inch, he worked his way along the length of her leg, taking time to stroke her stocking-clad knee, then her thigh, savoring her tiny mewls of pleasure, her shocked gasps. Beyond the top of her stocking, her skin was soft. So soft. He trailed his fingertips over it and she squirmed and groaned. Then, at last, he found her most intimate part, and her damp heat threatened to engulf him.

Daisy's fingers fumbled as she tried to unbutton his trousers, but Frank pulled away. "No," he rasped, when she complained. "This will be over too quickly if you do that."

As if it wasn't in danger of ending too quickly as it was. Frank didn't know how much longer he could hold back, though he was determined to try. She made another small noise of protest, which turned halfway through to a sob of delight as he stroked her, gathering her hot wetness. He played with the nub of her, bringing her higher, higher, before gently, carefully, pushing one finger inside her, then a second.

The lightning came thick and fast now, each dry streak striking the ground, each rumble of thunder coming quicker and quicker, louder and louder, more and more insistent.

Her muscles clamped around his fingers, tighter, faster, until, with a guttural cry, she shattered, arched her back and pushed herself closer into his hand as she gasped greedily for breath.

The rain came. Not soft and gradual, a summer shower, but hard and loud and attacking. Lightning hit, over and over. The thunder came in claps and bangs, no longer distant but here and now. Incessant.

Daisy screamed. Frank wanted to shout in triumph. It took all he had not to do so. Instead, he held her close as she came down to earth, and tried to ignore the pain in his own body. He wanted her so much, but he wouldn't just take. This was Daisy's first time. He knew enough to go slowly, to do what she needed him to do, and no more. If she didn't want it to go beyond this, he would abide by that, though every fiber of his being objected.

His heart raced until it was fit to burst. His breaths sawed, each one labored and hard won. Coherent thought was impossible. Every nerve was raw as his body pushed him toward her, seeking her, desperate for a release only she could bring...

NO! Enough!

With the last of his sense, he pulled back. To go further would be wrong. Frank could not, would not, betray her trust. Not when he could take himself in hand after she had gone. He had a feeling he'd be doing that a lot over the coming weeks and months. Every time he thought of her lying here, her body pulsing with her climax, the storm raging around her, within her, within him... Her eyes were half closed, and a small, shy smile played on her lips. She would be the death of him.

And if she was? So be it. Tonight, Frank would be a gentleman. He would treat Daisy with the respect due a lady. There would be no passing any point of no return. Even if he had to sit in this blasted summerhouse all night, waiting for the pain to subside and the ability to walk to return to him.

Daisy, however, had other plans. "Your turn," she whispered, her voice almost drowned by the rain shattering against the roof. Her smile was oh, so naughty as she reached once more for his buttons. Lightning flashed.

He tried to stop her. Truly, he did. She batted his hands away. He tried again, though even he had to admit his efforts were becoming half-hearted, at best.

Not so Daisy's. More determined than ever, she

played with the buttons again.

This time, he let her do it.

She reached inside his trousers, and her fingers curled around him. He bucked, an involuntary groan escaping him. Daisy grinned, victorious, and stroked her fingers, softly, gently, barely there as they traveled back and forth, swirling never-ending patterns over his skin, and running up and down the length of him. The torture was exquisite. His breath disappeared, his heart beat fit to explode. Every nerve was on end, every muscle tight.

"I want you," she whispered. "I need…"

"Are you sure?" he asked. He still knew enough to make certain of that. Although, God help him, if she said no now, he would probably expire.

"I'm sure," she answered. "Do it."

He pushed away her hand and moved onto her. Her legs wrapped around his hips once more, and his tip pressed at her core. A slight hesitation, then he pushed forward.

Her warmth sheathed him. It felt like home. He withdrew, and pushed in again, a little further. This time he met the resistance of her maidenhead. One more thrust and she let out a yip of pain. He stilled, holding himself rigid, waiting for her to adjust, though the effort nearly killed him. Outside, the rain lashed the rhododendron bush, rattling on the leaves, hiding them, covering their cries. Lightning lit the summerhouse, highlighting the desire on her face, the glaze in her eyes, the wetness glistening on her lips.

She moved again, encouraging him. Those lips found his. Her arms pulled him closer, held him tighter.

And then they were moving together, faster and faster, higher and higher, until she broke again, and this time, she took him with her.

Afterward, they lay on the sofa, listening to the rain. The lightning passed by, taking the thunder with it, until all that was left were the aftershocks, a few flashes of light, low throbs of sound.

He stroked her hair. She cuddled into his side. Frank had never felt such peace, such completeness. He almost wished he didn't have to report for duty tomorrow after all, wished he could stay here with her forever, the rest of the world be damned.

All too soon, the rain followed the thunder and lightning, and the first fingers of daylight prized their way into the cried-out sky. The world smelled new, fresh. Hopeful.

"Daisy?" he asked her.

"Hmm?" She turned and kissed his chest.

"You are my girl, aren't you?"

He felt her smile against his skin. "I am." There was happiness in her tone.

"You will wait for me, won't you?"

She sat up a little, so she could look into his eyes as she promised that she would.

"And when I come back, when this war is finished, will you marry me?"

Daisy looked astounded. "You want to marry me? But—my father is a chauffeur."

Frank didn't see why that mattered. "Mine's a shopkeeper," he answered. Walter Pearson might own twelve shops, all of them large and profitable, but when it came down to it, that was what he was.

She was bolt upright now, her blouse held under her hands, gathered against her breasts, hiding them from his sight. "He might see it differently," she said.

Frank shrugged. "He can see it any way he wants."

"But…"

"It's not his business. I'm not asking him to marry me. I'm asking you." He gave her an intense stare, trying to convey the truth in all he said. "I love you, Daisy Redmond. Will you wait for me? Till the war is over?"

Her smile deepened. "I love you, too, Frank. And yes, I'll wait for you. Till the end of time."

He kissed her again.

****

Thursday, 6th May 1926.

The engine grumbled as Frank climbed the hill back to the center of Tunbridge Wells. The end of time had come a little earlier than he expected, he thought, angrily. Why, he'd hardly got over the seasickness he'd suffered during the crossing to France before his mother wrote and told him Daisy had gone. She'd sent not one letter to him, though she'd promised many. She'd just packed her bags and left.

Now, Frank decided, he deserved to know why.

He'd asked why before, of course, when he'd written and asked his mother for details of Daisy's departure. Mother had said she didn't know what had happened, the girl had just gone, and that was that. And really, she'd added, it didn't matter why, did it?

"Yes, Mother, it does matter why," Frank murmured now. It mattered to him, even after all these years. He had a right to know why she'd left him with his heart shattered, the pain of it worse than anything the Germans might have inflicted on him. And now, he would find out.

Even if it re-opened the wounds.

Even if it killed him.

Chapter Four

Just before four o'clock, the butcher's lad stopped beside the picket line. The basket attached to the front of his bicycle held a large bag filled with small parcels, each wrapped in thick, cream-colored paper.

"Mr. Harold says to give you these," the boy called to Jerry. "He knows you aren't getting paid while you're out, and he thought this might help."

Jerry thanked the boy, took the bag, and was immediately surrounded by strikers, all eager to see what had been given, and to claim their share. Daisy held back. She would appreciate a gift from the butcher as much as anybody else, but she didn't want to get caught up in the jostling as they pushed forward, elbowing each other out of the way to be first in line.

"All right, all right," laughed Jerry. "Give me some air. It's pork chops, and there's plenty here for everyone." When nobody moved back, he continued, "They're staying in this bag until you give me some room."

The pickets grumbled and stepped back, though nobody went farther than they could get away with, and they came forward again when Jerry began handing out the parcels. Most got one packet, though some received two, with a cheerful instruction to "treat the missus and yourself tonight," or, to those who had children, "make a stew for the whole family out of these."

He worked his way through the crowd until he reached Daisy, who stood by the ticket office door. By now, his bag was almost empty, as was the picket line, since most of the strikers had taken receipt of the meat to mean it was time to go home for the day. Daisy was almost ready to leave herself.

Jerry winked at her. "Now, then, beautiful," he said. "I've got some chops here with your name on them." He reached into the bag and pulled out three packets, which he offered to her.

"Three?" she asked. She had watched him work through the pickets, and she was certain nobody else had been offered more than two, no matter how large their family.

He looked around at the remaining pickets, then lowered his voice so only she would hear him. "There's three of you, isn't there?"

"Yes, but…"

"A sick old man, and a growing lad. Pork chops'll do them the world of good." He thrust them at her, and instinctively, she grabbed them. He smiled and said, "Enjoy."

She didn't try to hand back any of the meat. She couldn't, for how could she deny her family a decent meal? Too often they'd made do with scrag-end, or pig's trotters, with mashed potatoes, stretched farther by adding oats to them. These chops would make tonight's meal seem like Christmas dinner. She smiled gratefully and put the parcels into her satchel.

From the ticket office doorway, Doris spoke, hopefully. "Is there one for me?" she asked.

Jerry gave the older woman a sunny smile. "Of course. In fact, I just happen to have two left. One each for you and your hubby." He handed her the parcels, then folded down the empty bag and asked her to store it in the office until they could give it back to the butcher.

"Time to go home," said Daisy, happy to be finished. Today's had been a long, long shift. After three days of showing solidarity with the miners and doing little else, Daisy could say for certain that time passed much quicker when one was actually working. Her feet and her back ached from hours of standing on the hard pavement, and if a fairy godmother granted three wishes now, she would ask for a long soak in a hot bath, followed by an evening with her feet up, and someone else to cook the dinner.

Alas, there were no wishes coming her way. Instead, she must now walk the two miles home, where she would cook that dinner, clean the house, make up the fires and prepare tomorrow's breakfast, before spreading the sheets and blankets over the bench that doubled as her bed, and lying down gratefully.

As for that long soak in a bath…those days were gone. For one thing, it was Thursday, and bath night was Friday. Besides, while the water might be steaming hot and clean when she first filled the tub, by the time Albert, and then Bertie, had used it to wash off the week's grime, it would be almost cold, and milky grey from the soap scum. The last thing she'd want to do was linger in it.

Still, a woman could dream.

She went into the greengrocer for potatoes, carrots and green beans to go with the chops, and headed for home.

Halfway along Monson Street she heard someone call her name. She turned and her eyes widened, while her mouth formed an O of surprise. Jogging toward her, one hand held up in a wave, and a wide grin splitting his face, came Frank Pearson.

"Afternoon," he said, as if it was the most natural thing in the world that they should meet.

"Good afternoon," she replied, because it would be churlish not to. After twelve years, she couldn't exactly rage at him, could she? The moment for that had passed, even if her anger had not.

That surprised her. If anyone had asked her, only this morning, how she felt about Frank Pearson and what he had done to her, she would have called it old news, something that hurt at the time, but which had no bearing on her life now. She certainly wasn't wearing the willow for him. She was far too practical to do that, for what good could it possibly do? Long ago, she would have said, her anger had dissipated, her heart had healed, and life had gone on.

It was unnerving to find that none of those things were true. In fact, it took all she had to remain calm, to walk at a steady pace and not give away, by the slightest tensing of her body, or the pursing of her lips or a tremble in her voice, that this man still had the power to affect her.

Not in the way he once had. Oh, no. Daisy was well and truly cured of that! It was a source of embarrassment to her now, knowing the way she had felt then. In her defense, she'd been little more than a girl at the time, and hadn't known any better.

You were eighteen years old! Many women of that age are married, with babies.

True. But, she argued with herself, she'd been a very young eighteen. Sheltered. Cosseted. Certainly not versed in the cruel ways of the world.

She knew better now.

"How have you been?" he asked, as if they were casual acquaintances, meeting by chance. Daisy did not believe for a moment that this meeting was by chance. His presence at the picket line earlier may well have been unplanned, but this…he had waited for her, and now he had ambushed her.

She wanted to be furious at him for it. Wanted to rail at him, tell him what she thought of him and send him on his way, his ears ringing, his head—and other body parts—shredded and handed to him in the same sorry state he'd left her heart. But they were on a public street, and Daisy would not cause a scene. The Pearson family may think of her as "the lower orders," but her father had always claimed otherwise.

"I brought you up to be a lady in the true sense of that word, my love," he'd told her many times as she was growing up. "So you hold your head high and be one, even when you're provoked into forgetting it."

She called on his teaching now. "I'm very well, thank you," she answered Frank's question. Her tone was polite, but frosty. Exactly as it needed to be. Belatedly, she remembered to ask him how he was, too.

Frank grinned. It was the same grin he'd sported when they were children. His mouth kicked up to one side, creating a dimple in his cheek, and his eyes sparkled with humor. For a moment, the boy she'd known shone from the man he had become. She had to bite the tip of her tongue and firm her chin to stop herself smiling back. He did not deserve to have her smile back.

He was tall, but then, he'd always been tall. He had topped six feet by the time he was sixteen, but back then, he'd been long and gangly, still to grow into his height.

Now, he had broad shoulders that filled his woolen jacket, and a wide chest. His legs were long and powerful, his stride sure. Beneath his trilby hat, she could see his dark hair curling near the top of his starched collar. All in all, he looked a gentleman about town.

Which was what he was. She would do well not to forget it.

"Would you care to join me for a cup of tea?" he asked, indicating the tea shop ahead of them. She could see, through its large window, the place was full, most of the tables occupied. There were women sitting together, chatting, and couples, some sharing the tender looks and shy smiles of sweethearts, while others maintained a decorous distance that said they were very much married and settled. A woman sat with two children, both eating biscuits, while she sipped tea. None of the patrons wore a worker's uniform, and Daisy knew she would feel out of place in there.

Although, there was no reason that she should. It was a modest tea shop with modest prices, and Daisy's money would be as good in there as anyone else's. If she had any, that was. For even without the loss of pay for the days of the strike, her money never stretched to fripperies like tea and cake in a tea shop.

"No, thank you," she answered Frank. She meant to sound emotionless, the way she would be when turning down help from a shop assistant. Instead, she sounded curt, her words clipped.

"Come on, Daisy," he cajoled. "Let me buy you a cup of tea. For old times' sake."

"I said no, Frank." Although she couldn't deny that a tiny voice inside her urged her to accept his offer, to take a few moments for herself and enjoy the indulgence.

The voice and its temptation made her angrier than she needed to be. She aimed that anger at him. Which was where it belonged, after all.

Telling herself she was justified, she turned to face him. Her heartbeat raced at the coming confrontation, and the skin on her face prickled, letting her know her color was up. She raised her chin, defiantly.

"Quite honestly, Frank Pearson," she said, keeping her voice low so the people nearby were not able to eavesdrop, "you have a bloomin' nerve, turning up and asking me to come for a cuppa with you, as if everything was hunky-dory between us, and you'd never done anything wrong in your life!"

As soon as she had said it, she regretted her outburst. A casual observer would hear and see nothing to alert them to her anger, but Frank would know of it, and that was the last thing she wanted. She wanted him to think she was indifferent to him, that his betrayal had been no more than a passing disappointment, long forgotten. Now, twelve years after the fact, her angry words would tell him it still smoldered.

He looked taken aback. "I have done nothing wrong," he said. "Not where you and I are concerned, anyway."

Ha! He could tell himself that all day long. "The really sad part is, you probably believe that," she said. "The great and mighty Pearsons could never be in the wrong, could they?"

A flash of pain and bewilderment passed over his face, but it was gone in an instant, replaced by a flat, impassive expression. If she hadn't been looking at him at that moment, she would never have seen it.

"That's a heck of a thing to say."

"It's all I can think of."

"Daisy…"

"Leave me alone, Frank."

With that, she pushed past him and hurried along the road, not quite running but not walking, either. Her eyes stung and the streetscape wavered, her focus lost in tears she was determined not to shed.

She reached the bend in the road and chanced a look over her shoulder. Frank stood where she'd left him, staring after her, his jaw clenched, face grim.

Blinking rapidly to clear her vision, she raced on, along the road, past the array of shops and their late afternoon patrons. Some turned to watch as she swerved past them, murmuring the words, "Excuse me," and, "Sorry," over and over again.

When he could no longer see her, she stopped and pretended to stare into a shop window, though she could not have described the display if her life depended on it. Despite her determination not to cry, her cheeks were tight with her tears, and the end of her nose tingled. She fumbled in her pocket for her handkerchief, then tried to wipe away the emotion without anyone being any the wiser.

"I have done nothing wrong."

How could he say that? Did he believe that having other people do his dirty work for him absolved him of blame?

Well, she didn't believe that. She blamed him for every single moment of hurt and shame she had endured.

Breaking a promise she'd made to herself years before, she thought back, remembering that time, the worst of her life.

****

Late November 1914.

Daisy sat on the edge of the overstuffed armchair, her feet together, hands demurely in her lap, trying to look like the lady her father said she was, when she actually felt more like a schoolgirl, summoned to the headmistress for a dressing down.

On another equally stuffed chair sat Sarah Pearson, Frank's mother. A small woman, both in height and build, Sarah looked even more like a child than Daisy felt. Her feet only just reached the lush carpet, although the woman's clothes were too expensive for any child to wear, the quality of the material excellent and the tailoring exquisite. Against her throat, Sarah wore a cameo brooch that had probably cost more than Daisy made in a month. Other than her wedding ring, and the jet combs holding back her neatly piled hair, she wore no other jewelry. Her hair was honey-blonde, the color slightly fading. She clutched her long fingers together, betraying nerves she otherwise hid well.

The chairs they occupied were covered in a busy pattern: large pink flowers of no genus Daisy recognized, and leaves in multiple shades of green on a cream background. They matched the sofa, two pouffes, and the curtains, which were drawn against the cold, wintry evening. Together with the dark carpet and the walnut credenza, side tables, and bureau, the chintz decor made what should have been a spacious room seem small, almost claustrophobic.

A fire burned in the grate, the only hint of cheer in the room. Frank's father, Walter, stood in front of the fire, his hands clasped behind his back, his body blocking the flames as if he begrudged sharing the heat with the rest of them. Tall and lean, his once-dark hair now almost completely iron grey, he looked like Frank but was without his son's good humor. His blue eyes were icy as he glared at Daisy, and she wished she was not facing him alone. If only Frank were here beside her, holding her hand and shielding her from this man's terrible countenance.

But Frank was in France. He must be by now. She didn't know for certain, because he hadn't written once since he left for basic training, though Daisy had written twice weekly, and sometimes more often, depending on what spare time she had, and how much she could afford in stamps. Working for Walter Pearson was never going to make a person rich, so every penny counted. And now that Dad had gone to the front line with the rest of the Pearson's Pals, Daisy had twice as many letters to send.

She had been surprised, shocked even, that Dad had made the cut for the Pearson's Pals. He was older than the men the government were recruiting, and he was not in the prime of health. Yet Walter had encouraged his participation, and the doctor employed to test the men's suitability for battle had passed him with flying colors.

All of which was by the bye. All that mattered now was that Daisy had been summoned to meet with Mr. and Mrs. Pearson, and there was nobody to come with her and support her.

That she might need support had been obvious from the moment her supervisor delivered the message to her earlier today. It was never a good sign to be summoned to see Mr. Walter, and for him to request her presence at his home, rather than in his office at the store, was even more alarming. All kinds of scenarios flitted into her head, none of them good. Was he about to tell her Frank had been killed? Although, why would he? To her knowledge, Frank's parents did not know of the bond between them.

Had her father been killed? Oh, Lord! She prayed not. But, no. Even that news would not have been enough to invite her into his private home. He would have sent her supervisor with the message, and his condolences.

For the briefest of moments, she wondered if Walter had learned of her condition. Then she brushed that fear aside. There was no reason he should know. The doctor she had seen was bound by rules of confidentiality, surely? Even if he were not, there'd be no reason for him to tell her employer, since she had scraped together the money for the consultation herself; Pearson's hadn't paid for it.

At nearly three months, she wasn't showing yet, not noticeably, anyway, although she'd had to wear looser blouses and let out the waistline on her skirt by a couple of inches. But it wasn't something that could be hidden forever and, Daisy knew, when her condition became obvious, there would be the most terrible hoo-ha.

She'd written to Frank ten days ago. She'd told him everything, sure that he would know what she should do until they could sort things out. He couldn't just pop over from France and make an honest woman of her there and then, of course, but if he told her to announce their engagement it would be better than nothing and, as his fiancée, she was certain to receive assistance from his parents.

Ten seconds after she was shown into the Pearsons' second best drawing room, she knew there would be no assistance from them. Sarah Pearson could not look her in the eye, and Walter glared at her as if she was the worst thing he had ever seen in his life. She was told to sit, then they maintained a frigid silence while their maid served tea, with no biscuits. That, in itself, was a most ominous sign.

Daisy picked up her teacup and sipped from it. Her hand shook, though not enough to slop the warm liquid over the sides, thank goodness. The idea that she should be worried over the minor social *faux pas* of spilling her tea struck her as absurd, and she fought to keep in the hysterical laughter threatening to explode from her.

"I am sure you know why you are here," said Walter. Ice dripped from every word, and he grimaced, as though they tasted rotten.

Hope flared within Daisy. Perhaps Frank had written to his parents and told them to help her, his intended wife. Daisy had no doubt that such an announcement of intent would not please his father. Walter had bigger ambitions for his sons than that one of them should marry the daughter of his chauffeur.

He's a shopkeeper. Frank's voice in her head was reassuring. Walter Pearson was not a duke or a prince, far above her touch. He was a tradesman, and the only real difference between him and Albert Redmond was the size of his bank balance.

But for now, she must answer his question. "No, I don't know why I'm here," she said. Carefully, she put her cup back in its saucer. Sarah bit her bottom lip and studied her tightly entwined fingers.

Walter moved to the bureau, pulled open a drawer and withdrew a letter. He took it from its envelope and opened it, dramatically. Daisy frowned. That looked like her handwriting, but she knew she had not written to her employer, so how…?

"I have come into possession of this," he said. "It is

from you, is it not?"

Daisy swallowed. The letter, she could see now, was the last one she had sent to Frank. It should be in France by now, with Frank. So why was it here, with Walter?

"How did you get that?" she asked. It wasn't really the most pressing question, but it was the one that first came to mind.

"It was sent to me so that I could deal with it," he said. And with those words, he brought her entire world crashing down.

Frank had not written to her in answer to her letter. Then again, he'd answered none of her other letters. She'd told herself he couldn't. He was kept busy. When he wasn't training, or fighting, he would be sleeping, exhausted. Besides, he was not his own man any longer. He couldn't just saunter into an office and grab a pencil and a sheet of paper, and he couldn't wander down to the local post office with the finished result. Dad hadn't written back more than a couple of times, either.

But not responding was one thing. Actively passing her letter to his father "to deal with" was quite another.

"When is the baby due, my dear?" Sarah Pearson's voice was soft, almost a whisper, but her question proved she knew what Daisy had written.

"Next June." Daisy didn't know whether she should sound ashamed or not. On the one hand, having a baby out of wedlock was never a good thing, although Daisy suspected she wouldn't be the only soldier's sweetheart in this predicament. On the other hand, she was not sorry that she and Frank had shared that wonderful night in the summerhouse, and she could not, truly, regret its consequences. This baby was a part of them both, a tangible symbol of all they meant to each other, and she welcomed it.

Well, it was a symbol of all she'd thought they meant to each other. She was less certain of it now. Why would Frank send her letter to his father?

Perhaps he had asked Walter to take care of her until he could come home and do it for himself. Yes. That must be what he had done.

"The date of the birth is neither here nor there," said Walter, testily. Sarah shrank into herself. Daisy was torn between feeling sorry for the woman and feeling afraid for herself.

"Sir, I…" she began, although she didn't know what she would say next.

Walter cut her off. "We are not here to chit-chat about babies," he said. "We are here to sort out the unholy mess my son has managed to make." He pursed his lips, making clear his distaste. "With Francis rather…preoccupied at the present time, it falls to me to clean it up for him."

Clean it up for him? Daisy's heart did a somersault, and her stomach churned. Heat filled her cheeks and it was all she could do not to jump to her feet and remonstrate with the man. Her baby was not a spillage from a mop bucket! *She* was not a dustbin a fox had knocked down and pulled apart!

"There are homes," Walter continued. "Good places. A mother stays in one of them, has the child and puts it up for adoption, then returns to her life with no one the wiser."

Daisy's mouth gaped open. Sarah Pearson gave a dainty sob.

"Naturally, as the baby's…" he cleared his throat, uncomfortably, "…father's father, I will pay the fees.

And, I daresay, I can support you for a few months afterward, while you establish your new life elsewhere. I am not unfeeling."

Daisy begged to differ. He was not exactly throwing her out into the snow, that was true, but how a man could suggest what he had just suggested as suitable treatment for his own grandchild—and then claim to have any compassion—was beyond her.

There was only one answer she could give. "No."

Walter stopped speaking, momentarily stunned. Sarah gasped and looked up, her eyes wide with shock and horror.

"No," repeated Daisy, emphatically. "That will not happen." She swallowed, hard, then raised her chin, meeting Walter's eyes. She refused to let him see she was intimidated by him. Even if she was. "I do not intend to put my baby up for adoption. And I do not intend to enter one of those places and allow the do-gooders of this world to take him or her from me."

To be honest, she wasn't sure where she stood on that point. It may well be that an unmarried woman of no steady income and who had not yet reached her majority, either, could not prevent the forcible removal of her child by far more powerful people than she. But she intended to fight tooth and nail to prevent it happening.

"My dear," said Sarah, "you cannot keep the child. You're not married."

"I will be." Daisy knew she could not say so, not truthfully, but she would not allow these people to best her without a battle. And, as her father had said more than once, a little bravado could carry you a long way.

"Not to Francis, you won't," stated Walter. "He is adamant that he does not want to know you."

Daisy felt the color drain from her cheeks. It wasn't true. She wanted to shout at Walter, to tell him he was a liar. But he had her letter. How could he have her letter if Frank hadn't sent it to him?

"Don't worry. You're not the only one who has incurred my wrath over this. I intend to ring a peal over the boy, too, although that will, obviously, have to wait until he's a trifle less occupied." He sniffed, contemptuously. "He always was the wildest of my lads. I should have reined him in long ago. But, in this at least, I am able to deal with it, so all is not lost."

Daisy rather thought that depended on where you sat.

"I recognize that the fault is, in part, mine. I indulged him too much, and allowed licentious behavior." He pointed an accusing finger at Daisy. "Which is the only reason I do not leave you to stew in your own juices. It takes two, so to speak, and Francis bears some of the responsibility for this. He's probably glad he's away. Hopes my temper will have cooled before he has to face me. I assure you, it will not have done. He will take his share of my disapprobation."

Sarah sobbed again, and put her handkerchief to her lips.

Walter rolled his eyes. "My wife has a soft heart. Which is, no doubt, where my son gets his. You should know, Miss Redmond, that even now, when you have sought to entrap him…"

"I did no such…"

He held up a hand to stop Daisy's outburst. "Sought. To. Entrap him," he repeated, more forcefully, "he feels some responsibility toward you."

Daisy seethed. She did not say anything. She did not

trust herself.

"Because of his finer feelings, I shall deal leniently with you. I shall not send you packing with a flea in your ear and my boot at your backside, as you deserve. I have offered to pay for a room in a mother-and-baby home…"

"And I have said no." Daisy's voice quivered as anger, shock and horror warred within her. Frank did not want her. He didn't want their baby. He was not prepared to honor his promises. But that didn't mean she, too, would turn her back on the life they had created.

She knew it wouldn't be easy. With no husband, she would be vilified, branded a fallen woman. Her friends, most of them at least, would turn their backs on her. Employers would not consider her for vacancies. It went without saying that Walter would terminate her position at Pearson's. Even so, she knew she would keep her child, would struggle on, and do her best. And Frank Pearson and his father could like it or they could lump it.

"As you say." Walter nodded in answer to her refusal of the mother-and-baby home. "In which case, I'm prepared to find you rooms to let, away from Fieldhurst, of course. I will pay the rent on those rooms for the first year. I suggest you tell your new neighbors your husband is in France; I leave it to you to decide at which point the tragic man becomes a casualty of the war. It will salvage your reputation to some extent, and enable you to find work when the baby is born. I will also furnish you with a character, and the equivalent of six months of your father's wages, to enable you to live until you are established. Your father doesn't need his salary while he's drawing army pay, and I'm sure he would want you to have it. I think I am being more than fair."

Daisy stood and curtseyed. "More than fair, sir." She

tied the strings of her bonnet and fastened the buttons of her coat. "Thank you for seeing me." She walked from the room with her head held high.

The servant who opened the front door gave her a sympathetic smile, and surreptitiously pressed an envelope into her hand. "From Mrs. Pearson," she whispered. Then she closed the door with finality.

Daisy did not cry until she reached her own home, the home she would have to leave now that Walter had terminated her employment. She threw herself onto her bed and sobbed for over an hour, for herself, for the baby, for what Frank had done, the dreams he had shattered.

After her tears were spent, with her head aching fit to burst and her eyes hot and raw, she opened Mrs. Pearson's envelope. Inside was ten pounds, and a note. It read, "For the baby."

It made her cry all over again.

Chapter Five

Thursday, 6th May 1926.

Daisy stood in the corridor of the boarding house and ran her fingertips over her cheeks, checking they were no longer wet with tears. Her skin felt rough and dry, but there was little she could do about that. She hoped her eyes were not puffy, and wondered if she might blame any redness on the late spring breeze.

The corridor was long and narrow, its wooden floorboards bare and uneven, the walls painted in what had once been white but now was the color of old, over-used linen. Here and there were scuff marks left by countless residents, along with grubby hand prints and, in one corner, a mottled dark patch where the damp seeped in. Behind her, the narrow wooden stairs, their treads worn down in the middle, led to the ground floor. At the far end, the corridor turned back onto itself with an equally narrow staircase to the second floor. The smells of boiled cabbage and musty damp coated the whole.

She reached the door of one of the two rooms her family rented. The wood was old, the paint chipped, and a simple lock sat above the round door handle. Pasting a bright smile onto her face, she put her key into the lock and went inside.

Her father sat at the dining table, which was pushed

underneath the window to catch the maximum amount of light. Beside him sat Bertie, her son. The child rested his elbow on the table top, his cheek against his upturned hand. In front of him was an exercise book and a piece of paper. He chewed the end of his pencil, his face puckered in thought.

To one side of the table was the area Daisy referred to as her kitchen. It consisted of another, smaller table, on which was a wash bowl, soap, and stiff brushes, as well as two trivets for resting hot pans upon. Beside the table was a small stove and, above that, two cupboards.

Along the wall beside the door was the only other furniture in the room, a bench covered by three cushions—a sofa by day, Daisy's bed at night. Her pillows, sheet and blanket were folded neatly underneath the seat. A single curtain hung at the window, ready to be drawn when the night grew dark.

In the corner opposite her kitchen was another door. It led to the second of their two rooms, where Bertie and Dad slept.

"Evening," said Dad, in the same welcoming tone he used every night. His voice, which had rung clear and strong when she was growing up, now had a husky breathless quality, a legacy of his time in the trenches.

Bertie looked up. His dark hair was tousled and his shirt collar slightly skewwhiff, but his face was clean, which wasn't always the case. He wore short trousers that were getting shorter by the day. His socks were rolled around his ankles, revealing bruises on his shins to go with the graze on one knee.

He smiled. "I've nearly finished my homework, Mum."

Daisy had impressed upon him, from his first day at

school, the importance of doing well. Not for her son the low wages and long hours to be had at places like Pearson's. Nor would he join the ranks of easily exploited workers at the bus company. If Daisy had her way, he would do well in his studies, earn a place at the grammar school, and go on to a respected career, in a solicitor's office perhaps, or a bank.

"He's a clever lad," said Dad, now. "I can't make head nor tail of that stuff." He ruffled Bertie's hair, stood up and made his way to the kitchen. Every step seemed to cost him, his back stooped slightly, his shoulders hunched. He moved as though his body was too heavy for him, though he was a shadow of the man he had been, thin to the point of emaciation, his clothes hanging, far too big for him.

"How was your day?" he asked.

"Fine." Didn't that word cover a whole gamut of events and incidents? She reached into her satchel and pulled out the well-wrapped parcels of meat. "We have pork chops for dinner."

Dad frowned.

"The butcher gave them to everybody on the picket line," she explained, knowing Dad was wondering how she'd afforded them, and hating that she sounded so defensive. She pushed her smile back into place. "We'll have a feast tonight." Tomorrow, too, if they were careful.

She hung her coat and hat on the hook on the door, then busied herself in her kitchen, peeling potatoes and preparing vegetables.

"It's going well, then?" asked Dad. He lit the stove under the kettle, while she poured water from a jug into a pan to cook the potatoes.

"I suppose so. I've never been on strike before, so I can't tell. But the miners are still out, and the mine owners haven't backed down, so we keep going."

Dad reached into the cupboard and pulled out cups, a teapot, and a tea caddy. "I wish you weren't out there, my love. These things have a way of turning nasty." He measured three spoonsful of tea leaves into the pot.

"It's all very good natured." Mentally, she crossed her fingers and told herself it wasn't a complete lie. The majority of people were supportive of the strike, although there had been more objections voiced today than on previous days.

"Yes, well. It may be, for now. But sooner or later, there'll be trouble. There always is, when rich bods stand to lose something. I don't like to think of you stuck in the middle of it." He stared at the kettle, which made a soft roaring sound as the water heated. She chopped the vegetables and said nothing.

Because he's right, isn't he?

She used the knife to sweep the diced carrots, green beans and peas into the saucepan, then cut up the potatoes. As she worked, she saw, once again, Frank Pearson, standing by his van, surrounded by the threatening mob of strikers, and she shuddered.

There *had* almost been trouble today. If it hadn't been for Frank's charm and Jerry's quiet authority, it could have been nasty. Next time, it might be.

She knew she should mention today's events to Dad. If she didn't, somebody else was bound to do so, and then he'd be upset, not only at what had nearly happened, but that she had held it from him. If she told him now, she could make sure he heard what she needed him to hear, and put his mind to rest.

So, she took in a deep breath and said, far too cheerfully, "I saw someone today. Someone I haven't seen in years." She gave a trill little laugh. It sounded false to her own ears. "If you stand on the pavement long enough, the whole world passes you by."

"Oh, yes? Who was that, then?" Dad poured the boiling water over the tea leaves and put the kettle to one side so she had room on the stove to cook everything.

Daisy hesitated for the briefest of seconds, before she said, "Frank Pearson."

Dad stilled. He stopped stirring the tea in the pot. Without the clatter of the spoon against the ceramic, the room was too quiet, the only sounds in it the bubbling of the potato water heating up, and the tiny scratch of Bertie's pencil on the page of his exercise book. Somewhere in the rest of the house, another tenant slammed the door, and footsteps ran, quick and bright, along the corridor.

Her father's chin jutted as his mouth tightened, and a muscle jumped in his cheek. "That black-hearted dog," he said, at last. "He should show his face to me, not you."

Bertie's pencil stopped scratching and he looked up.

"Dad," said Daisy, in a low-voiced warning. She flicked her eyes toward Bertie, to remind him of the boy's presence.

"I'd whip him up the street and back down again, given half a bloomin' chance," continued Dad, as if she hadn't spoken. His eyes were dark, his brow lowered. The wheeze, which was always present, grew more pronounced with every breath.

"Dad!" she whispered, and gestured with her eyes once more. "Be quiet."

"I will not be quiet! It needs saying, and I don't care

who hears it. The man's a blackguard. How he's got the nerve to show his face is beyond me." His chest moved up and down, faster and faster, each breath catching, the wheeze singing as air struggled to reach his lungs, his sentences broken into smaller chunks between each inhale.

"There's no need for you to get upset…"

"There's every need! The way he treated you! The way they all treated you. They left you high and dry, with never a thought for how you were doing. And he didn't even have the courage to face you himself! A spoilt, selfish coward, that's what he is! Just like all the bloody Pearsons. Excuse my French, but they're enough to make a saint swear."

"Mum?" Bertie sounded small, unsure. His grandad rarely showed his anger, and it unnerved the boy to see it now.

"It's all right, love," she answered, her own voice deliberately gentle. "Start packing that away and lay the table."

"So, what did he have to say for himself?" demanded Dad. "Bet it wasn't 'sorry,' or 'can I help you,' or anything like that."

"We didn't really speak. He just said hello, and…"

"He should be at your feet, begging your forgiveness!" His barked words ended on a choked cough. "Mine, too!" He panted now, as though he'd run up Mount Pleasant Road, at speed. "He ruined your life. He…"

"That's enough."

"Mine as well, I shouldn't wonder." More coughing. More wheezing. "Makes sense. They wanted rid of me, because…" He fought to take in another breath. "He knew I'd have him…" Another. "He knew…"

The cough wracked his body. His face was red, his chest heaving with the effort of inhaling, only for his lungs to expel the air in yet another cough.

He leaned against the wall, his strength gone.

"Grandad?" asked Bertie.

"Run and fetch the doctor, Bertie," said Daisy.

Bertie grabbed his jacket.

"Don't you dare," said Dad. "Sit down, boy."

"But Grandad…"

"Do as you're told!"

"You need…"

"Don't fuss, woman!" He grabbed the paper bag she'd carried the carrots in and bunched it so the opening at the top was narrow. "Don't need no doctor," he wheezed. He put the narrowed opening over his nose and mouth and began to breathe from the bag.

Bertie looked from his grandfather to his mother, uncertain which one to obey.

Daisy bit her bottom lip and watched the sturdy paper of the bag move in and out in time with Dad's breathing, the crackle of it drowning his wheezing fight for more air.

She was torn. She wanted to call the doctor, have him check Dad, give him medication to open his airways, but she didn't want Dad any more agitated than he already was, and if she called for help he didn't want, it might well make him worse.

If only she hadn't mentioned Frank. If she'd said nothing…No. That would have done no good. Too many people had seen Frank near the picket line. The near-fight with Charlie had been noteworthy. Someone was bound to tell Dad about it. Not only that, but Frank had called her name. That would not have gone unnoticed, either.

She could only hope nobody had seen her with him later, in Monson Street. That would just about finish her father off.

The sides of the bag moved more slowly now, in and out to a healthier rhythm, each inhalation deeper and more measured than the last. Dad wasn't slumped against the wall anymore, though he didn't look steady on his feet.

"Sit down, Dad," she said, careful to make it sound like a request and not an order.

He moved across the room, his footsteps shuffling, as if it was too much effort to pick up his feet, his back even more bowed than usual, and he sat at the table.

The bag's sides moved at the rate of a normal person's breathing now. Relieved, Daisy turned to Bertie. "Finish laying the table," she said, trying to sound nonchalant. With a quick glance at his grandfather, Bertie did as he was bid.

Dad took the bag from his face. "See? Don't need no doctor." He gave her a weak smile. "There's better things to spend your money on."

She gave him an exasperated look, then turned back to the stove.

"Suppose it was too much to hope that no-good you-know-what offered you an apology?" he asked, but his voice was even now, devoid of his former agitation.

There had been no apology. If there had been, she wouldn't have accepted it. It would have been too little, far too late. What was done was done.

I have done nothing wrong. Not where you and I are concerned.

71

Frank had seemed confused, hurt even, as if he believed himself unjustly accused. But how could he think that? The man wasn't stupid. He knew right from wrong. And what he had done to Daisy, the way he had behaved toward her, well, that was wrong, no matter how you sliced it.

"We didn't speak, as such," she answered her father, crossing her fingers over the handle of the spatula she used to turn the pork. "He just passed the picket line and I saw him."

"Why would anyone apologize to Mum?" asked Bertie, carefully laying out the knives and forks.

"It doesn't matter," said Daisy, and she glared at her father, daring him to gainsay her. His return glower was mulish.

"Did he insult you?" continued Bertie. "Clive's dad got cross when a man insulted Clive's mum, and he punched him on the nose. Do you want me to punch this man on the nose?"

"No, I do not!"

Daisy glared at her father, who quickly stopped chuckling at his grandson's question. She picked up the teapot and put it in the middle of the table with an irritated snap, then carried the cups over, along with the milk jug.

"Punching people never solves anything. And you," she pointed her finger at Dad, "should think before you speak."

"Nothing but the truth," he muttered.

She gritted her teeth and moved back to the stove.

"Those high and mighty Pearsons," he mumbled. "Think they can treat anyone any way they like. Well, the day's coming when everything will change. Mark my words. It's already happened in Russia, hasn't it? A few years back now, but it took hold. Don't know what we're waiting for."

"No politics at the table."

Dad harrumphed, but he said nothing more.

They ate their dinner in silence. Daisy had been looking forward to the meal but, after their quarrel, the food tasted like ash and she had to force it down.

Afterward, she washed up the plates and pans, cleaned the room, then put Bertie to bed.

"You don't have to tuck me in, you know," he said, as she did just that. "I'm nearly eleven now. I'm practically a grown up."

"Is that so?" She fought to keep the smile at bay. He wouldn't appreciate seeing it.

"I can leave school soon. I'll get a job, and I'll look after you. I won't let any black-hearted dogs insult you."

Daisy sighed heavily. She was going to have to have strong words with Dad. "First of all," she said, in a voice that brooked no argument, "you are not leaving school. You are going to pass your exams and go to the grammar school."

"But…"

"No buts. I don't need you to look after me, and you'll get a much better job when you're older, if you stay on. It's not up for discussion, Albert Francis Redmond, so don't even try."

He pouted but said nothing.

"And secondly, nobody insulted me. Your grandad's just being silly. He gets like that sometimes, when he's feeling under the weather. Now, go to sleep and I'll see you in the morning." She bent down and kissed his cheek, although the look on his face told her he'd rather she hadn't. It sent a shiver of regret through her. Her little boy was growing up too fast.

Back in the main room, she stared sternly at her father.

He looked up from his perusal of the newspaper, his face a study in innocence. "What?"

"You need to curb your tongue when Bertie's present."

He rolled his eyes. "I spoke the truth."

"It isn't his fight."

"It's his father."

"That's not the point."

"Isn't it? Sooner or later, he's going to know…"

"I don't see why he should."

"Of course he will. You only have to look at him, Dais. He's the spitting image of Frank. More's the pity."

"Bertie doesn't need to know. As far as he's concerned, his dad died in the war, and that's an end to it."

"Like I was supposed to?" He folded the paper neatly and put it on the table. "I don't know why I buy this rag. There's nothing in it of any note."

"You were not supposed to die."

"It's what Walter Pearson wanted."

She threw her hands up. "That's ridiculous."

"Is it? I wasn't supposed to go to the war at all. I wasn't what the army wanted. Too old, they said. Too sick. But that man forced me into the Pals anyway, and then paid the doctor to pass me fit. He wanted me on that front line, out of the way. And when I didn't have the decency to die, like a good little soldier…"

"For goodness' sake! There's no talking to you when you're like this. Why would you even think…?"

She breathed out, carefully. "Walter Pearson is a stupid, selfish man. Other people don't matter to him. And being my dad made it difficult for you to carry on in his employ. But that doesn't mean he wished you dead. He didn't wish anyone dead. He just wanted the glory of sending soldiers. He wanted everyone to think he was wonderful without actually doing anything himself. Same as always."

"He wanted rid of me," Dad insisted. "He knew I'd fight for you, protect you, if I was here. He knew I wouldn't have let him treat you like he did. So he got rid of me first."

"That doesn't even make sense! When he sent you and the others off to France, he didn't know about me and Frank. He certainly didn't know I was expecting Bertie. So why would he have got rid of you?"

"He knew."

Dad was not going to back down from this. He'd made up his mind about what had happened, and there was no arguing with him.

She gave up. "Forget it. Just…forget it."

Daisy pulled out her sheet from under the bench and turned the seat into a bed, signaling the conversation was at an end. Dad got up, mumbled a good night at her, and shuffled away to the room he shared with Bertie.

When he'd gone, she sat on the edge of her bed, her head in her hands. "I wish I could blame this on you, Frank Pearson," she whispered. "But honestly? I can't. Because he's as bad as you are."

Chapter Six

After Daisy had left him in Monson Street, Frank returned to his Bentley and drove home. He'd bought the sleek two-seater four years ago, having promised it to himself as soon as he'd saved enough money to buy it. His father had called it a waste of money, and a financial drain, with its thirsty three-liter engine. To be fair, Walter was correct; it was a drain, and with petrol currently at a shilling and sixpence a gallon, he didn't take it out as often, or as far, as he would have liked, but Frank would never admit that. Just like he would never admit that its major selling point had been Walter's opposition to it.

The engine gave its usual throaty roar as he drove from Tunbridge Wells to Fieldhurst, but he was in no mood to enjoy it, nor the stares of people as he passed, the fresh freedom of the wind against his cheeks, or the firm feel of the steering wheel under his leather-gloved hands. The countryside roared by in a blur of colors: the green fields where sheep and cows grazed; the muted honey shade of almost-ripe early wheat; the bright yellow of rapeseed. Trees lined the road, dappling the tarmacadam and causing a stroboscopic effect that made him squint.

Daisy had been angry with him. He hadn't expected that. He'd expected her to be reluctant to see him. Embarrassed, perhaps. Guilty. But angry? Anybody would think she had been the one betrayed and cast aside, not him.

"What is it with women?" he asked as he drove along Fieldhurst High Street. His sisters often used dizzying displays of logic to confound him and his brothers. They could tie a man's mind into a Gordian knot and make sense out of nonsense when it suited them. But for Daisy to have the right to her anger, she would have to outdo all their wiles, twisting logic until it entered the realms of Lewis Carroll's Wonderland: so turned about it looked backward.

He shook his head, pushing away thoughts of her as he parked in the large graveled area in front of the house. There was space for half a dozen cars, although the only vehicles here at the moment were his father's sedate Bentley, gleaming where the chauffeur had buffed it as if his life depended on it, a roadster belonging to Ray, and a smaller, less showy car that Frank knew was driven by Richard Irwin, a somewhat earnest young man who was courting Frank's sister, Dorothy. There was no sign of Harry's car, which was disappointing. He'd hoped to speak to him and discover what Harry wanted. Although, if it was urgent, his brother would have made more effort to seek him out at Ramslye.

The house, which had been owned by his mother's family before Walter acquired it, was not overly grand. A large, red brick building, it had been built in the mid-nineteenth century and boasted myriad lead-light windows and a forest of chimneys on the roof. The oak door in the center of the building was flanked by tall, red-leafed bushes. Nearly as high as the door frame, they were a source of pride to his mother, a notoriously unsuccessful gardener. She had grown those bushes from seedlings with, she said, very little help from the gardeners. A small lawn lay to one side of the driveway, an ornate bird bath in its center, and a row of trees shielded the property from the prying eyes of passersby.

The front of the house was a study in understated elegance. It called out that this was the home of somebody successful, but it wasn't showy. Only when one moved behind the building did one see the full extent of Walter Pearson's estate, and his wealth.

The back of the property was vast. French windows in all the ground floor rooms led onto a terrace of grey flagstone, bordered by marble balustrades. Stone steps went from the terrace to a manicured lawn surrounded by well-stocked borders. The summerhouse sat on the lawn, its base designed to rotate so the doors could face in whatever direction was wanted.

Beyond the lawn was the park, carefully wilded and flanked by wooded areas, and a lake on the far side. Well, Walter called it a lake. To Frank, it was a larger-than-normal pond, filled with carp and home to a family of ducks. There was a rowing boat there, though the width of the lake hardly warranted it. Growing up, Frank had, more than once, referred to it as "the pond" and "Dad's water folly," earning himself a clipped ear each time Walter heard him.

After the lake came farmland and a small estate of tiny houses, tied cottages for those employed in the house and gardens. Daisy had lived in one of those cottages when her father was Walter's chauffeur.

"If only…" Frank whispered.

If only Albert hadn't been killed. If he'd lived, Daisy might not have felt the compulsion to leave here.

Then again, if Frank hadn't gone off to fight… He

huffed a sardonic laugh. "If ifs and ands were pots and pans," he murmured as he got out of his car, slammed the door, and went to Harry's rooms to make sure he wasn't there.

Harry had a suite of rooms on the ground floor. They had been adapted for him when he returned from the war, his legs, hips, and pelvis shattered beyond repair. It had been the only thing Walter was willing to do for him, the only way he'd ever tried to make life easier for his youngest son, who had, as far as Walter was concerned, only himself to blame for his injuries. Frank suspected the rooms had been adapted more to keep Mother happy than for Harry's sake.

There was nobody there now.

"Are you looking for Harry?" called Mother along the corridor. "He and Reggie have gone to the theater. Was it urgent?"

Clearly not. "It can wait."

Mother nodded. "Did you have a good day?" The question was impersonal, delivered in a way one might ask a passing acquaintance.

"Yes, thank you," he replied, in the same offhand manner.

"I'm about to take tea. Care to join me?"

Frank followed her into the smaller of the two drawing rooms. It was comfortable, lacking the ostentation of the bigger room, which was intended for receiving and impressing guests. This was Mother's room, homey and cluttered, with its chintz furniture and abundant knickknacks.

He sat on the overstuffed sofa and stretched his legs out in front of him. Mother sat on one of the two matching armchairs and poured tea from the Crown

Derby pot into matching cups. She added a lump of sugar to her cup and poured milk into both before handing one to Frank.

Mother sipped her tea, leaving the slightest smudge of lipstick, a pinker shade than the red roses painted on the side of the cup. "Were you busy today?" she asked. "I imagine the strike has cut down the deliveries you and Harry make?"

"Some. But there is still work."

"Your father has been in a snit all day over it. He can't sell what isn't coming in." She took another sip of tea and nibbled on a Marie biscuit. "He says things are getting out of hand."

Frank couldn't really argue with that. Although everything was still manageably civil, there had been a distinct hardening of attitudes today, and that would only get worse the longer the strike went on.

"He suggested I stay in the house until it's over. I should send a girl to do the shopping and such, he says."

Because, of course, it was acceptable for a maid to go into an increasingly fraught situation you wouldn't subject your wife to.

But pointing that out to Mother would serve no good purpose. So he kept his face bland and said, "It isn't that bad. There are some problems. There are always hotheads jumping on any bandwagon." He thought of Charlie Taylor, whipping up his colleagues. "But they're few and far between."

"You are safe?"

"Of course. There's no danger at all." He smiled. Mother didn't need to worry over this, and he didn't like lying to her, so he changed the subject. "I bumped into an old friend today." His voice was too bright and cheerful, considering the encounter with the old friend hadn't been particularly uplifting. Still, Mother would enjoy hearing of it. She'd always liked Daisy, and if her letters to him at the time were anything to go by, she'd been upset by her departure.

"Oh?" She raised an eyebrow in query.

"Someone I haven't seen in years."

"How lovely. Was he someone from your army days?"

"No. In fact, it wasn't a he. It was a lady."

He realized his mistake as soon as he said it. Mother's smile was suddenly brighter. Sarah Pearson lived in hope that her children would marry and provide her with grandchildren before she was too old to enjoy the little darlings. She had completely misinterpreted Frank's words, and he needed to stop her now, before she wove a fantasy future out of his clumsy phrasing.

"You know her, too," he said, quickly. "Daisy Redmond. Albert's daughter."

Frank expected his mother to be delighted at his news, to ask how Daisy was and reminisce about when they were children. He was shocked, therefore, when her smile fell and her face greyed, her eyes huge and round, swimming in sudden tears. Her hands shook, and she had to put her tea on the table before she spilled it over herself. The dainty cup rattled loudly in its saucer. Her hand went to her throat, and her fingers pressed into the sides of her cameo brooch, hard enough to leave indentations in her fingertips.

"Mother?" Frank knelt beside her and rubbed her hand. He didn't know what good that would do, but it was all he could think of. "Are you all right? Do you need something?"

She didn't answer. She simply stared at him, as if he was a strange apparition she could make no sense of.

"Do you need the doctor?" he asked.

At that exact moment, his father called from the doorway, "What the devil is going on?"

Frank faced Walter, who looked from his wife to his son, confused and annoyed. Frank hoped, rather than believed, his father's annoyance was aimed at whatever had upset his wife, but he knew it could as easily be because Mother's distress disrupted Walter's plans.

Walter opened his mouth to say something more, but closed it again when Mother spoke. "Daisy," she whispered. "He saw Daisy."

At that, Walter took over. He pushed Frank aside, calling to the maid, and when she arrived told her Mrs. Pearson was unwell and should be put to bed and given a restorative draught. The maid helped Mother from the room and up the stairs.

As soon as they had gone, Walter closed the drawing room door with a decided snick and rounded on Frank, his eyes filled with venomous fire. "How dare you upset your mother?" he demanded. "Thoughtless boy! I won't have it, do you hear me?"

"I did no such—"

"Clearly, you did. Look at her. She's a nervous wreck!"

"All I said—"

"You said enough! Honestly, Francis, will you never learn to think before you speak?"

Frank stared, dumbfounded. He was used to Walter's admonishments, but this time he knew he'd done nothing wrong. Said nothing wrong. Why would his father act as if he had?

Walter took a deep breath to calm himself. "The trouble with your mother," he said, "is her soft heart. She's always had a soft heart. She feels things more deeply than she should."

What did that have to do with Frank seeing Daisy?

"She gets upset, even after all these years, about the losses we sustained in that terrible war. Which is commendable of her, don't you think? Fitting that a lady should have sympathy for the brave soldiers?"

"What has…?"

"Thirty men joined the Pearson's Pals, you know. Thirty. Every last one of them a man to be proud of. And we were proud." Walter sighed. "Twenty five of them did not return."

Frank knew that. They had died at the Somme, along with thousands of others. Killed for a few feet of land, most left to lie where they fell, never even afforded a proper burial. For the past five Novembers, Frank had marched along Fieldhurst High Street, his poppy proud in his lapel, in tribute to each and every one of them.

He'd known most of the Pals. They'd been the lads he played with as a child, the ones who'd faced him on the cricket field and drank beer with him at the pub after the game. He missed them. In their honor, he had donated as much as he could afford to the fund for a memorial, which was planned for the town center.

"Your mother grieves for them," Walter went on. "Including Albert Redmond."

He moved to the drinks cabinet and poured himself a whisky, then held up the bottle, silently asking Frank if he wanted one. Frank nodded, and Walter poured another glass.

"Albert was a particular favorite of your mother's.

Did you know that? He used to take her shopping in Tunbridge Wells, and drove her to Eastbourne when she wanted to visit the seaside. Sometimes, it seemed he was more her chauffeur than he was mine."

Frank sipped his whisky.

"She took it hard when he didn't come back. And now, you…mentioning Daisy, it's brought it all back for her. Surely you can see that?"

Not really. Mother must see the relatives of other men they'd lost without going into a decline. Frank couldn't see why the mention of Albert's daughter would be any different. Unless…was his father saying…?

No! Frank would not believe his mother was the type of woman who would break her marriage vows. And Walter was certainly not the kind of man who would have tolerated it, or forgiven her if she had.

"It was more than just the loss of a well-liked man, if you really must know."

Walter took a big gulp of his drink. He stood, one hand in his pocket, glass in the other, his face grim. "It was the way the girl treated us after…" He pursed his lips. "She demanded money from us."

"What?" That didn't sound like Daisy, at all. She'd never been interested in his family's money. At least, not that Frank had noticed.

"Saw an eye to the main chance, mercenary little baggage."

That couldn't be right. If Daisy had wanted the Pearson money, she would have waited and married Frank after the war. Provided he survived and came back to her, that was. There'd been no guarantee of that. Whereas, he supposed, a payment from Walter, money safely in her hand…

"Said she wanted recompense, if you please," Walter continued.

"Recompense? For what?"

"Her father's loss, I presume. We gave her something, of course. Six months of Albert's wages. Then, when she'd got her pound of flesh, she moved away. Your mother was terribly worried about her."

Deep in thought, Frank stared, unseeing, at the picture on the wall. It was one of Mother's favorites, a watercolor of Ashdown Forest in springtime bloom, created by a local artist she supported.

Walter drank the rest of his whisky and said, "Don't mention her to your mother again. I don't want her upset."

What else could Frank do but agree?

He was still pondering what his father had said when he changed for dinner. None of it made any sense. The Daisy he'd known would never have done what Walter accused her of. Perhaps the loss of her father had pushed her into an abyss where everything was topsy-turvy and people behaved in ways that were completely out of character.

Although that didn't seem right either. However he looked at it, he couldn't believe Daisy would have done such a thing. But then, why would Walter lie?

As he shaved, an entirely plausible scenario came to him. Walter would have needed the Redmonds' cottage for his new chauffeur. Had he forced Daisy to leave her home? Frank could see him doing that.

Surely Mother would have stopped him? Sarah Pearson was in awe of her husband, and she kowtowed to him over most things, but when she truly wanted something, she stood her ground. It happened so infrequently that when it did, she invariably got her way. Frank could imagine her refusing to allow Albert's daughter to be made homeless. Perhaps, in a compromise with his wife, Walter had given Daisy what she needed to start life anew.

That was certainly more plausible than the tale Walter had spun.

But if that was what had happened, why would him seeing Daisy have upset Mother? Wouldn't she be overjoyed to hear of her?

Frank growled in frustration. He was no nearer to understanding it all now than he had been in the drawing room earlier.

And really, what did it matter? Daisy was gone. He should put her from his mind, the way she had clearly put him from hers. He had managed without her quite well for the past twelve years. It would be no hardship to manage for another twelve.

There was no reason to suppose their paths would cross again. Especially if he took care to see they did not. She'd made it plain that was what she wanted. It was what he wanted, too. And on that note, he headed down, looking to share a drink and some meaningless banter with his brothers before dinner was served.

Frank was at the top of the stairs when he heard Walter greeting someone in the hall. Had his father invited someone to dinner? With Mother feeling unwell, surely he would have cancelled the invitation, or at least, postponed it?

He peered over the banister and saw Police Superintendent Morten being ushered into Walter's study. It wasn't strange to see him here; William Morten was a friend of Walter's, and had, on occasion, provided security for Pearson's. But Morten was not Walter's only guest tonight. There were two others with them: a man Frank didn't know, and William Chilvers. Chilvers was Reggie's father, and a bitter rival of Walter's. There was usually nothing but animosity between them. Frank could imagine no circumstance in which one would invite the other to dinner.

So why was Chilvers here now?

Only one thing came to mind. William Chilvers' daughter, Reggie, was betrothed to Walter's son, Harry. Frank knew neither father was happy at the match. Were they planning to sabotage it? Perhaps even to sabotage the couple's business? If Superintendent Morten was also involved, it could prove dangerous for them and their fledgling company. And if the two men were planning something to hurt the couple, Frank needed to know so he could warn them.

There was a way to find out what they discussed, although Frank hesitated to use it. The study was next door to the morning room, and the two fireplaces lay back to back. As children, Frank and his brothers had discovered that if they moved the damper in the morning room in a certain way, they could hear everything that was said in the study. It had mostly been done for fun, although it had once saved Frank and Ray a good hiding when they aborted a piece of mischief after hearing Walter say he would be working at home that day.

Those were the antics of childhood, though. Eavesdropping as an adult was not the same thing at all. But for Walter Pearson and William Chilvers to be in the same room as each other…

And if he learned their meeting was not about his brother, of course, he would simply close the damper and walk away.

He raced to the morning room. It was large and airy, its French windows facing southeast, perfect for catching the sun's midmorning warmth. The walls were covered in pale green paper, decorated with delicate flowers picked out in gold. They matched the gold-and-green velveteen furniture, and the shades of the Tiffany lamps dotted about the room. The curtains were a darker shade of green, as was the rug covering the middle of the polished hardwood floor. A bureau and several small tables were made of dark wood, as was the surround of the fireplace. Tiles either side of the hearth built pictures of golden flowers on a pale green background, and a small set of fire tools stood to one side of the cold grate.

Frank leaned over, pulled the damper at the back of the grate, and carefully maneuvered it. Immediately, sounds from the study came through. He heard the chink of glass on glass, liquid being poured, and the rattle of ice cubes being disturbed.

"Not for me," said Superintendent Morten. "I'm on duty."

"Very commendable," said a voice Frank did not recognize. Presumably, that was the unknown man he had seen in the hall.

"Let's get on, shall we?" Walter sounded testy. "The half hour gong for dinner has been sounded. I want to be finished with this before my family starts gathering."

The other men murmured their agreement.

"I think we're all agreed, are we not? This strike has gone on for far too long."

"It's only been three days." That sounded like Chilvers. Frank had only met the man a few times, but, like Walter, he had a certain presence. One did not forget him, or anything about him.

Walter huffed. "Shouldn't have lasted a day. The government had no business pandering to them."

"The strike is legal," pointed out Morten.

"An issue for parliament, at another time. Our immediate problem is this particular walk-out. Every day those idle louts withhold their labor costs us dearly."

"I rather think that's the idea." Chilvers sounded unbothered.

"Three days is not a long time," added Morten. "The miners have been out a lot longer."

"I am not interested in the miners," Walter snapped. "I am not a mine owner, so I'm not losing money on an investment, and, at this time of year, I don't envisage needing to order coal, either. Their petty dispute, in and of itself, does not affect me."

Frank clenched his jaw. Trust Walter to see the issues only as they pertained to himself.

In one respect, though, Frank could put his mind to rest. It sounded as if this was simply a meeting of businessmen, bemoaning their lost profits and wondering what the world was coming to. Morten's presence was an anomaly, but perhaps he'd invested in their businesses. Improper, to be certain, but not unheard of. There were worse things a police superintendent could do.

The main thing was, the meeting wasn't a threat to Harry. Frank reached in to close the damper, but stopped when Walter continued: "I'm concerned about this strike, in this area. It needs stopping, and those upstarts need to be taught a lesson. One they won't soon forget."

Frank's hand hovered over the damper. That did not sound good.

"What do you propose I do?" Morten sounded whiny. "I've assigned a militia of special constables to keep them in check, as per Whitehall's instructions."

"Fat lot of good that did. Most of them sympathize with the strikers."

"The OMS has the armed forces on standby to help maintain basic services," said Morten, referring to the Organization for the Maintenance of Supplies. "But I can't call the army in without good reason. Union members taking part in a lawful strike is not a good reason."

"Lawful!" Walter sounded furious. Frank could imagine him—standing, stiff-backed and rigid-necked, his face puce, eyes sparking angrily. A muscle would jump in his cheek and a vein would pulse in his temple. There had been times, in the past, when Frank had watched his father's temper transform him like that, and worried the man would have an apoplexy. Now, he realized that, far from being damaged by it, Walter thrived on such anger.

"Those good-for-nothings should get back to work. We must make them get back to work!"

"How?" asked the third businessman.

"Good question," said Chilvers.

A very good question. Frank leaned nearer.

"Have you heard," Walter asked, "of something called R Company?"

Superintendent Morten moaned. "Oh, God!"

Frank agreed with Morten. Whether the businessmen drinking Walter's Scotch had heard of them or not, Frank knew something about R Company, and what he'd heard of them turned his blood to ice. A private army of vicious thugs led by an ex-army officer called Ralph Roberts, they saw nothing wrong with bringing violence down on those they decided deserved it. Which, from what Frank could work out, was everybody who didn't agree with them wholeheartedly.

Surely his father was not suggesting they be brought to Tunbridge Wells?

The door to the morning room opened. Frank whirled, startled, and saw Ray, grinning broadly. Frank breathed his relief and closed the damper, regretting he could hear no more.

Ray sauntered further into the room, his eyes sparkling with mischief. "Tut, tut, tut, little brother," he said. "Bit old for that caper, aren't you?"

Frank went for a shrug, which was not as nonchalant as he hoped.

"Hear anything interesting?"

For a moment, Frank toyed with the idea of telling Ray what he'd heard. His brother would be as appalled as he was at what Walter proposed.

Or would he? Ray worked for Walter, managing one of the stores. From what Frank could tell, he loved his job. Of all the Pearson children, he got on best with their father, and everyone expected him to take over, if and when Walter retired. He might think Walter's actions were justified in defense of the company profits.

"Nothing," he answered Ray's question. "I thought he might say something that would be useful to Harry's business, but they're just sharing drinks."

"Which, in itself, sounds like a good idea. Joe's pouring them out in Mother's drawing room as we speak. Coming?"

Frank nodded and followed Ray from the room. Tomorrow, he would seek out Jerry Balcombe and tell him what he'd heard. Forewarned was, in this case, definitely forearmed.

Chapter Seven

Friday, May 7th, 1926.

The picket line was awash with rumor when Daisy got there just after nine. She had taken the opportunity to walk Bertie to school, something she was rarely able to do with her work shifts. Her son had been less than thrilled at having to walk with his mother, but he had accepted it, albeit with bad grace.

"The other lads'll think I'm a baby, with my mum walking me to school," he had grumbled.

"Or, they will think you're a gentleman, escorting a lady on her way."

"Mum…" He elongated the word to three syllables.

"We're going the same way," she pointed out. "How would it look if you had to walk three paces behind me?"

Bertie shrugged. "You could walk behind me."

"Not in a hundred years."

In the end, she agreed not to hug or kiss him at the school gate, which proved a satisfactory compromise.

She was still chuckling over his objections when she reached the ticket office. Most of the others were there already, huddled together, discussing something they clearly felt was important.

"I heard they routed a huge group of strikers in London," said Henrietta, her eyes wide with gleeful shock. "Battered and bruised, some of them were."

"This isn't London," said Doris. "We don't have that sort of thing in Tunbridge Wells."

"I'd like to see them try it here." Charlie pushed his left fist into his right palm.

"Everyone should just calm down," said Jerry. He gestured with his hands, palms down, to emphasize his words. "We've got enough to go on with, without getting excited over rumors."

"It's not rumors," argued Henrietta. She and Jerry stared at each other for a moment. He looked exasperated, while she glared angrily at him. Then she turned away, deliberately putting her back to him, and said, "Have you got that kettle on yet, Doris? I could murder a cuppa."

"Give me five minutes," said Doris, and she went into the office.

Jerry shook his head, and walked away to talk to someone else.

"What's going on?" asked Daisy, taking her place next to the other clippies.

"Some people got roughed up in London by strikebreakers," answered Henrietta.

"*Organized* strikebreakers," said Matt Fuller. "R Company. Thugs and rabble rousers."

"They can't be all that," sneered Charlie. "Bunch of upper-class twits and chinless wonders, I reckon."

The other men laughed and added disparaging remarks about the thugs. The clippies shared eyerolls.

"It's all very well," said Henrietta. "But what if they come here? I don't want to be involved in a fight. Even with chinless wonders."

"Don't you worry, Henny," grinned Matt. "I'll look after you."

"Yeah," said one of the other clippies. "But who's going to look after you, Matt Fuller?"

The talk became a good-natured trade in insults. Daisy stopped listening, her attention snagged by the man approaching the picket line, as bold as he could be.

Frank Pearson.

What was he doing? Had yesterday not been enough for him? He had to know he wasn't welcome, and he could hardly rely on Jerry to help him again.

She hoped he wasn't here because of her. He'd tried to speak to her last night, and she'd walked away. No, that wasn't true. She hadn't walked away. She'd run like a coward, refusing to talk to him, refusing to have anything to do with him.

Wouldn't he take the hint? Was he stupid enough to risk his safety simply to talk with her?

The men saw him as he reached Jerry. Some jeered. Others called him names that would have had their mothers washing their mouths out with soap. Jerry glowered at him, annoyed and unwelcoming.

Go away, you numbskull! Before you get hurt.

Daisy stepped forward. She didn't know why. Perhaps she thought she could make him leave. She could do little else to help him, not if he insisted on putting himself in harm's way.

Jerry moved to stop him coming closer. "What are you doing here?" he demanded, his voice low, but not so low that those nearby couldn't hear.

"I've come to warn you," said Frank, not looking in the least intimidated.

"Ooh, look," hooted Charlie, and he pushed his way through to them. "The boss's son is getting all tough and heavy-handed. He's come to warn us."

Behind him, men laughed.

"Warn him back, Charlie," called one.

"Send him packing," said another.

As if Charlie needed encouragement. Daisy willed Frank to leave while he still could.

"Get gone, Pearson," said Jerry. "Look at them. They're spoiling for a fight and you're about to give it to them."

"I'll be gone in a minute," promised Frank. "First, I need to tell you…"

Charlie had circled behind Frank, and now, he pushed him. Frank stumbled. Matt stopped his fall, only to push him back at Charlie.

"For God's sake, you idiots!" muttered Frank. "I'm trying…"

"Idiots?" The grin fell from Charlie's face. He had been about to push Frank back to Matt, but now he grabbed Frank's lapels. Frank did not raise his fists in return, which was, Daisy thought, the only reason a fight did not start there and then. Behind Charlie, men who had been jeering now looked decidedly sinister.

"Let him go, Charlie," said Jerry. "Frank, get out of here."

Neither man took any notice.

"You come here, thinking you're the big I AM, swaggering around and calling us idiots?" Charlie's voice carried. He was playing to his crowd.

Jerry tried to push between them, but he couldn't. The special constables seemed to be occupied with something else. They didn't even look at what was happening here.

"I'm trying to help you," answered Frank.

The men moved nearer, hemming him and Charlie

in. Two of them grabbed at Frank's arms, holding him in place. Matt stood behind him, fists clenched.

Daisy had to stop this. Nobody else would. Jerry had tried and failed. She didn't know what she could do, or how she would do it, but she had to try. So she pushed forward, squeezing between the bus drivers and mechanics, all of them burly, and ready, and angry.

"What do you think you're doing?" she asked Frank. It was all she could think of. She hoped it would work, that her intervention would shock both him and Charlie, and make them stop.

Charlie responded first. "Stay out of this, Daisy."

"I will not! Look at you. Both of you. All of you." She raked her glare over all the men, who had quietened. "You all think you're so big, and strong, and tough."

Frank and Jerry both said her name in low, warning tones.

"I've seen tougher meringues."

"Dais…" Frank's voice was soft.

"And if you're so tough, Charlie Taylor, why do you need them to hold him for you?"

"I don't," argued Charlie, defensively.

"They think you do. They think it's going to take four of you to go after one man."

"He's tricky, Daisy," argued Matt. She glared at him. He swallowed, but continued speaking, though his tone was less strident. "He's like his father."

"I am *nothing* like my father," insisted Frank.

Daisy ignored him. He was not the immediate menace. Instead, she concentrated on Matt, and the men who held Frank. If they backed down, stopped giving him support, Charlie might walk away too.

"Talking of his father," she said, "you think he's

going to stand by and let you duff up his son, and then do nothing about it? You think that's how Mr. Pearson works? You're fools if you do. You might bruise Frank up a bit, give him a black eye or something. But you will all go to prison. Mr. Pearson will make sure of that."

She had no idea whether Walter Pearson could have these men thrown into prison or not. If he was able to do so, she suspected he would. The men clearly thought the same, because they let go of Frank's arms, and they, and Matt, backed off. The rest of the crowd didn't seem quite so gung ho any more, either. Charlie had even let go of Frank's lapels, although Daisy wasn't ready to count her chickens just yet. It could still flare up again.

"Let's all calm down," said one man.

"We don't want trouble," said a second.

"I'm not here for trouble," Frank told them. "I'm here to tell you about…"

"Keep it to yourself," snarled Charlie. "We aren't interested. You're trying to scare us into giving up."

And, just like that, another spark threatened to ignite. Desperate to keep the flame at bay, and to show her even-handedness, Daisy rounded on Frank. "You never learn, do you?" She stared into his eyes, willing him to see sense, to do what she wanted him to do. "You need to be on your way."

He didn't move. His stare held hers. His eyes were an icy blue today, tiny flecks of navy and silver within them, making them seem as deep and vast as the sky. His lashes were long and thick, and there were laughter lines at the edges, seeming more pronounced because his skin was tanned from driving the van. Already, stubble darkened his jaw. This close to him, she could smell the citrusy tang of his cologne, the mint of his toothpowder, the starch in his shirt collar, and that certain something that was, simply, Frank. She wanted to stay here, next to him, to take in all that he was, to savor the moments that he was so close.

Which was why she had to move away. She lowered her eyes, cleared her throat, and took a half step backward.

"You need to get out of here, too, Daisy," he said, his voice deep and low, and oh, so tempting. "You and the other ladies. It isn't safe for you here."

Charlie bristled. "Are you saying we can't take care of our women?"

Oh, for crying out loud! What was the matter with these men? Charlie was spoiling for a fight, and unless Frank left, now, he was going to get one. But Frank didn't seem in any hurry to leave. Which meant Daisy was going to have to make him go.

She turned to Jerry. "I'll be back soon." Jerry nodded. Daisy took Frank's arm and pulled him into the road, the only way around the crowd of belligerent men. "Let's go," she said.

For a moment, she thought he wouldn't come. Even as she tugged on his arm, she saw him glower at Charlie, defiant to the last. Then he glanced at Jerry, who gestured with his eyes that Frank should leave. Frank gave Jerry the slightest nod, and allowed Daisy to lead him away.

Charlie made clucking noises like a chicken. Other men jeered. Some shouted that Frank was under the thumb. Thankfully, he ignored them and walked away with Daisy.

She didn't let go of his arm until they had rounded the corner into Monson Street. His van was parked there, across the road from the tea shop. She led him nearer to the vehicle, then stopped and turned on him, hands on her hips, jaw clenched tight.

"What is the matter with you?" she hissed. "Does your brain not work? Do you hanker after a beating? Because that's what you were going to get, what you could still get, if you keep riling them like that!"

"I wasn't trying to rile them. I wanted to warn them. At the very least, they should make sure you ladies are out of the way. It's not safe."

"It never is." Frustration fizzed and bubbled inside, building, threatening to explode. "Where do you get off, telling me what's safe and what isn't, anyway? Life isn't safe. Not for us, the ones outside your ivory towers."

He looked taken aback. "Daisy…"

"I don't see or hear hide nor hair of you for twelve bloomin' years, and then here you are, throwing your weight around, telling people what to do. Well, I don't need it. I don't need you."

"Daisy, it's not…"

"If you say it's not safe for us 'ladies' one more time, Frank Pearson, I will crown you! You think—all of you think—" She pointed back over her shoulder at the men they'd left at the picket line. "You think we clippies need protecting, like some delicate drawing room roses. We don't. We can take care of ourselves, thank you very much! What do you think we do every single day of the week? We get on those buses, with men who…" She huffed. "Never mind."

Frank's eyes were sharp and hard, his focus completely on her, whatever mission had brought him here forgotten. "What men? What do they do?"

"Nothing."

Frank narrowed his eyes at her. "What do they do?"

"Nothing," she insisted. He continued to stare at her. She sighed, heavily. "They try, all right? They don't get far."

"Try what?"

"It doesn't matter."

"Does to me."

She growled her frustration. "If you must know," she said, realizing telling him was the only way she could end this, "they say things. They think they're clever. We ignore them. Now and then, if they go too far, we say something back. Make them look small, make their mates laugh at them. Like I said, nothing."

"Is that all of it?" He raised one eyebrow. It was a look she remembered from their youth. It meant he was not convinced he had heard everything, and he was determined to do so.

"Some get…handsy."

His jaw gritted and his lips thinned, his cheeks darkening, even as his eyes became icier.

"Oh, get down off your high horse," she said. She didn't need his anger, or his outrage. It was too little, too late. "We take care of it." In spite of the anger and frustration she felt toward him, she grinned. "Sixpences in a bag are quite heavy, you know. Sometimes, they manage to slip out of our satchels and fall in customers' laps. Land hard enough to wind a man. He might have to sit on past his stop, until he can walk again. And he has to pay the extra fare."

Frank closed his eyes and shook his head, as if he didn't quite believe it, but his lips twitched. "You are more than enough to give a man nightmares."

"My bag of sixpences is."

He fought the smile. Nonetheless, it was enough to

101

defuse her anger.

"Anyway," she said, her voice calmer now, more even. "That's not the point, is it? The real issue is, why are you here? You said you wanted to warn us about something? All right. Tell me, and I'll pass it on to Jerry."

All trace of humor left him. "Tell him R Company are coming. He'll know what I mean, and he'll know what to do about it."

Daisy frowned, thinking of what the others had discussed earlier. "R Company? Aren't they that private army lot from London?" She frowned, perplexed. "Why would they come here? This is Tunbridge Wells, for goodness' sake! We're a sleepy little town in Kent. Not exactly the grand metropolis."

"They'll come here because..." He looked ashamed. "Someone might have invited them."

It did not take a genius to work out who he meant. "Your father."

He nodded. "And others. I heard them last night, talking about it. Look, I don't know how real the threat is. Some were more keen on it than others, so it might come to nothing. And even if they do decide to, I don't know if any of them can even get in touch with Ralph Roberts. But I do know Walter, and...better safe than sorry, eh?" He smiled, sadly. "It would kill me if anything happened to you."

His gaze left her eyes and traveled to her lips, then moved back up again. His eyes were notably softer now, and they spoke to something within her, a yearning for what might have been, perhaps; a memory of what they had once had.

Daisy's heart skipped a beat and her breath stuttered,

as if it caught on something. Her mouth felt suddenly dry and, unconsciously, the tip of her tongue touched her lips, moistening them. His eyes darkened, and there was no mistaking the desire within them. It answered to the longing building within her.

He moved closer. She could see the individual lashes around his eyes, the laughter lines on his skin, the first hints of silver woven into his thick black hair. The air around him seemed to shimmer. Her breasts heavied, her nipples coming erect, rubbing against the soft cotton of her chemise. An ache built in the pit of her belly, an ache she hadn't felt since that night in the summerhouse, when…

She gasped and stepped back. Surely, he hadn't been about to kiss her? Here, on a public street? One of the busiest streets in town, no less. She would never have lived it down if he had.

People might have accepted her story that she was a war widow. They might not have made too much of the fact that she used her maiden name, even though most married women changed theirs. But there was only so much that could be covered by a nod and a wink. If she were seen kissing in the street, acting the wanton with a man so far above her touch as Frank Pearson, the gossips would have a field day. And then what?

Daisy would lose her job, that was what. The RedCar Bus Company would not stand for moral turpitude in one of its employees. More than that, her father would be disappointed in her. He would be shamed, perhaps even ostracized by his friends. While Bertie…

Oh, Lord! Bertie. She had to make sure his life wasn't ruined before it had properly begun.

She cleared her throat. "Thank you for telling us," she said. Did she sound stiff? Or was it her imagination?

Frank nodded. "It was the least I could do." His voice was stilted, and he, too, had to clear his throat. It made her glad to think he was as affected by what had nearly happened as she was.

"I know you can take care of yourself," he continued, carefully. "You can protect yourself from lechers and sleazes. But this is different. These people won't just grope you. They'll use fists and feet, lengths of chain, iron pipes, even knives. They'll do real damage, Dais. And I don't want to see you hurt."

She thought back to Henrietta's words. *I don't want to be involved in a fight.* Did that mean…?

"They would hurt women?"

Frank shrugged. "From what I've heard, they don't care who gets hurt. But I do. I care about *you*. I don't want anything to happen to you. I know you don't want to hear that, but it's true."

Daisy didn't know what to say to that. He cared about her?

Did he mean her, personally? Surely not. After all, he had made his indifference to her more than plain twelve years ago, and had reinforced it with every year that passed with no attempt to contact her, to see how she fared, or, more importantly, how their child was growing. So, no, Frank did not mean her, personally. He was talking generically. He was, at heart, a gentleman, and as such, he wouldn't like to think any woman might be subject to violence.

Which was commendable. She shouldn't feel disappointment that she was just one of many he sought to protect. And she didn't. Truly. She was glad he didn't have special feelings for her. If he did have, it would complicate things. Daisy didn't want that.

Yes, his eyes had held desire for her just now. There'd been no mistaking it. He had leaned in, as if he was drawn to her on an invisible thread. He'd wanted to kiss her. But that was only lust. It had nothing to do with finer feelings and emotions. Thank goodness.

"Thank you for the warning," she said. She needed to get away from him, to put aside the swirling confusion he'd created within her, the maelstrom of feelings churning through her, threatening to destroy her, nerve by agonizingly exposed nerve.

"You're welcome." He smiled, sadly. "If you need anything…"

"What is your problem, Pearson?"

The belligerent shout made Daisy jump. Frank looked up, sharply, then narrowed his eyes. She turned, then groaned as Charlie and Matt approached. From the cock-of-the-walk swaggers, and the grim expressions on their faces, they still hoped for a fight.

And she'd thought a kiss in the street would be bad!

Frank moved forward, putting himself between her and the two men. Did he mean to protect her? That was silly of him: she wasn't the one in danger here. Deftly, she sidestepped and put herself in front of *him*.

"You think," Charlie challenged Frank, ignoring the protective two-step she and Frank were engaged in, "because your dad's got money, you can give our girls a hard time?"

Daisy squared her shoulders. Not only was she unwilling to let them attack Frank, she was determined they would not use her as their excuse. "Stop it, Charlie," she said. She kept her voice low, not wanting to attract more attention from passersby than Charlie already had done. "He's not giving anyone a hard time. But you need to hear what he's got to say."

Charlie's lip curled. "What do you see in him?"

Matt joined in. "Yeah. What's he got that we haven't?"

How long have you got?

Charlie moved closer until he was only two feet in front of Daisy. His glare fixed on Frank, and Frank's hand touched Daisy's shoulder. He was probably preparing to move her aside, but his touch sent an arc of energy thrilling through her. It shocked her, but at the same time, it enthralled her, made her want more.

Which was ridiculous. Absurd. She did not want more of him. She wanted him to go away and never come near her again.

And yet…

Charlie spoke again, bringing her attention back where it belonged. "You have no right. Coming here, making a nuisance of yourself, pestering our women."

That was more than enough. Daisy poked Charlie in the chest with her finger, startling him into silence. Beside him, Matt looked shocked, less sure of himself.

"He was not pestering me," she said. "And if he had been, I can fight my own battles."

"Daisy," murmured Frank.

She wasn't sure if he was warning her about putting herself in danger or if he was objecting to her defense of him. Either way, she ignored him. "You keep your noses out of my business," she warned Charlie and Matt.

"We don't want to see you hurt, Daisy," said Matt. It was a whine, the sound of a man trying to justify his actions.

Behind her, Frank sighed, wearily. "Look, I don't want to fight you."

Charlie laughed. "'Course you don't. You don't want that pretty face of yours rearranged."

"Stop it," hissed Daisy. "Stop it, now!"

"He needs teaching a lesson," said Matt, though she noticed he hung back a little, so that, although he looked as if he stood at Charlie's side, he was actually behind him, a cheering spectator rather than a willing fighter. "It's because of the likes of him the strike got started in the first place," he continued.

"Frank is not a mine owner," she argued.

"He's cut from the same cloth. Given half a chance, his lot would increase our hours and cut our wages, just like they have."

The two busmen stepped forward again. Frank stood his ground.

Daisy looked around for help, for something that would stop this. The street around them was clear of other pedestrians now, though the people sitting at the tea shop window tables were watching, avidly. As was the waiter. Further along the road a man stood in his shop doorway, arms folded across his aproned chest, attention fixed on them. He made no effort to intervene.

Then she saw something that gave her hope. Hugh Burgess walked toward them, his briefcase in one hand, a rolled-up umbrella in the other. Daisy knew Hugh well. Now a bank manager in Fieldhurst, he'd attended the same school as both Frank and her, although he'd been in a different year to them. Back then, he'd had a reputation for fairness and common sense that saw him elected Prefect and, eventually Head Boy. Today, that reputation still stood. It meant that, unlike many bank managers, he was well respected, liked even, by people like Charlie and Matt as well as by his wealthier customers.

Perhaps his presence would be enough to stop this madness.

Her hope faded a little, though, when she glanced to the street behind him and saw three policemen come round the corner. Their uniforms marked them as regular constables, not specials like the ones at the picket line.

Daisy wasn't sure if the presence of the officers would be good or bad. On the one hand, their presence might be enough to stop the fight before it began. But what if they decided Charlie and Matt were hotheaded troublemakers? What if Frank complained that they'd threatened him? Which he was entitled to do, since they had. It boded ill for the two idiot bus drivers. Walter Pearson's son would be believed above them, and his welfare taken seriously. Charlie and Matt would be arrested on his say-so, which would be catastrophic, not just for them personally, but for the local strike in general.

"Good morning, gentlemen," said Hugh, as if he had come across friends on a Sunday stroll.

Charlie and Matt nodded an uncomfortable greeting at him. Daisy saw the moment they noticed the policemen, who now stood in a line, blocking the pavement. The officers had clearly assessed the situation, and were more than ready to intervene.

"I'm sorry to interrupt, but Frank and I have a meeting," said Hugh. He smiled, pleasantly, and tipped his hat at Daisy. "Good day to you, Mrs. Redmond," he said, before holding out a hand for Frank to shake. "Sorry I'm late, Frank. Have you been waiting long?"

"No. Only just got here," replied Frank. He glanced quickly at the constables, then turned his attention back to Charlie and Matt. He grinned, broadly, and held out his hand, as if to friends. "It was good to see you both. We must catch up some other time."

Charlie frowned, confused, but in an instant, his face was impassive again. "Yeah," he said, and he shook Frank's hand. "Good to see you, too, mate. You take care."

The policemen looked disappointed.

"You coming, Daisy?" asked Matt.

She wanted to say no. She wanted to stay here, with Frank. Which was absurd. For one thing, it seemed he had a meeting with Hugh Burgess, and anyway, why on earth would she wish to spend more time with him than she had to? She needed to get back to the picket line and tell Jerry about R Company. And then, she must put Frank Pearson from her mind completely and concentrate on the life she now lived. Without him.

With one last glance at him, she followed Charlie and Matt back along the road, toward the Opera House that stood proud on the corner, and to the bus companies' ticket office beyond it.

They walked in silence. The police officers watched them but made no move to follow. And all the way, she felt Frank's eyes on her too, marking every step of her progress.

Chapter Eight

Hugh would never know how grateful Frank was for his timely intervention. He'd had no idea how he was going to defuse the situation and ensure Daisy's safety, not just from the bully boys out for his blood, but from herself. She had willingly put herself in the line of fire there.

Did she believe she was indestructible? Frank had wanted to shake her, to rattle some sense into her. He'd wanted to stand in front of her, like some knight errant, wielding his protective sword and slaying all her dragons. He'd wanted to grab her hand and run until the danger could no longer find her. And yes, he knew what running with her would look like. But to keep Daisy safe, he would willingly be branded a coward.

The police officers turned from watching the strikers return to the picket line.

"Everything all right, Mr. Pearson?" asked one.

"Tickety-boo," said Frank. There was the slightest tremble in his voice, a consequence of the adrenaline surging through him. It would be gone in a moment.

"Looked a little unfriendly, there," said another officer. "We can haul them in, if you like. You say the word, we'll make sure they never bother you again."

Frank knew very well that if he gave these officers the nod, Charlie and Matt would be dragged to the station without ceremony. There they would be questioned, or worse. After which, they'd be charged, and convicted before the week was out. With criminal records, they would be unemployable in this area, and thus forced, once they left prison—for he had no doubt it would be a custodial sentence—to move away. The fine, upright denizens of Tunbridge Wells would no longer be affronted by their shameful, thuggish presence. So what if their families were left to struggle, forever tainted with the label of kin to convicts?

The officers watched him eagerly. They were clearly keen to teach a lesson to two men who had forgotten their place.

Well, not today. Not at his instigation.

"It wasn't unfriendly," he said. "Anything but. We're old mates."

The officers' faces fell.

"I can attest to that," said Hugh. "We were all at school together. I have a lot of good memories involving those chaps."

"If you say so, sir." The officers bade them good day and continued their patrol.

"Not unfriendly, eh?" asked Hugh, when they'd gone. "Could have fooled me."

Frank shrugged. "Just banter. You know how it is. Pretty lady, a couple of stags…" He gestured at the tea shop. "Can I buy you a cup of tea?"

"I think you'd better. Since we just told the world and his wife we have an appointment."

It was as they followed the waiter to a table at the back of the shop that Frank realized something. Two somethings, actually. Firstly, Hugh had not been surprised to see Daisy, so he'd obviously known she was living in this area. And secondly, he'd addressed her as

Mrs. Redmond.

Mrs.

Redmond.

That she truly was married should come as no surprise to Frank. She'd left here to marry her new beau after a whirlwind romance, after all. Apart from which, it made sense that she would be married, even if not to said beau. Daisy was a beautiful woman. It was only to be expected that some lucky man would have snapped her up.

But...*Mrs. Redmond*?

Redmond was Daisy's maiden name. What were the odds that she'd found a husband with the same surname? Redmond was not a rare name, that was true, but it wasn't as common as, say, Smith, or Jones. So the likelihood of her meeting and falling in love with a man with the same surname as herself was, Frank would have thought, infinitesimal.

But if she hadn't married a man called Redmond, why had Hugh addressed her as Mrs. Redmond? She didn't strike Frank as one of those suffragists, who insisted that keeping their own surnames after marriage proved their independence.

Mrs. Redmond.

There was a story behind that name, and Frank was determined to discover it. But he'd have to do it surreptitiously. It would do neither of them any good to draw attention to his interest in her. A casual remark, an encouragement to Hugh to say more about her, an innocuous conversation filled with information he could take or leave...

Who was he kidding? Hugh Burgess was nobody's fool. He'd see through Frank's questions in a heartbeat.

Frank would have to think of another way to learn about her.

They sat and gave their order for tea and sandwiches. When the waiter had gone, Hugh said, "Be careful, Frank. Charlie and Matt are trouble. They were trouble at school, and, I daresay, they'll be trouble when they draw their old-age pensions. If they live that long. People like that always risk running into someone bigger and harder than they are."

Such as R Company.

Another reason not to have had them arrested. If the vicious group did descend on Tunbridge Wells, Jerry would need every man he could get. He just hoped the shop steward had the sense to send the women home before everything kicked off.

"What brings you into Tunbridge Wells, anyway?" asked Hugh, as he poured the tea.

Frank gestured at his van, parked in the street outside. "Deliveries. We aren't unionized, so we keep working. What about you? Why are you here? Not that I'm not grateful you came along when you did, but I'd have thought, at this time of day, you'd be hard at work in your office. Or have bank managers joined the strike now?"

That made Hugh laugh. "Striking bank managers? That would divide public opinion. I've taken the morning off. I'm here looking for Florence bloody Chilvers." His eyes hardened and his jaw tensed. "The silly little madam…she's only gone and joined the strikebreakers."

For an instant, because it was uppermost in his thoughts, Frank thought he meant she'd thrown in her lot with R Company. Then he realized that was absurd.

"The strikebreakers?"

Hugh rolled his eyes. "Would you believe she's working on a bus?"

Frank laughed, partly in relief that she wasn't mixed up in something dangerous, and partly at the ridiculous idea that Florence Chilvers, fashionable party girl, would ever be seen wearing a clippie's uniform, risking the ruination of her long red nails as she punched tickets and collected sixpences from the hoi polloi.

"I'd pay to see that spoiled little minx get up before noon just so she can ride a bus. Next thing we'll hear, she's leaving parties before the milkman comes."

"There's more to her than that." Hugh bristled at Frank's derision.

Interesting.

"Although," Hugh continued, "I can see why you would say such a thing. She does seem to enjoy making people think she has air where her brains should be." He sipped his tea and reached for a sandwich. "Thing is, she's out of her depth with this. She thinks it's a lark, but it isn't. With every day the strike goes on, things get more and more fractious. Tempers are starting to fray, and sooner or later..." He grimaced, as if he tasted something rotten. "Florence should not be in the middle of it."

She's not the only one.

Frank wished he could make sure Daisy stayed away from the picket line. He didn't want her anywhere near the looming danger. She wouldn't thank him for getting involved, though. She'd made that clear. Didn't want his help, in any way, shape or form.

He knew she was angry with him, although he didn't know why. To his knowledge, he'd done nothing wrong.

She was the one who left. *She* was the one who broke *his* heart.

Which was by the bye. Whether it made sense to him or not, her wishes were clear. She didn't want him, and he would do well to put her from his mind.

The best way to do that was to occupy his thoughts with something else. Thankfully, in his attempt to come to Florence's rescue, Hugh had given him exactly what he needed.

"Why you?" he asked.

Hugh frowned. "Why me, what?"

"Why have you taken the day off to look for Florence Chilvers? Seems to me, she has a perfectly good father, and a brother. Why aren't they looking for her?"

Hugh shrugged. He didn't quite manage the nonchalance he clearly aimed for. "They seem to have given up on her. Whatever she does, as long as she doesn't bring the family name into disrepute, they let her get on with it."

Frank picked up an egg-and-cress sandwich. Cut into quarters and shorn of its crusts, it looked delicate and insubstantial. He popped it into his mouth in one bite. "They know her best, I suppose. Perhaps they know what they're doing."

"Perhaps," Hugh conceded. For a moment he looked troubled. Then he brightened, his smile too wide. "So, I hear you've been driving for Harry? How are things going?"

****

Daisy, Charlie and Matt rejoined the group outside the ticket office. She wanted to scold both of them roundly, but there was little she could say. She could tell them not to fight her battles, but they wouldn't listen, and really, she wasn't certain she wanted them to, not in the grand scheme of things. She might have made light of it for Frank, but some of the bus passengers she'd mentioned were more than a little aggressive when their overtures were rebuffed. While it was true that a bag of coins landing in the groin area might deter most, there was still the odd one or two for whom she needed the driver to come to her aid. If she told them now not to help her and they took her at her word…best to say nothing.

The three constables came out of Monson Street and walked purposefully to the picket line. The special constables stood straighter, and tried to look as if they were working. Charlie stiffened, as if he expected something to happen and was prepared to resist.

The constables eyed him and Matt but they didn't approach them. Instead, they gave them a warning glare, then passed by.

When they'd gone, Matt blew out the breath he'd been holding and murmured, "I thought they were going to…you know."

"Yeah," said Charlie. He looked thoughtfully from where the constables had gone, back toward Monson Street.

"His dad would have," pointed out Matt.

"Yeah," repeated Charlie.

Daisy left them and told Jerry what Frank had said.

"Blasted Walter Pearson," muttered Jerry. "Why does he have to be so…" He huffed, frustrated. "I suppose we should be thankful his son's still got some decency left in him. Enough to warn us, anyway."

"That isn't fair, Jerry. Frank Pearson is a decent man."

"He's Walter Pearson's son."

"Doesn't mean he's like him."

Jerry did not seem convinced. But then, she thought, why should he be? More than a few of those who now worked for the bus companies had, at one time or another, suffered at the hands of Walter Pearson. And there was no denying that Frank's lifestyle was possible only because of Walter's money. He didn't buy those bespoke suits on what he made as a delivery driver.

Besides, Daisy knew to her cost that the chip could be as hard, as ruthless, and as cold as the old block when it suited him. He was just cleverer about it, more careful not to show his dirty hands to the world. He'd been quite content to stay in the background and let Walter be the one to see her off, had he not?

She wondered what would have happened if Frank hadn't been stranded in France, up to his ears in muddy trenches and German bullets. If he'd been here, if he'd learned about her pregnancy face to face, would he have dealt with the problem himself? Or would he still have hidden in his father's shadow, taking himself off while Walter did what he did best?

Daisy would never know. And what did it matter? Whoever had delivered the coup de grace, the outcome would have been the same. The Pearsons would have been rid of an embarrassing problem, and she would have been unmarried and pregnant. She would still have had to raise Bertie on her own, her father would still have been turned off, their futures would be just as ruined.

"I suppose we should give him the benefit of the doubt," said Jerry, pulling her back from her thoughts. "He did warn us. That's something in his favor." He stared across the road, his brow furrowed and his lips thinned as he thought. "Hopefully, the thugs won't come."

"Hopefully not," she agreed.

"From what I've heard, they like publicity, so they'll probably want to stay where they'll make the newspaper headlines. London, or Manchester. Birmingham, even."

She nodded, although she wasn't sure she agreed with him.

"Then again," he went on, "if somebody paid them to come…" His voice trailed off. After a moment, he sighed, heavily. "You clippies should go home. Doris, too."

"What? No!"

"Yes," he argued. "I can't have you here. If any of you should get hurt…"

"We're part of this, Jerry. You can't—"

"I can. And I will. For the good of everybody."

"But—"

"You'd be a distraction. Give them the upper hand. We, these men here, they'd be worrying about you, trying to protect you, which would tip the scales. We couldn't fight like that, and more of us would get hurt."

Daisy couldn't argue with that logic. "You don't fight fair, Jerry Balcombe."

He grinned. "Maybe fighting dirty will see us win. Come on. Let's tell the other clippies."

Ten minutes later, the women had agreed to leave. Some were openly happy about being relieved of picket duty and spoke of all the things they could do with their unexpected free time. Others made objections, but none of them fought too hard to stay.

Daisy headed for her home, which meant walking along Monson Street.

Frank's van was still there. He must still be meeting with Hugh.

"Must be nice," she mused, "having the bank manager come to see you rather than being summoned to his office."

As she approached, Hugh came out of the tea shop. He touched the brim of his hat to her. She smiled back, and he walked away.

Through the window she saw Frank, sitting at the back of the room. She watched him pour a cup of tea, and she felt the almost irresistible urge to go in to him—because she wanted to thank him for not having Charlie and Matt arrested, that was all. Oh, and perhaps she'd tell him he had been daft to come to the picket line in the first place, that he could have sent a message instead. Although, she could see why he wouldn't want to involve anyone else, particularly any of his father's employees, in what Walter would surely consider a betrayal.

On behalf of her fellow strikers, she ought to thank him for the warning, too. It would be churlish not to.

All in all, then, there were myriad reasons for going inside to speak to him. Not one of which was her desire to be close to him. Of course it wasn't. She didn't want or need to spend time in his company.

Before she could talk herself out of it, she went into the tea shop. She waved off the waiter and pointed at Frank, implying that he expected her, then weaved between tables where nicely dressed people enjoyed tea and sandwiches, scones with cream and jam, shortbread, and sponge cake.

Frank stood to greet her. "Join me," he invited. "I was about to order a fresh pot."

Daisy should say no. She should turn on her heels, walk out of the shop, and hurry home, where a mountain of tasks awaited her.

"Thank you," she said, and she sat down. He gestured to the waiter to bring more tea, then offered her a sandwich. She took it and nibbled, savoring the soft white bread, the creamy egg-and-cress filling.

"I thought you'd be long gone by now," she said, between bites. "Don't you have to get your 'non-union' deliveries done?"

Frank tapped his nose as if joining her in a conspiracy. "I'm taking a break."

"A perk of working for your brother? Since most workers don't get that option."

Why was she goading him? There was no need to be rude. She was being unreasonably argumentative, and he didn't deserve it.

He didn't take umbrage at her words, or her tone. "True," he said, with a rueful smile. "But then, most workers get paid. I don't, so Harry can't complain if I take a little time off, can he?"

The waiter brought a tray with a fresh pot of tea, new cups, and scones with dishes of clotted cream and strawberry jam. Feeling decadent and spoiled, Daisy decided to enjoy every mouthful of this unexpected treat.

"Thank you," she said again, as she helped herself to a scone.

He waited till she had slathered it in jam and cream and taken a bite, then gestured at the teapot. "Shall you be mother, *Mrs.* Redmond?"

Daisy felt the color drain from her cheeks. He'd emphasized her title, drawing attention to her supposedly married state. Which meant he knew it was a lie! Her heartbeat sped up and her hand shook. She picked up the teapot and tried to pour without spilling as she worked out what he knew, and how.

It was obvious, really. He'd heard Hugh call her Mrs. Redmond. He wasn't stupid. It wouldn't have taken him long to work out the truth.

As her bank manager, Hugh knew she was single, but he had never made anything of the fact she called herself Mrs., never called her out on it. A gentleman to his fingertips, Hugh had simply addressed her the way she wished him to, showing no censure. And, in so doing, he'd helped to preserve both her reputation as a respectable woman, and her dignity.

But Frank…now that he knew the truth, would he be discreet and nonjudgmental, like Hugh? Or would he expose her lie? Would he tell the world she was a wanton, that Bertie was— Oh, Lord! Bertie!

"My first thought was, of course you'd be married," Frank said now, cutting through the fog of her terror. "It makes sense that you would be." He grinned but there was no humor in it. "It explained a lot." He took a scone and cut it in two. "Your reluctance to talk to me yesterday, for instance, and your refusal to have tea with me last night. I could see why you would avoid me, or any man, if there was a jealous husband in the background."

She concentrated on the scone on her plate, so that she didn't have to look at him, so he wouldn't see the guilt and shame and fear in her eyes. On the edge of her vision, she saw him spread jam and cream on his own scone and lift it to his mouth.

"It also explains why you never wrote to me, after you promised you would. It would hardly have been appropriate, would it? A married woman writing to another man."

He put his scone back onto his plate without having taken a bite.

She glanced up and saw the muscle jump in his cheek. His jaw was so tense, she thought it might shatter.

"It was somewhat lowering," he continued, "to know you didn't waste any time, after I'd gone, before you gave yourself to someone else."

Daisy gasped. "I did no such thing!" she protested. "I would never…" She waved off that accusation and went for the one that had really hit home. The truly unjust one. "As for not writing any more, what would have been the point?"

You never wrote back. Not one single letter. Not so much as a postcard. Until your reaction to my final letter, that is, and even then, your reply was not addressed to me.

"Doesn't matter," he said, waving away her indignation. "It's all done and dusted now."

That depends on where you stand.

"My ego is not so great that I couldn't accept you'd found someone you liked better," he went on, his voice no more than a whisper, keeping the conversation private. "These things happen." He swallowed. "But then I heard Hugh call you Mrs. *Redmond*. And I wondered, what were the odds of you marrying a man with the same surname as your own?"

She squared her shoulders, defiantly. "It does happen."

"But it didn't, did it?" His eyes were chips of ice, a cold, cold blue that froze her to her soul.

This was worse than anything that had gone

before… The agony of abandonment, the lonely birth and the struggles of being a single mother, the lies she'd had to tell to protect herself and her son. Then, later, the heartbreak of watching Dad suffer too, knowing it was because of her.

All of that paled next to this. For if it became known that she'd never been married at all, that Bertie was, in fact, illegitimate…

His life would be ruined. Everybody would look down on him, as if he was somehow dirty. Diseased. His friends would be forbidden to play with him. Even if he passed their exams, the Grammar School would refuse to take him, which meant he would never gain those valuable qualifications, never reach for that wonderful career she'd dreamed of for him. To say nothing of the bullying he would endure! The shame he would face.

Worst of all, the person threatening to bring all of that down upon him was his own father!

Not that Frank would be bothered. He hadn't cared a jot for what became of his child in 1914, and he wouldn't care now. It would be useless to ask him to keep his silence for the sake of his son. But there had to be something. Some reason that would make him keep her secret. What could it be? At this moment, she could think of nothing.

"What do you do when people want to meet the esteemed Mr. Redmond?" he asked. "How do you put them off?"

I say what so many other women must say these days. "I lost him in the war."

Frank flinched. "That's cold."

"It's true." In a way. Frank may not have died in France, but he was lost to her. And to everyone else, from what she could see. The open, friendly youth she'd known had disappeared, had been replaced by a hard and cynical man. The boy he had been would not have turned his back on her and their child, would not have left her to the tender mercies of Walter at his sanctimonious finest.

The man in the trenches had.

So yes, she could honestly say she'd lost him in the war.

He picked up his scone and took a bite, and looked her directly in the eye. She stared back at him. She couldn't have looked away if she tried. It was as if his gaze had captured hers and refused to set it free.

"Did you tell Jerry what I said?" he asked.

Relief flooded her. He wasn't going to make anything more of her marital state. For now, at least.

"I did. Thank you for it. And…" She cleared her throat, uncomfortable, as she continued, "thank you for not having Charlie and Matt picked up, too."

He shrugged. "They didn't do anything to be picked up for. And it's true what I told those bobbies. We were friends at school." He frowned. "I don't know why they dislike me so much now. My status as a non-union delivery bloke notwithstanding, to the best of my knowledge, I've given them no cause."

That was an easy question to answer. "It's because of your father."

He rolled his eyes and clicked his teeth. "As I keep telling everybody, I am not my father."

"The trouble is, they see you working for him—"

"I don't work for Walter. I used to, I grant you that. But I stopped doing so, months ago. I work for Harry now. You remember my little brother, Harry? He's set up on his own—much to Walter's disgust. If it's any consolation to all of you, Walter is as angry with Harry as he is with all of you strikers put together. If not angrier. And because I'm helping Harry, he's angry with me, too." He chuckled. "To tell the truth, it's one of the reasons I enjoy my job so much."

"Why doesn't your father like the idea of Harry having his own business? I'd think he'd be proud of him."

"Harry proved him wrong."

She frowned, perplexed. That made no sense.

Frank's smile was sad. "Harry was…damaged. In the war. He walks with sticks now. To Walter, that makes him useless. Worse than useless. A drain and a liability. By starting his own business, and making a success of it, Harry proved Walter wrong. Walter does not like to be wrong."

"That's terrible!" Daisy felt for Harry and all he'd been through. She remembered him as a boy of twelve, full of life and mischief, the fastest of the brothers, winner of all their races, useful on the cricket pitch and the football field. It was upsetting to think all that had been taken from him, and along with it, his father's regard.

"It's how things are," said Frank. He bit into the second half of his scone. "How long have you worked on the buses?"

They talked of this and that: her work, his, mutual friends and past acquaintances. She was careful not to mention Bertie. Frank hadn't wanted to be a father from the first, and he made no effort, even now, to ask how his child fared, so reminding him of the boy would do no good, and might bring significant harm.

For the same reasons, she didn't mention her father. Walter had turned Dad off, thrown him on life's scrap heap. She didn't subscribe to Dad's theory that he'd been forced into the Pearson's Pals to get rid of him and isolate her in the first place. That was, to Daisy, a conspiracy theory too far.

For one thing, as she constantly pointed out to Dad, the Pals had already gone to war when Walter learned of her pregnancy. He hadn't known of her courtship with Frank, of her hopes in that direction, so why would he have pushed Dad away? It was just coincidence.

Over the next hour, their conversation was mellow and civilized. His eyes danced with humor as he spoke, and his smile showed readily, dimpling his cheeks and drawing her further and further into a world where they were friends once more, where past hurts were forgotten, no longer valid. Around them, people came and went. Tables were cleared, new cloths laid, new customers served.

It was only when she looked up and saw the time on the grandmother clock on the wall that Daisy realized how long they'd been here. The waiters were now preparing for the lunchtime customers, and the day was more than half gone. The thought that she could have spent so much time with Frank Pearson and not even noticed, left her suddenly flustered, and feeling guilty.

"I have to go," she said. "Thank you for the cream tea."

"It was more cream elevenses." He grinned.

"Thank you, anyway." She stood. He got to his feet, put enough money onto the table to cover the bill and a generous tip, then followed her from the shop.

Outside, she held out her hand, formal and final. "It

was nice to see you again, Frank."

"I'll walk you home."

"No." That was the last thing she wanted. Dad had been angry enough last night, just at the thought of her seeing Frank in passing. How he would be if he saw Daisy walking with Frank, his attention exclusively on her... The very idea would probably be enough to kill him.

Frank looked as if he might argue. Then he nodded, and shook the hand she offered.

"Goodbye," she said, firmly.

"Au revoir," he replied. He bowed over her hand, as if he would kiss it. Her heart stuttered but, at the last minute, he let go. Even through her gloves, her hand suddenly felt chilled.

He sauntered across the road to his van. Within moments, he had cranked the engine, climbed in, and driven away.

Daisy didn't know any more whether she was relieved or disappointed.

Chapter Nine

Frank finished the few errands he had for the day, picking up produce from farms and delivering it to local shops and taking orders from the shops to various houses. There wasn't much to occupy him.

There could have been. Harry had had a chance to make quite a profit from the strike. From the first day some of the affected companies, who usually ran their own delivery fleets, had tried to recruit him to fulfill their orders. Harry had turned them down. He knew those firms would not bring repeat business. Once their workers returned, they would have nothing more to offer him, and he had no interest in breaking the strike for a short-term monetary gain, a decision both Reggie and Frank had endorsed wholeheartedly.

So until the railway began transporting goods again, allowing Harry to return to business as usual, there would be little for any of them to do and Frank's time was, for the most part, very much his own.

Today, most of that time was taken up thinking of Daisy. He found himself going over every moment they'd been together in the last couple of days. He looked at it all from every angle, examined every nuance.

She'd stood up for him at the picket line today. He didn't think he'd needed her to do so, but she had anyway. Did that mean she still cared for him? Or would she have done the same for anyone? She certainly hadn't wanted to talk to him last night, although today she'd sat with him for more than an hour and had seemed happy to do so.

He'd been both surprised and relieved to discover she wasn't married. He'd wanted to ask why not, but he'd known, instinctively, that she wouldn't tell him. Even so, he wondered. Had she been abandoned by the man she'd left Fieldhurst with? Had she changed her mind? Had the man even existed in the first place, or had he been a convenient excuse? Why would she need a convenient excuse?

More than that, why would she now pretend to be a widow? There was no reason, not a single one Frank could think of, which explained her lie.

If the "new love of her life" had, in fact, never existed, why had she left home in the first place? What had so upset her that she fled from all she knew? Whatever it was, why hadn't she shared it with him? She had to know he would have helped her, if she'd but written to him.

But she hadn't written to him. Not once.

Receiving letters from her would have meant everything to him. He would have read them eagerly, then re-read them, time and time again, until the paper was worn thin from his handling of it, and the ink faded so the words could no longer be seen. Then he would have read them again from memory. Her letters would have reminded him of all he was fighting for, all he had to come home for.

He remembered the mail orderly, bringing the sack of letters into the barracks every week during their training. Every week, Frank had stepped forward, as eager as everybody else to see what had arrived. Some men collected sweet-smelling envelopes and walked back to their bunks with wide grins. Others took away letters from mothers, sisters, daughters.

Some men had no letters at all. Frank had asked his sister, Helen, to write to one such soldier. Oscar Carson had had no family, no sweetheart, nobody to write to him. Helen, irrepressible and irreverent, had been the perfect foil to Oscar's quiet demeanor, and her letters had, as Frank hoped, transformed him. His face lit up every time the mail orderly read out his name. Frank didn't know what had happened to Oscar after they left basic training, didn't know if he had survived the carnage they were fed into. Helen had never mentioned him in the years since, so he supposed not.

Meanwhile, Frank himself grew used to disappointment. As the weeks went by with no letter from Daisy, he became more and more despondent. He'd not been without correspondence entirely; his family was far too large for that to happen. He'd had letters from his mother, and from his sisters. There'd even been occasional missives from Harry, although his youngest brother had been a poor correspondent.

But from Daisy there had been nothing.

At first, he made excuses for her. She had a job which took up a lot of her time. She cared for her father, and that filled her spare hours. Not everybody was good at keeping up with correspondence. She was being discreet, not wanting friends and neighbors to discover their courtship. Maybe she thought he hadn't meant it when he asked her to write.

He'd written to her. Daisy didn't reply. He sent the photograph she'd asked him for. She never acknowledged it. Weeks went by with no word from her.

Then came Mother's letter, telling him Daisy had left him, left Fieldhurst, left everything. Gone to who-knew-where with her unknown beau.

What would have been the point?

Had she already met the man she ran away with when she came to Frank that night?

Immediately, he dismissed the idea. Daisy wasn't like that. If she'd had a beau, she would have been faithful to him. She would not have given herself to Frank. Anyway, Frank would have known if she'd met someone at that time. She would have told him, or one of his sisters.

On top of which, she'd clearly never married the fellow, or she wouldn't be calling herself Mrs. Redmond now.

Doesn't matter. It's all done and dusted.

That's what Frank had said today. But it wasn't done and dusted, and it *did* matter. He needed to know what had happened between that night in the summerhouse and her leaving. He couldn't settle until he did know.

How was he to find out, though?

There was only one way. He had to ask her. She might hem and haw and try to tell him nothing; she could be stubborn, as he'd learned to his cost more than once throughout their childhood. But Frank could be stubborn too, and he wanted to know. He *needed* to know.

Frank had lived the last twelve years not knowing, and had thought everything was all right with that. It was only when he saw her again that he realized it wasn't. He'd been less than whole all this time, going through the motions of living, grinning when he wasn't truly happy, going out when he didn't really want to party, spending time with women he didn't care for. A restless, rootless soul. If he could speak to Daisy, ask her what had happened and learn the truth, maybe he could put it behind him, move on, and rejoin the world.

He would do it today. He had to. Otherwise, this empty darkness within him would continue to grow, a canker eating away at his heart and his soul, slowly killing him. He would go to her now and…

He couldn't. He didn't know where she lived.

The realization was like a lightning bolt shooting through him. He jolted, swore loudly, and slammed his hand against the steering wheel.

Frank didn't know where Daisy lived. He couldn't just go to her home, knock on her door and ask her to talk to him. Which meant he must wait, endure another sleepless night of not knowing, before braving the rancor of the picket line again…

Except Daisy was no longer on the picket line. Jerry had, rightly, sent the women home until the threat of being attacked by R Company louts had passed. Lord knew when they'd be able to return. And he couldn't wait indefinitely to ask what he wanted to ask her.

Frank sat at the roadside and pondered his problem. That he needed to find Daisy was a given. It needed to be sooner rather than later. Today, preferably. But he didn't know where she lived.

However, he did know some things about her. For example, he knew she lived within walking distance of the town center because, if she hadn't, she would have joined a picket line nearer to her home. There were plenty to choose from. Frank had driven past lines in High Brooms, Southborough and Pembury, as well as Tunbridge Wells itself. Her presence at the town center picket considerably narrowed the area where she might live.

He also knew she walked home along Monson Street, which meant she must live in Camden Road, or in the rabbit warren of streets off it. So that was where he should concentrate his search.

He put the van into gear and headed along the road toward those streets.

What are you going to do when you get there?

The thought niggled. It was a good question. He couldn't just set off, look around the streets, and expect to be successful. That idea was absurd. Beyond absurd. Even so, he didn't stop driving but trundled down the long road and away from the middle of Tunbridge Wells.

Monson Street, with its shops and offices, became Camden Road, where the last few of those shops quickly turned into houses. Some were small, square, semi-detached homes with tiny front gardens, well-cared-for patches of grass behind neat hedges, a hyacinth bush in one, roses in another. These were the homes of office workers, bank cashiers and solicitor's clerks.

Then came long rows of terraced houses, the homes of lower-paid manual workers, with front doors that opened directly onto the pavement, narrow sash windows, and sharp slate roofs.

Any one of those could be Daisy's home. Not only here on Camden Road, but on at least ten other streets surrounding it. So many dwellings. How on earth would he know which one was hers? She was hardly likely to be standing outside on the street, patiently waiting on the off chance that he'd show up. Nor would there be a big sign in the road, surrounded by neon light bulbs and flashing the words, "Daisy lives here."

"You're a fool, Frank Pearson," he chided himself,

even as he laughed at the silliness of that image. "Might as well give up before you become a laughingstock."

Still, he drove on.

Slowly, he made his way down Camden Road. He drove past the houses with their whitewashed steps and gleaming knockers and their proudly polished windows. Past the pubs and the Working Men's Club and the few tiny shops that existed so far from the other retailers. A few people were on the street, shopping, running errands, chatting with neighbors.

Of Daisy, he saw nothing.

Nothing, that was, until he came to the primary school at the end of the road. And there she was, waiting at the gates with a handful of other women.

****

Daisy had come back to an empty home. Bertie was still at school and Albert would be at the Working Men's Club, enjoying a glass of beer and a game of dominoes while setting the world to rights.

She started on the household tasks that normally crowded her evening. Perhaps, having done them early, she'd have time tonight to reinforce the pockets on Bertie's school trousers, which were decidedly strained from everything he stuffed into them. Both he and Albert also had socks that needed darning, and her Sunday dress needed mending. A hundred other chores sprang to mind, all things she never had time to do. Perhaps today she would catch up a little.

While she cleaned, thoughts crowded her, all concerning Frank Pearson. She tried to block him out by planning how to stretch their food so that not getting paid wouldn't leave them starving. She tried not to think of how their only income for the duration was Albert's meager war pension. It would cover the rent, which was a relief, but it would pay for little else.

Another reason to despise Walter Pearson. After the years of service Dad had given to that man, he deserved a company pension now. Especially since his unfitness for work was because he'd served with the Pearson's Pals.

Of course, thinking of Walter brought Frank straight back to mind.

She thought about their time in the tea shop today. They'd been, for the most part, friendly and civil, although there had initially been some animosity between them. Much of that centered on the strike, and on what she saw as a provocation by him, turning up at the picket line and pushing at the tempers of men like Charlie Taylor and his followers. He'd known or, to her mind, he should have known the likely effect his presence would have on them.

But there'd been more. More than her anger and exasperation at his foolhardiness.

Because he'd been angry, too. Angry at her pretense of being a married woman.

Why he should be angry over that was a mystery to her, though. What had he expected her to do? He must have known she wouldn't give away her child; surely his father had told him she'd turned down the Mother-and-Baby home? And his own common sense should have said that, having decided to keep the baby, any mother worthy of the name would protect it from the taint of illegitimacy.

She'd kept her maiden name, simply changing her status from Miss to Mrs. The ruse would have fooled nobody in Fieldhurst. It hadn't fooled Hugh: he'd simply gone along with the lie. Some of those she worked with in Tunbridge Wells probably knew as well, but none of them had said or done anything to expose her. In some ways, the war made it easier for women like her to overcome their shame. After the terrible loss of life on the battlefields, stories of husbands one could not produce were accepted much more readily, and everybody turned a blind eye, for which Daisy was very grateful.

Anyway, married or not, widowed or not, she didn't see how it was Frank Pearson's business! He should be thankful for her lie, not condemning it. It meant he didn't have to own his part in her shame, he didn't have to acknowledge her child as his, and he didn't have to face the disapprobation of the guardians of morality.

So why had he been so angry?

"Men!" Daisy would never understand them. Was his ego bruised by the fact that another—fictitious—man took credit for the child he'd fathered? Had his pride been battered because she hadn't gone to her knees and begged him for help? As if she would ever do that again, after he'd happily handed over her last letter to his father!

Which led to another mystery. Why had he accused her of never having written to him? He had to know she'd written two dozen times, at least, before that fateful last letter. She couldn't believe he'd not received a single one of those other letters; it wasn't likely that more than one or two of them would have got lost in the post. The chaos of the war and the constant mass mobilization of men might have delayed delivery at times, and it was possible that, occasionally, something would go astray. But every last one? That just wasn't possible.

You never wrote to me, after you promised you

would.

How dare he accuse her of that? How dare he pretend she had been the faithless one? Anger boiled within her. It made her scrub harder at the stove, until the sugar soap displaced the thin layer of grease that day-to-day cleaning had not quite removed. She wrung out the cloth and started to rinse the soap off.

Something about Frank's words did not add up. What he'd said made no sense. And the way he had said it…it was almost like an accusation. He'd seemed…hurt.

"I *did* write to him," she murmured, and she wiped the rinsed cloth over the stove again, clearing off more of the soap. "Just like I promised. Until he made it impossible."

For how could she have written again after he'd sent her last letter to Walter and completely broken her heart? Why would she have even tried to contact him after that? The trust she'd had in him had been shattered by his actions, her love for him betrayed, her dreams crushed. Yet he'd expected her to write again, as if nothing had happened?

"Expect away, Frank-bloomin'-Pearson," she muttered. "I had better things to think about at the time than you." She finished cleaning the stove and set about making the floor shine.

All afternoon she kept herself busy. The floor was scrubbed. The windows gleamed, and the rag rug was thoroughly beaten against the outside wall. The food for tonight's supper was chopped and ready in the pot, the tiny fire swept out, beds remade and the sheets parceled up, ready for the laundry, although they wouldn't be collected until Monday.

None of her busy work was enough to rid her mind

of thoughts of Frank. Nor could she come up with answers to her questions. None that made any sense, anyway. And the least sensible thing at all was him. Twelve years after the events that had changed her life—and Bertie's—Frank, the least affected of all of them, was still angry! Angry enough to accuse *her* of faithlessness. She couldn't, for the life of her, think why he'd do such a thing.

And now she had a headache, to boot.

She needed fresh air. A walk to clear her mind and push Frank-blasted-Pearson out of her thoughts. The clock on the mantel showed a quarter to four. Bertie would finish school in fifteen minutes. The lad would hate to see her at the gates, of course, but she needed the time outside, and meeting him was the perfect excuse. He would just have to lump it for today. Besides, he was a good boy. When she explained about her headache, he wouldn't mind so much. She hoped.

On that thought, she grabbed her coat and hat from behind the door and left the room.

At the school gates, she joined with a group of women, all waiting for their children to come out. She saw Jean, whose son, Clive, was in Bertie's class, and greeted her with a broad smile.

"I was feeling bad about coming to meet Bertie," she said. "He says he's too old for that. But if you're here, too, he can't complain at me, can he?"

Jean shrugged. "I wouldn't normally come, but they were talking at the butcher's earlier. Seems like there might be trouble brewing, so for the next few days, at least, I'll be here making sure Clive comes straight home."

"Trouble?" Daisy swallowed. It was true then? The

thugs from London were coming. She had hoped it was all just a story. Now she sent up a silent prayer that, if those men did come, the police would protect the people on the picket lines and nobody would be seriously hurt.

"Yeah, trouble," Jean answered. "I'm not sure what's going to happen, nor where or when. But I don't want my Clive running about, getting in the middle of it all. Lord knows, that boy can find enough trouble on his own without someone handing him more."

Daisy felt sick. This should not be happening here. Well, she supposed, it shouldn't be happening *anywhere,* but it certainly should not be coming to sleepy, leafy Tunbridge Wells.

In her mind's eye, she saw the strikers—men she cared about as colleagues and friends—bloodied and broken by professional troublemakers. She saw those troublemakers strutting through the streets, armed and menacing, frightening everybody and taking pleasure in doing so. Nobody would be safe.

Oh, God! The quicker she took Bertie home and got him safely indoors, the better. She would keep him in for the whole weekend. He could complain as much as he liked, but he wouldn't sway her. She wondered if she could force Dad to stay at home until the danger was past, too. Chances were slim to none on that, but she'd try. And at least he'd be warned.

Then there was Frank. Frank Pearson, whose father had summoned those thugs in the first place. He should be safe. But he'd warned the strikers. He'd stood up against his father, when push came to shove, and done the decent thing. Would that make him a target?

Of course it won't. He's a Pearson. They won't touch him.

If only she could be sure of that.

She bit her bottom lip, her mind playing a dozen nightmarish scenarios in which he was hurt, or worse, by the louts from London. Her breaths came short and sharp and the beat of her heart sounded loud in her ear, pushing away the everyday sounds of the street.

Jean spoke. Daisy smiled and nodded, though she had no idea what the woman said. All she could think of was Frank. She willed him to be sensible. To stay off the streets, out of the way of R Company. She prayed his name would be enough to keep him unhurt.

Her thoughts must be stronger than she imagined because, suddenly, there was the man himself, striding along the pavement toward the school gates, acting as if he didn't have a care in the world, his eyes on her, and that oh-so-enticing grin deepening his dimples.

She blinked to vanish the mirage. Twice. But when she opened her eyes, he was still there, coming ever nearer.

"He's a bit of a sheikh," murmured Jean, using the slang term for a handsome man that had become popular because of the Rudolf Valentino film. "You lucky thing, you." Discreetly, she stepped away, although not quite so far that she would be out of earshot.

Daisy watched him approach.

"Good afternoon," he said, grinning broadly, as if it was perfectly normal to see him here and her heart wasn't beating eighteen to the dozen while her cheeks burned. All coherent thought momentarily left her head.

"What are you doing here?" she managed, after the briefest of hesitations.

From the corner of her eye, Daisy saw Jean, who looked shocked at her unwelcoming tone. But then, Jean didn't know Frank. A handsome man he might be, but that was all surface. Underneath, he was rotten, the sort of man who would leave a woman high and dry. He didn't deserve a welcome.

"Currently," he answered her question with a wink, "I'm admiring the view."

Smooth, Pearson. Luckily, Daisy had heard it all before, so she ignored his comment. "Have you been following me?" she asked instead. She narrowed her eyes into a glare of accusation.

"No," he said. "Not following you, exactly. Although I did hope to see you."

Then he seemed to realize where they were. He frowned at the school. "Why are you here?" he asked, and he sounded genuinely perplexed.

Daisy swallowed. Cleared her throat and swallowed again. She wanted to say it was none of his business and send him on his way. To rail at him that he hadn't been interested before, so why would he be now? She wanted to shout that he knew very well who she was waiting for, and him standing there, looking innocent, was not going to fool her or anybody else. At the same time, she wished she could run. Just grab Bertie and race home, where she could lock the doors until this man had gone away again and life could return to normal.

A couple of streets away, a church bell struck the hour. Seconds later, the school bell clanged discordantly in the playground, and children poured noisily from the old stone building. The boys wore grey sweaters over once-white shirts, grey shorts, and grey socks wrinkled around their ankles, showing off bruised shins and grazed knees. The girls were, for the most part, tidier, their dresses an array of colors under neatly buttoned cardigans. Most of them wore white socks, and their shoes were less scuffed than the boys' were. Some of the boys stuffed their arms into gabardines as they hurried across the playground, running for the gates as if they had to get out of there before the teachers changed their minds and herded them all back inside again.

Frank stared at Daisy, clearly waiting for an answer. She didn't have the chance to give it to him.

"Mum? Mum, is it all right if I go to Clive's house?"

Clive implored Jean to allow it, and Jean made excuses about coming another day.

"Please, Mum?" begged Bertie. "Can I go?"

"No, you can't." Fear made Daisy's voice sharper than she intended.

"Mum…" He stretched the word out.

"I said no," she told him, in a much softer tone. "Don't argue with me, Bertie. We have to get home, and that's all there is to it."

But Bertie wasn't listening. He was staring in disbelief at Frank, who stared right back. Both of them stood silent, shocked.

Well, Bertie was shocked. But Frank—Frank was far more. Frank was absolutely furious.

Chapter Ten

Frank knew, the moment he saw the boy, that this was his son. There was no mistaking it. Not only did the lad have Frank's ice-blue eyes and the same dark hair that wouldn't stay flat on his scalp, but he looked exactly like Harry had when Frank went off to war. Even down to the dimple on his chin.

For a moment, he could say nothing. Do nothing. Even his thinking stalled, the only thing in his head the two words beating, over and over, like a tattoo: *My son. My son. My son.*

Daisy had had his son. More, she had run away to have him, gone to Lord-knew-where, invented a husband to give her respectability. She'd proclaimed herself a war widow rather than let Frank be a father to his boy.

Why? Was Frank that bad? Did she find the idea of making a family with him so abhorrent that she would do so much to avoid it?

She hadn't seemed to find him abhorrent that night in the summerhouse. She had lain there, her hair fanned out across the sofa, her blouse open and pushed aside so he could reach her breasts. Her skirt was discarded, pooled in the doorway where it had fallen from her. Rain beat loud and insistent on the roof, its steady rhythm interspersed with the loud claps and bangs of the thunder. Lightning streaked the sky and glittered in her love-misted eyes. In that moment, with the world exploding around them, he'd asked her to wait for him.

"I love you, Daisy Redmond," he'd said, injecting every last piece of himself into the declaration. He stared at her intensely, wringing himself dry, giving her all his feelings, all his truth. "Will you wait for me? Till the war is over?"

She smiled at him. "I love you, too, Frank. And yes, I'll wait for you. Till the end of time."

The end of time! Hah! Daisy hadn't even waited until the end of the year.

Had she known she wouldn't wait, then, that night? Had she planned her escape even as she dressed and left him there?

That night grew sharper now, more vivid in his memory. He could smell the burning electricity of the lightning, the hot, damp violence of the rain, the lust on her body. He felt the satin smoothness of her skin, the soft cotton of her underclothes, the tops of her stockings…

God! He hadn't even taken the time to remove her stockings!

He'd undone her blouse and pushed it away, devoured her breasts with his eyes, his hands, his mouth. He had undressed her, yes, but only as far as he'd needed to expose her to him.

And as for him…his shirt was open, too. He could see himself, his chest uncovered to her exploring fingers, his back, his shoulders, his arms, still hidden. The buttons on his trousers were undone…he fought back the small groan of realization. He'd taken her without even removing his trousers!

She'd been a virgin. *A virgin!* And he had rutted with her like a…like a…

Frank was thoroughly ashamed of himself. A girl's first time should not be a clumsy fumbling on a summerhouse sofa, with his family less than a hundred yards away, ready to discover them at any moment! Her first time shouldn't have been so rushed that neither of them even removed their boots! Granted, Frank was only eighteen years old himself, still a boy, largely untried, certainly inexperienced.

Now he was making excuses for his behavior! Because, whichever way he looked at it, he had treated Daisy badly that night, and he should be ashamed of himself. He *was* ashamed of himself.

But his poor behavior did not excuse hers.

He had a son!

They'd made love only the one time. It had never occurred to Frank that she would fall pregnant. Everybody said a girl couldn't fall pregnant on her first time and, foolish boy that he was, he never questioned that. He blithely went to camp, where he trained briefly before being shipped out to France, his waking mind filled with drills and rules, quick lessons in how to shoot properly and what to do when faced by the enemy, along with even more quickly learned lessons on how to avoid the sergeant-major's wrath. New mates. New brothers. New situations.

But every night when he fell into his cot, he dreamed of Daisy. He saw her clearly, saw her sweet smile, the way her mouth turned up at the ends and her nose wrinkled just the tiniest amount when she laughed. He saw the desire in her dark eyes, the languid pose of her delectable body, heard the tiny cries of pleasure she made when he touched her. His dreams left him hard and wanting, wishing he could dive into Walter's lake and let the cold water sluice the need away. It was a miracle none of his mates noticed.

Then again, maybe they had. Maybe they were all fighting the same battle with their dreams, and each ignored the others so they'd be ignored as well.

Frank was disappointed when no letter came from Daisy. He'd written to her, full of hope that she would reply. When she did not, he made excuses for her. He told himself that tomorrow he'd see her handwriting on the envelope, smell her perfume sprayed onto the paper. Tomorrow. Or the next day. Or the next. He'd hoped, and hoped.

Right up until his mother wrote and told him the truth.

Some of it, anyway. Mother had told him Daisy was gone. She hadn't said anything about a child. Probably Mother hadn't known. Frank doubted Daisy would have confided such a thing to her. His mother was old school, proper to the core. Very much a lie-back-and-think-of-England type of woman. She would never have understood the passionate heat of a moment on the eve of uncertainty.

Walter, on the other hand…had Walter known the truth? Was that why he'd said Daisy asked him for money? Why the hard, cold businessman gave the young girl six months of her father's wages?

If Walter knew the truth, then he had lied to Frank. First, he'd lied by omission, not apprising his son of the facts. Then, last night, he'd lied outright. Which, in itself, was not a shock to Frank. He knew very well Walter Pearson did and said whatever it took to get him what he wanted. Other people's feelings were inconveniences to be glossed over. It saddened Frank to realize that this was so true to his father's character that not only was he not surprised by it—he wasn't even disappointed.

But Daisy…Daisy had said nothing, either. She had borne Frank's child and told him nothing. She'd made no effort to say anything. There'd been no letter from her. Not even one to tell him goodbye. Even now, all these years later, she had still said nothing. They'd spent over an hour in the tea shop today, reminiscing, catching up on each other's lives. And, in all that time, she'd made no mention of her son, *his* son, at all.

Frank's jaw tightened. His teeth gritted together and his spine straightened to the point of pain, and there was a sickly, roiling anticipation in his stomach.

They needed to talk, he and Daisy. He wouldn't leave until they did so. He was adamant about that, even though she stood before him now, her eyes big and begging, her cheeks pale, her lips unnaturally dark. A few feet away, her friend watched. The woman's face was a mixture of speculation and feigned indifference. Other women stood around, too, though they had collected their children and could—should—have moved off by now. Instead, they stayed where they were, watching him, watching Daisy.

Everything around him seemed clearer somehow, more pronounced, like one of those stereographic photographs where parts of the image jump to the fore, giving it more depth and making it more realistic. The sky above him was a gunmetal grey, the clouds rolling against each other, over each other. A breeze skittered along the street, kicking up grit and dust from the pavement and the gutter, coating shoes and making the air taste dry. Boys called out. Girls whispered in friends' ears. A car drove past, its engine growling grumpily.

Cold air brushed Frank's skin and softly ruffled his hair.

There was a tug on his arm. Frank looked down, startled, and saw the boy staring up at him, his fingers closed around the hem of Frank's sleeve, confusion swirling in his eyes.

"Who are you?" the child demanded. There was a belligerent set to his jaw and he squared his narrow frame, as if preparing to fight this man who had so clearly upset his mother. "Who are you?" he repeated, more insistently.

How was Frank supposed to answer that? *I'm your father?* How could he say that, right here, right now, completely out of the blue? He didn't know what Daisy had told the boy about his parentage. Presumably, the lad had been fed the same lie she'd told him—that his father had died in the war. Was it fair to the child to gainsay his mother? To ruin whatever notions he had, not just of his "heroic" absent father, but of the mother who'd brought him up, nurtured him, cared for him?

For she had cared for the boy. Frank could see that. The child's clothes were not expensive, but they were in good order. He didn't seem undernourished, and he didn't have the attitude of a child who was insecure in a parent's love. If anything, he looked more secure in that love than Frank had ever been, for all the material advantage of being Walter Pearson's son.

If Frank was fair to the boy, and to his mother, he couldn't tell him, here and now, that he was his father. He might never be able to tell him.

Then again, how was that fair to Frank? Did he not deserve something, too? This was his son! Surely, he deserved that to be acknowledged? He deserved to get to know the boy, to claw back some of the years he'd already lost.

Frank glanced around. This was not something they could resolve here. There were too many people nearby. People who would gossip, people who would put two and two together and, in this case, make four. They'd probably already done so, on the basis of the resemblance between Frank and the boy. There was no need to feed the fire any more than his mere presence already had.

So he didn't answer the boy's question. Instead, he smiled at him in a way he hoped would reassure the lad. Judging by the suspicious scowl he got in return, it didn't. So be it. It wasn't the boy he needed to have this out with anyway.

Frank shifted his attention from the child to Daisy. "We should go somewhere quieter," he said, keeping his voice low so the other women wouldn't hear him. "Somewhere we can talk."

****

Daisy swallowed. Her mouth was dry and her throat painful, and inside her chest, there was a hard, cracking sensation. The world crashed around her, the future blown to smithereens, and there was nothing she could do to stop it. She wanted to run, as far and as fast as she could. To grab Bertie's hand and race for all she was worth until they left Frank far behind, so he couldn't find them, couldn't use that look of disgust and fury he aimed at her now.

But this was the real world. Daisy could not run from this. Not anymore. She must meet him head on, face his anger, and show him anger of her own. For yes, she *was* angry with Frank. Still angry, even after all these years, that he'd so easily cast her aside, so cavalierly shed himself of responsibility. That old anger only grew when she saw, in the set of his jaw and the fire in his eyes, that she had upset him.

She had upset him? By keeping her son?

There was no other reason for the way he was glaring at her now. Just a few moments ago, he'd been smiling, affable. He'd been keen for her company, even charming. Then he had seen Bertie…

Was Frank seriously surprised that she'd kept her son—their son—with her? He knew her better than that, or he ought to have done. He had to have known, or at least suspected, that she would not give up her baby no matter how much pressure was brought to bear by the mighty Pearsons.

Clearly, Walter hadn't told him of her decision to turn down the Mother-and-Baby home. Why not?

The answer came in an epiphanic flash. Walter had been set a double task: make the problem of Daisy go away, and get rid of the inconvenient baby she carried. He had succeeded in the first, to the extent that Daisy left Fieldhurst and started a new life in Tunbridge Wells, a bigger, more anonymous town where she had, apparently, been out of sight and out of mind. No longer a concern, no longer a reminder of a moment's foolishness.

Walter had, however, failed in the second part of his mission: getting rid of Bertie. The usually irresistible force of the man's will had hit the immovable barrier of Daisy's determination, and he'd been unable to push through. He would not have wanted to admit that, especially to his son. So he'd allowed Frank to spend the last twelve years in ignorant bliss, never knowing that, one day, he might be confronted with his callous misdeeds.

None of which was Daisy's concern.

She pressed her lips together, raised her head, defiantly, then stared back at him with eyes that felt as hard and angry as his were. Frank could glare at her all he liked. He could rage that his will had not been done, and lament that the facade of the good-humored, well-intentioned charmer had crumbled, revealing to the world the brutish cad who had walked away from his responsibilities.

Daisy didn't care. All she cared about was getting through the rest of this afternoon, with as little damage as possible to herself and Bertie. She needed to let Frank know, in no uncertain terms, that he was not now—nor ever would he be—part of Bertie's life. That he was not obligated to them in any way and he could safely return to his life of carefree comfort.

But she couldn't tell him that here. Not with Jean and the others openly listening, watching, hoping for gossip. That could not happen. Not anymore than was already inevitable. Daisy could probably talk her way through what the women had already seen and surmised, and she would do so. She would salvage enough of her reputation to protect Bertie.

To do that, of course, she had to get Frank out of the sight of these women and away from here as soon as she possibly could.

At the same time, she must shut down all of Bertie's questions before he had any chance to ask them. The child stared at Frank, confused and frightened. He had to have seen what Frank must also have seen: the likeness between them was marked. Nobody could mistake it, nobody could see the pair of them together and not know they were closely related.

Although that did not mean people—Bertie— needed to know that Frank was his father. Related, yes. But Bertie also looked like Harry, and Harry was only an uncle. If she could pass off Frank as an uncle…

Lord, but the lies were never-ending. They piled, each one adding to a wall, hiding and protecting the one behind it. Then again, what was the alternative? Tell Bertie this was his father? How could she do that? After all the times she'd told him, and everyone else, that she had lost his father in the war.

Daisy had, she realized now, always been careful to word it thus. She'd "lost" his father. She had never once said Bertie's father had been killed. It was almost as if that was some sort of talisman; if she didn't say he was dead, she didn't make him so. A strange superstition, like never crying off an obligation with the excuse that you were ill, because then you *would* become ill.

The absurdity of that had her struggling not to laugh at herself. Becoming ill because guilt at your lie ate at you and made you ill was one thing. You couldn't make someone else die because you said they'd been killed. Who did she think she was? God?

Besides, the distinction was mealy-mouthed, and she knew it. Lost? Killed? Both sounded like the lies they were. And whichever word she used, the truth was now going to hurt her son. She could see it, chipping away at his innocence, turning his trust in her to a pile of rubble.

Head high, refusing to be cowed by Frank, or by the women nearby, Daisy walked along the road toward her home. Bertie walked at her side. He said nothing, as if he sensed now was neither the place nor the time, though the look on his face said there'd be questions aplenty later.

He didn't hold her hand. Then again, he hadn't done that willingly for a long time. He was too grown up for such childish nonsense, even when she could see, by the way he chewed at his bottom lip and kept glancing at Frank, that he was feeling far from grown up. He was a scared, small child whose world had imploded, and for that, she hated Frank. Hated Walter. Hated herself.

In just a few minutes, they reached the place she'd called home since November 1914. Once she turned down the Mother-and-Baby home, Walter had found this place for her, paid the first year's rent, then walked away and forgotten her.

He wanted her to leave the area, said he had friends in Buckinghamshire who would find her a cottage. Daisy refused it. She didn't want to move so far from everything she knew. She wanted to be nearby when— she always said *when*, not *if*—her father returned. Tunbridge Wells wasn't Fieldhurst, but it was near enough to be familiar. Dad would be able to find her here.

Walter had objected. Of course he had. He wanted her gone. It was liberating to realize he couldn't force her to go. Once he'd terminated her employment and agreed terms, he no longer held any power over her. The lesson came hard to him. She saw it in his displeasure, in his tense jaw, the jump of the muscle in his cheek, the rigidity of his shoulders.

He tried to force her to his will, but he was careless. He drew up his agreement with her, but he hadn't dotted every *i* and crossed every *t*. Daisy took petty delight in besting him. It wasn't something to be proud of, not really, but even so, a victory over Walter Pearson was to be savored.

He tried to coerce her with threats to Dad. But it was because of Dad she wanted to stay close. When he returned, he would want to be near Daisy and her baby. He certainly wouldn't want to be the reason she moved away. If he came home and she was gone, he would have left Walter's employ to follow her anyway, so Walter's threat to fire him was toothless.

Finding her the rooms in this boarding house had been Walter's last act of revenge. He deliberately found a building that was run down, in need of repair. Then, as now, its walls had been patched with damp, which darkened some bricks and left others the brighter red they were supposed to be. Here and there, between the bricks, there were gaps where the mortar had crumbled away. The door looked solid enough, but it sagged on its hinges, and there was a gap at top and bottom where daylight shone in. Daisy suspected the wood of the door was kept in one piece only by the layers of paint the landlady's son applied with monotonous regularity. The sash windows didn't fit properly either, and they rattled on a stiff breeze.

However, for all the building's faults, the interior was kept clean, and the landlady herself was a decent woman who had been nothing but kind.

All in all, Daisy thought now, Walter could have done much worse by her.

Not that Frank would see it like that, of course. She looked up at the three-story building and envisaged it through his eyes. Narrow and tall, rundown. Mold grew under the eaves, and there was a strong smell of damp. Although the door gleamed, the windows were not so well cared for, and the paint on them bubbled and peeled, exposing bare wood. The garden path was uneven, some slabs sunken, some cracked, and the well-scrubbed doorstep was worn in the middle.

Daisy glanced at Frank and saw the disdain on his face. Did he think this wasn't where his son should be raised? Did he believe she was an inadequate mother who hadn't done right by Bertie? Would he use this place and its obvious flaws to take her child from her?

She tamped down the panic at that thought. He wouldn't do any such thing. Frank hadn't wanted anything to do with Bertie before. Not in 1914, when the baby had still been an abstract concept, something growing within her, easy to dismiss. And not in the years since. Not once had Frank made any effort to seek her out, to discover how she fared, to learn what had happened to his child. So why would he want to involve himself now?

Still, she wished she hadn't brought him here. She wished they could have gone somewhere else. Somewhere that would have made him believe she was doing well, that she and Bertie had thrived without him.

But where else was there? There was nowhere else. She couldn't have walked him back into town to a tea shop. Not only could she not afford that, but the tea shops would be closing now. Besides, they needed privacy for this talk. Bad enough Bertie would be there, hearing everything, without others eavesdropping too. At least, if they were at home, Bertie could go into his bedroom to do his homework, giving her and Frank a modicum of space.

On that thought, she pushed open the front door and led Frank up the stairs to the first floor, to the home she, Bertie, and Dad now shared.

****

Frank stared at the house, astounded. This was where Daisy lived? He could have given her and her son so much more than this. They could have lived in comfort, with more than enough for their needs. She wouldn't have had to work, either.

What was so wrong with him that all of that was not enough to tempt her?

The stairs she led him up were steep and narrow, uncovered wooden treads and a loose banister to hold on to. The walls in the hallway had once been white but had faded to grey over the years, and there were obvious patches of mold where wall met ceiling. The floorboards on the landing were uneven, and they creaked when he walked on them. There was the faintest hint of soap in the air, mixed with the musty dampness.

Daisy unlocked a door halfway along the landing and pushed it open. She ushered the boy inside, having to take his shoulder because he was so intent on staring at Frank. The boy's eyes were narrowed with suspicion, and his whole body tensed. He looked as if he was about to spring an attack on Frank, even though he was less than half his size.

Guided by Daisy, the boy went inside. She followed him, then stood, holding the door open in silent invitation for Frank.

The room was barely ten feet squared. It was light, thanks to a sash window taking up almost a quarter of the outer wall. Beneath the window was a table, surrounded by three chairs. To the side of the table was a kitchen area with a cupboard on the wall, a stove, and facilities for washing up and for preparing food. Beside the door was a wooden bench made homey by the cushions spread over it. Underneath the bench Frank saw blankets and sheeting, neatly folded, along with a pillow. Did that mean it doubled as Daisy's bed? He looked around again. If this was the only room she had to live in, he supposed it must do.

But if she slept there, where did the boy sleep? They couldn't both fit on that narrow seat, even if the boy had still been young enough to share his mother's bed. Did he sleep on the floor? Or did he use the bench while Daisy took the floor?

Shame washed over Frank. He should have looked for Daisy. When he returned after the war, he should have tried harder to find her, to make sure she was all right. He'd taken far too much for granted. But then, why would he not have done? She'd left him and, he'd been told, married another man. Daisy certainly had never written to him to say otherwise.

His justifications felt hollow. Having offered for her and been accepted, he'd had a duty to care for her, and he should have made sure she was all right. Frank had failed her.

Daisy crossed to a second door in the far corner and opened it. He felt some relief that they had access to two rooms. The pair of them were not living exclusively in this one small space.

"Bertie," she said, in a tone that reminded Frank of his childhood nurse. It said, "I'm in charge, I'm telling you to do something, and I will brook no opposition, though I expect you will try." Absurdly, Frank wondered if the voice came naturally to a woman with children in her charge. True, he'd never heard his mother use it, but then, Mother had never taken charge of the children. Why would she, when Walter could afford to employ nurses?

"Bertie, please go to your room, and do your homework," said Daisy.

Bertie. His son's name was Bertie. No doubt in memory of her father.

"But, Mum…" Bertie began.

Daisy said nothing. She stood, hands on hips, eyebrow raised above a "don't-argue" stare.

"Yes, Mum," said the boy. He dragged his feet but went into the room. Daisy closed the door behind him.

And just that suddenly, she and Frank were alone. Unchaperoned. Not even by a boy of… what was he? Ten? Eleven? A quick calculation told Frank he must be eleven, or near to it.

Daisy cleared her throat, pulling Frank from his musings. She moved from Bertie's door to the tiny stove in the opposite corner. "I can…" She cleared her throat again, removing the nervous huskiness from her voice. "Would you like a cup of tea?"

That left Frank more unsure than ever. He didn't know the protocol for this. Did he say yes, pretend this was a social call, and keep everything on a superficially civilized level? Or did he decline, and act as though this was a business meeting?

Should he accept? He could see for himself that Daisy had very little. Tea was not as expensive as it had once been, not in relative terms, but if you lived hand-to-mouth in two rooms, was it a luxury? If he said yes, would he take something she couldn't really afford to give? If he said no, would he insult her?

Before he could decide, the door behind him opened and he heard a man's tread. Frank whirled around, expecting to see Daisy's…husband? Lover? The man who had taken Frank's place in Bertie's life.

For the second time in less than half an hour, he was rendered speechless. He stood rooted to the spot in shock, his eyes painfully wide, his mouth gaping open. For there, in the doorway, was a man he'd thought had died more than ten years ago, at the Somme.

Albert Redmond.

Chapter Eleven

The man in front of Frank was older than he remembered. Of course he was; it had been twelve years since he'd last seen him, but this man had aged far more than that. Shockingly so.

Albert Redmond, Walter's chauffeur, had been a portly man, his uniform jacket always stretched over a sizable paunch. That paunch was gone now, and instead of a robust man, Frank faced a thin one. Emaciated, even. His shoulders were stooped, as if standing straight required too much effort. It accented his sunken chest, while his lined face was an unhealthy grey. His hair was still thick, but where it had been a deep chestnut, similar to his daughter's, it was now a dull carrot color, streaked through with white. He had a slight wheeze, and he smelled of beer and tobacco, although the tobacco smell came from his clothes, not his breath. His eyes were rheumy, and his nose too long for his face, thanks to the lack of flesh below the skin of his cheeks.

It took Albert a second or two to recognize Frank, presumably because Frank was the last person he expected to see here. When recognition came, however, it was immediately followed by a loathing anger.

The feeling was mutual. Daisy might have left Frank, she might have hidden his son from him, but this man had done far worse. He had allowed Frank's mother to believe that he'd died, that his death was a result of her husband's actions in forming the Pearson's Pals, which, somehow, made it her fault, too.

Sarah Pearson had grieved this man's loss as she would have grieved a family member. She'd been so upset that even the mention of his daughter's name last night had sent her to bed with a migraine.

How could Albert have been so cruel as to allow that?

Before Frank could voice his shock, anger, and disgust, though, Albert's temper exploded. His face changed from grey to a mottled red and his eyes lit with unholy fire, while spittle formed on his lips and his whole being quivered. He raised an accusing finger toward Frank and called him a name Frank had never heard outside a barrack room.

"Get out!" he shouted. For someone who looked so frail, his voice was strong and clear.

"Dad," said Daisy.

"Get. Out!"

"I brought him here," argued Daisy.

"You'd no right," Albert told her. "He's no right to be here."

Frank took a breath, his first for an eternity, as the shock left and feeling rushed back in.

"He shouldn't be near you," he yelled at Daisy. "You owe him nothing!"

Daisy said something Frank didn't catch, because his attention was drawn to the door to Bertie's room, which opened slowly. Frank's stomach flipped. The child didn't need to hear this vitriol. He shouldn't be subjected to such anger, especially when his mother was in the thick of it. The thought occurred that this might be a normal scene in Bertie's life. That sickened Frank.

"He should be flogged," Albert said.

Which made no sense. Frank had done nothing to deserve a flogging. Unless one counted getting Daisy pregnant. Her father would have been angry at that. But Frank had planned to marry her. It wasn't his fault he'd been denied the chance.

Bertie stood in the doorway, clutching the jamb. His eyes were wide and frightened, and Frank felt guilty. This was his fault. He shouldn't have come here and upended the child's world. If he'd left well enough alone... He wished he could turn back the clock. Then he could drive by the school, refuse to stop when he saw Daisy, and avoid everything that had happened since.

A moment later, Daisy saw Bertie. She crossed the room and shooed the child away. "Do your homework," she commanded. "Stay in there till I call you."

The boy looked as if he would argue, but in the end, he said nothing. He simply glared at Frank, his face murderous. Frank's heart broke.

Daisy pushed Bertie gently into the room and shut the door, then turned back. Her father's torrent of abuse had stopped, not because he'd run out of things to say, and not because his anger had run its course, but because it had turned into a fit of hacking coughs and tight wheezes. His complexion went from red to purple, and there was a blue tinge to his lips.

Instinctively, Frank stepped forward to help him, though what he could do, he didn't know. He didn't have the knowledge to deal with this, though he'd seen plenty of men afflicted in the same way, when he'd visited Harry in the hospital. Those men's lungs had been ruined by mustard gas. It seemed Albert's were the same, and Frank could not stand by and watch him struggle.

Before he reached him, though, Daisy pushed Frank away and did the job herself. Just as well, thought Frank, now he thought about it, because his attempt to help would surely have further fueled Albert's anger and made things worse.

"Calm down, Dad," soothed Daisy, as she guided him to a dining chair. "Breathe slowly." As she spoke, she slowed her own breathing, demonstrating what she meant.

Albert wheezed and panted, though he did try to slow it down. Daisy handed him a paper bag. He held it over his lower face, the open end crunched around his nose and mouth. The sides of the bag billowed in and out as he breathed, then rebreathed the air inside it.

He took it away from his face and glared at Frank once more. "Why is he here?"

Daisy steered the bag back to her father's face. "I invited him. Breathe, Dad." She looked over her shoulder at Frank. He thought she would tell him to go, but she didn't. "Make yourself useful." She nodded at the kitchen. "Light the stove and fill the kettle from that jug. I take it you can do that?"

Frank bristled at the implication that he was useless, but he moved to the stove and carried out her orders.

"He's trouble, Dais," said Albert. His breathing was still not normal, but it didn't sound critical anymore. "You shouldn't have brought him here."

The bag rustled as she pushed it back to his face again, and told him to breathe. Frank opened the cupboard and found the teapot and tea caddy, then measured tea leaves from one to the other: a spoon for each drinker and one for the pot. His only hesitation was wondering how many drinkers there would be. He wasn't sure Albert would want Frank drinking with them.

In the end, he put a spoonful in for himself. If he was denied the chance to drink it, Daisy could have a second cup. She would probably need it.

"Hasn't he hurt you enough, girl?" asked Albert.

Frank frowned. What did Albert mean? What did he think Frank had done to hurt Daisy? He'd done nothing to hurt her. Well, yes, he'd got her pregnant and he hadn't married her, but then, he'd hardly been in a position to do so at the time, and it wasn't him who had run away afterward. He would have hoped that both Daisy and Albert knew him well enough to realize he would not have abandoned her deliberately. He would have put things right, if she'd given him the chance.

"We're just going to talk, Dad," she said.

Albert gave a wheezy chuckle which held no humor. "Bet he said that the last time, too."

Frank turned to see Daisy's face burn scarlet at her father's crude words. He wouldn't stand for anyone treating her that way. Not even her father. He opened his mouth to remonstrate with the man, but changed his mind when he saw the look Daisy gave him. Outwardly calm, her eyes were filled with a morass of emotion. She was upset and angry, uncertain and scared.

Albert, on the other hand, was suspicious and angry, and ready to jump in and start the fight all over again.

Daisy shook her head, silently pleading with Frank to remember Albert was a sick man. Frank took a deep breath and calmed himself before he spoke.

"I don't want to cause trouble," he said. "But that is my son in there. You can't deny it."

"I'm not—" began Daisy.

Albert cut her off. He jumped to his feet, his face reddening again. "Your son?" he demanded. "Your. Son? You lost the right to call him that when you sent your dad to do your dirty work for you!"

He coughed and pushed the paper bag to his face again. Over its rim, his eyes bored into Frank's, and Frank saw how much Albert hated showing him his weakness.

"Dad!" Daisy was angry now, too. Angry at Albert. She had clearly not wanted him to say what he'd just said. And anyway, his words made no sense. What dirty work?

"Couldn't do it yourself," panted Albert, between inhalations. "Had to hide behind his coattails, didn't you?"

"Dad, that's enough!" Daisy said, at the same moment that Frank asked, "What do you mean?"

Albert overrode them both. "Not that he minded. Oh, no! Not Walter Pearson! Did it willingly, he did. Gleefully."

"Did what?" Frank felt like he had slipped into some sort of fevered dream, the kind where nothing makes sense and everything whirls around like a carousel, spinning far too fast and out of control.

Daisy shoved the paper bag to Albert's face again.

Albert pulled it away. "Don't you come the innocent with me, you lying bastard! Excuse my French, Dais, but he's enough to make a saint swear. And I'm calling him no more than what he is." He glared at Frank. "It won't work with me. I'm not green enough to fall for your lies."

"I never lied—"

Albert threw out a laugh that ended in another cough. Daisy pushed the bag at him. He inhaled and brought it away again. Behind Frank, the kettle began to roar dully.

"You come here, large as life and twice as ugly. I don't know how you have the nerve." He mimicked Frank, nastily. " 'That's my son.' As if it makes any difference."

"Enough!" Daisy insisted. Albert glanced up at her and, for a moment, stopped his diatribe, though whether that was because she'd told him to or because he needed to catch his breath Frank could not have said.

For himself, he struggled to make sense of it all. He did understand Albert's anger that Frank had fathered Daisy's child outside wedlock. Frank was certain he'd feel the same if he had a daughter. But he hadn't lied. There hadn't been any "dirty work." And what had it to do with Walter?

Albert drew breath and began again. "Did you think Walter would do the decent thing? Pay her off properly? See she was all right? Of course you didn't. You didn't care. Chip off the old block, that's what you are."

Frank had had enough. This conversation made no sense. It was time to slow it down, inject some rationality, although his anger at being called a chip off the old block didn't help. He took a breath and pushed past that.

"What has Walter to do with anything?" he asked. It seemed the most pressing question, since Walter's involvement seemed to be the catalyst for Albert's anger.

"Mum? Grandad?" The little voice was high pitched with fear.

Daisy turned, saw her son in the doorway again, then rounded on both Frank and Albert. "Now look what you've done," she accused, her voice low, which emphasized her anger. She turned back to Bertie. Frank saw the strained smile she gave the boy. It pulled at her cheeks, but did not trouble her eyes. "Go back to your room, Bertie," she said.

Bertie's bottom lip quivered but he lifted his chin, defiantly. "What's happening? Who's he?" He glanced at Frank, then back to Daisy. "Is he my dad?"

"I'll explain later," promised Daisy. "Now, do as I say."

"But…"

"Do as your mother tells you," roared Albert.

The boy gasped and jumped, but he didn't run. Daisy opened her mouth, fury in her eyes, directed at Albert. Before she could say anything, though, Albert redirected his anger to Frank. "And you," he shouted. "Get out! Go on! Run back to Daddy! See if he can fix it for you again, why don't you? Who knows? He might actually succeed in killing me this time."

"Dad!" Daisy's voice was a mix of horror and anger.

"Grandad!" Bertie sobbed.

Frank could say nothing. He was too stunned.

"Go on!" yelled Albert. "Get out!" He began to cough again, more ferociously than before. He lifted the bag to his face himself, not waiting for Daisy's intervention, which told Frank he was getting worse. Every breath the older man took was labored, although that didn't stop him glaring as if he wanted to knock seven bells out of Frank. Frank suspected a large part of his rage was frustration that his body wouldn't let him do exactly that.

Meanwhile, Bertie stood resolutely in his doorway. He was distressed and angry, worried for his grandfather and his mother. He clearly hated Frank, blaming him for everything. The child was frightened, but determined to stand his ground. Frank felt a surge of pride rush through him. Pride that this young lion was his son. Even though he'd had no hand in raising him, or shaping him in any way.

Daisy was crying, the tears openly flowing over her cheeks. She rubbed at the tip of her nose with the back of her hand, not even bothering to look for a handkerchief.

As for Frank, he was in turmoil. He didn't know which way to turn, what to do or say for the best. What questions to ask. His head ached and his neck and shoulders hurt from the rigidity in them. The only thing he did know was that there would be no more talking today. Not between him and Daisy. Certainly not with Albert. The man looked one bout of anger away from an apoplexy. Frank didn't want that. He could not be responsible for that. Which meant a tactical retreat was his only option.

"I'll go now," he said. "We'll talk another time."

"You'll leave her alone," said Albert.

Frank didn't answer. He turned and walked from the room, pulling the door closed behind him, and leaving the little family to sort themselves out. He would seek out Daisy when her father wasn't there, with his unreasonable anger and outlandish accusations. It would probably be for the best if Bertie wasn't with them, either. Although that hurt. Now he knew he had a son, Frank wanted to spend time with him.

Perhaps Daisy would permit that, once everything else was resolved.

He caught his breath and let his heartbeat slow before he made his way to the stairs to leave. An elderly lady, presumably the landlady, stood at the bottom. She held a poker in her hand and she brandished it at Frank like a cosh.

"What's going on up there?" she asked. "Who are you? You don't belong here. I run a respectable establishment, I do."

Frank came further down the stairs and the woman took a step back, the only hint that she felt any fear. "I've sent for the police," she said. Something in her tone told Frank she hadn't. She wouldn't want the police here, hinting at disorder within her walls. Not unless it became absolutely necessary. Reputation was everything, even for the owner of a seedy boarding house.

He didn't want them called, either, so he held up his hands in the universal sign of surrender. "I'm leaving."

She pressed herself against the wall, the poker gripped tightly, ready for her defense. Frank ignored her. He glanced back up the stairs, as if he would be able to see Daisy, or Bertie, through the walls. His heart hurt, and there was a lump in his throat as big and hard as a piece of coal.

Frank had been hurt before. Of course he had. How could he not have been? He'd gone through four years of hellish war. Four long years, watching men he loved like brothers fall, while the world shattered.

Then there had been the heartache of losing Daisy the first time. The pain of that had brought him to his knees.

Add the months when it seemed Harry would die from his wartime injuries, and the years of healing his youngest brother had struggled through afterward.

Heartbreak, and worry, and devastation.

Not once, in all those times, had he felt as lost and

alone as he did right now.

"Don't come back," called the landlady. "This is a respectable establishment."

He didn't answer as he walked away.

He was halfway back to Camden Road when he heard the click-click-click of someone running in heels. He looked over his shoulder and saw Daisy. Her face was pink with exertion, and her hair poked out from under a hat that looked to have been jammed on her head in a hurry. Her coat was unbuttoned, and she wasn't wearing gloves.

Frank stopped. He watched as she caught up to him, then stood, catching her breath.

"There was a time," she breathed, then swallowed, "I could have run that and more."

Despite the misery of the afternoon, Frank laughed.

"It's not funny," she said.

"You're getting old, Daisy."

She gave him an old-fashioned look. "Same as you are."

"I'm not the one wheezing like an old Puffin' Billy."

"You're also not running up the road in Louis heels."

He grinned. She grinned back, no doubt remembering the years when such teasing banter was *de rigueur* between them.

After a moment, though, the smile fell from her face and she huffed out a deep breath. "We still need to talk," she said.

She was right. They did need to talk. But they would be better off somewhere more private than the street. The trouble was, where could they go? Frank would not be welcome at Daisy's home. Albert had made that clear.

Even if he hadn't, Frank didn't think the landlady would take too kindly to his reappearance.

To his knowledge, there were no tea shops in the immediate vicinity, and the ones he did know of would be closed now, since it was after five. He wouldn't feel comfortable having a heart-to-heart in a pub, where privacy was not guaranteed. Besides, in a pub in this neighborhood, they were likely to encounter strikers, men who would see Frank as the enemy, and he had better things to do than sidestep trouble every few minutes.

There really was only one place where they could talk, candidly and without listeners.

"Let's go and sit in my van," he said, then winced at the way it sounded.

Daisy chuckled at his obvious discomfort. "You know how to treat a girl, don't you?"

"I meant—"

"I know what you meant. Where is it?"

"Near the school."

Chapter Twelve

They walked, side by side, without speaking. Her heels clacked against the pavement, brisk and businesslike. As she walked, she buttoned her coat, so that she looked more the respectable woman she was and less the hurried hoyden.

Frank fought the urge to take her hand in his. Which was absurd. They had never walked hand in hand, even when they'd been friends—more than friends. Still, the desire to do so now was strong enough that he clasped his hands behind his back so he couldn't reach for her. She thrust her own gloveless hands into her pockets, and he wondered if she felt the same urge to touch him, to be closer to him.

Immediately, he dismissed the idea. Daisy had shown no inclination to be close to him on the other occasions when they'd met this week. She hadn't even been pleased to see him, so she was unlikely to want to touch him. It did him no good whatsoever to pretend otherwise.

The van sat on the side of the road, next to the school fence. The playground was empty and forlorn, the building dark against the fading light, no sign of the life and noise and exuberance of the children who occupied it by day. It gave this part of the road a sad, dejected atmosphere, which made him shudder. It seemed to go with the mood of their coming talk.

He helped Daisy into the passenger seat, then climbed in on the driver's side of the vehicle. The crank handle lay on the bench between them, solid and heavy, and he wondered, briefly, if he should put it out of her reach. With the dagger looks she'd given him, and the anger Albert had poured on him on her behalf, he wasn't certain she wouldn't try to brain him with it.

Though why would she? Frank hadn't done anything to warrant such treatment. Nor had Daisy ever shown him she had a violent side. Then again, Albert had always been affable and easy to get along with in the past.

Speaking of Albert was as good a place to start as any. "I was shocked to see your father today."

Daisy frowned. "Why? Where did you think he lived?"

Frank opened his mouth, then closed it again. It didn't seem the best thing to say to the man's daughter: *Your father is supposed to be dead.*

"Where did you think he lived," she repeated, when he didn't answer, "if not with me? It's not like he had any other family to go to, is it?"

"Um, no." Frank shifted, turning toward her. "I'm sorry, I—I expect this sounds crass, but I was told he'd…died."

Daisy's eyes widened with shock.

"In the war." Frank cleared his throat and wished he hadn't started this.

She took a moment to compose herself. Took a few deep breaths. Folded her arms across her chest, and stared through the windscreen. Her chin trembled. Frank wanted to say he was sorry, but he wasn't sure what he'd be apologizing for. He *had* believed Albert had died.

That *was* what he'd been told. Although perhaps he shouldn't have blurted it out like that. He could have been more diplomatic.

Thank God he'd learned the truth before he'd gone all the way and offered his condolences.

After a moment, Daisy nodded. Her voice was calm. Unnaturally so. "He survived."

Frank nodded. Survival in itself was something of a miracle. Albert had been at the Somme. So had Frank. Images of the place rushed through him now, forcing him to remember.

The trenches, carved across the landscape like scars on a flogged back. The stretches of land between them, covered with barbed wire and trellises, and pocked with craters. The mud, sucking and thick, water seeping into everything, dripping down the walls, soaking a man's clothes so he was never dry, never warm. Men with trench foot: cold, wet feet that itched and tingled, then turned numb and heavy before they swelled to twice their normal size and blistered, festering and gangrenous. The whooshes and whizzes of incoming shells; the bangs and crashes as they exploded; flashes when the guns fired; the moans of the sick and the dying; the sickly stench of blood and pus, urine and dysentery. The ribald jokes and ripe language of men who wouldn't be there to repeat them the next day. The piercing shrill of the officers' whistles, signaling it was time to climb up into that no-man's-land and let the enemy use you for target practice. Advance. Retreat. Advance. Retreat. And, at the end of it, you would be exactly where you were when you started. If you were lucky.

Oh, yes. Survival was a feat, in and of itself.

"Most of the others didn't survive," Daisy

continued, in her flat monotone. "The Pals, I mean. They…"

"I know."

"Dad nearly…" Her voice shook then, and she took a deep breath. "Mustard gas."

Frank closed his eyes. He knew about mustard gas. The noxious fumes that choked, while the chemicals burned and blistered the skin, damaged the eyes, and ate at a man's lungs. It had never been used on Frank and his company, for which he thanked God, because he'd seen plenty of men who had suffered its effects. They'd been wracked by coughs, left with asthma and other respiratory complaints, unable to walk more than a few yards without breathless exhaustion. That Albert had suffered that, was still suffering, from what Frank had seen, was appalling. The man needed help: good care, clean air, a dry home free from anything that might exacerbate his problems.

"The mold in that boarding house can't be good for him," he said, although he hadn't meant to voice his thoughts aloud.

Daisy bristled. "It's a roof over our heads."

"I didn't mean—"

"We can't all live in nice big houses with large, airy rooms."

"I just meant…look, I can help…"

"No, you can't." She glared at him, her eyes filled with venom.

It took him aback, and he swallowed. "Daisy—"

"We are not charity cases," she hissed. "I work to pay for what we have. And, together with Dad's war pension, we get by. We don't want any handouts from you, thank you very much."

Frank opened his mouth to argue further, but closed it again without making a sound. It would do him no good to speak. Daisy had a look about her, a defiant tilt of her head, pursed lips, and a spark in her eyes telling him that if he pushed this, she would only grow more determined.

Anyway, something wasn't right. It didn't make sense. Frank had spent enough time in Walter's offices to know what his retired workers were paid. They weren't wealthy, not amongst the highest paid pensioners in the land, but they had enough to be comfortable. Which meant…

"Albert's company pension on its own should buy you somewhere better than that."

Daisy sniffed. "Yes. Well." She turned her head and stared out of the passenger window.

It didn't add up. Albert had been a good father to Daisy and, Frank was willing to bet, he'd be a good grandfather to Bertie. He wouldn't want them to live in a place like that if he could do anything about it. So why couldn't he do something?

His war wounds were chronic, of course. They would need ongoing treatment and medicine. Was his medical care so expensive the family had had to give up on other necessities to pay for it? Albert had used a paper bag to regulate his breathing today, and Daisy had offered him no medication to alleviate his symptoms. Did that mean he didn't have any medicine to help overcome his condition?

If they were doing without for lack of funds, it was a disgrace, and a blight on the Pearson name. Walter had put together the Pearson's Pals and sent them to fight; if they returned damaged, he had a duty to care for them.

He'd been quick enough to recruit them, after all. He'd even paid the men a bonus for signing up, and "making him proud."

But Albert…Albert should never have been one of them. Walter should never have accepted him. Once he had, he should have been prepared to pay for the consequences.

Which wasn't to say Albert shouldn't own his share of the blame. He had signed up for the fight, after all, though Frank had never understood why. True, just about every man in England had wanted to play his part, but Albert Redmond was no hothead, and he must have known his physical limitations. So why…?

"Why did your dad volunteer?" he asked.

Daisy gave a humorless laugh. "Depends what you mean by 'volunteer.' "

What did that mean? "Are you saying he was forced to go?" Frank could not believe that. Even Walter wouldn't do that.

Daisy gave Frank a stare so cold he almost expected icicles to form on the steering wheel.

"Are you saying he was forced to go?" Frank waited for her to deny it. She had to deny it. It could not be true.

He stared at her, willing her to say that no, Walter had not forced Albert to sign up. The longer she didn't reply, though, the more his doubts grew, and the more he dreaded the answer.

"Let's just say he was strongly encouraged," she said, at last.

A moment went by. Two. Frank didn't know what to say. He could barely think. His stomach bubbled and churned, and a deathly cold crept over him. It seeped into his bones, froze every nerve and sinew. He couldn't even shiver.

Outside, the breeze rattled, pushing eddies of dust through the air. The sun was setting now, bathing the street in a golden glow that gave it an otherworldly beauty it could not possess in full daylight. People walked by, laughing together as they hurried home from work. The world went on, as if nothing had happened to upend it.

If Daisy was telling the truth, Walter had not just knowingly accepted an older, sickly man into his regiment. He'd actively encouraged him to join.

Disgust warred with disbelief. Frank took several deep breaths, willing himself not to be sick. His chest was tied in knots, and his throat burned. He wanted to rail and curse, to shout that it wasn't true. It couldn't be true.

But, whispered a voice in the back of his head, *it sounded true*.

"I didn't know," he said.

She gave a quick laugh of disbelief.

That angered him. Insulted him. That she could think he would have stood by and allowed such a thing to happen was…how could she think that?

Clearly, she did.

"Come on, Dais," he snapped. "You know me better than that!"

"Do I?"

Rage colored her cheeks and glittered in her eyes. Her face hardened, and her shoulders shook, her breath quickened, and her hands formed into fists in her lap. He half expected her to fly at him, and braced himself to ward off her attack. He glanced at the crank handle, lying between them, worried she might pick it up, swing it, and brain him. And if he had been complicit in Walter's crime, Frank wouldn't be able to blame her.

"I thought I knew a lot of things," she said. Her voice was quiet, but it sounded to him as if she shouted. "I thought your dad was a decent man," she went on. "Hard, perhaps. Exacting. But not a murderer. Not a…" She breathed out, heavily. "I thought I knew a lot of things."

"You should have gone to my mother." Frank hadn't been there to help her and Albert. He'd already been at the training camp when the Pals were recruited. But his mother had been there. Daisy could have spoken to her. And yes, he realized Mother deferred to her husband in most things, but she would not have stood by while—

"Your mother knew." Daisy's words were little more than whispers. They detonated in his head like bombs.

No! That was not true. It couldn't be true. Frank could believe such things of his father—Walter Pearson was a self-interested man who had no concern for anybody else. He would happily send someone to die if it benefited him. But Mother was different. She was softer, more caring. More…humane. She would never have countenanced this. And if she'd been unable to stop him going, she would have made sure Albert was looked after on his return. To say otherwise went beyond belief.

He opened his mouth to say just that, but Daisy beat him to it. "I won't say your mother wanted my dad to go to France," she said, flatly. "She probably didn't. But she did nothing to try to stop him going. She did nothing to try to stop your father sending him." Her lips thinned. "None of you did."

That was unfair. What could Frank have done? He

wasn't even living in Fieldhurst when the Pearson's Pals were formed. By the time he knew Walter had gone ahead and acted on his idea, Frank was long gone, the property of His Majesty's Army, with no power to affect anything other than the daily survival of himself and his mates. Sometimes, not even that.

A fatalistic calm swept over him then, and he found himself wondering what all of this mattered now. What purpose did it serve? In Frank's opinion, this entire conversation was twelve years too late. Nothing could be done to change what had happened to Albert, and to the other men who'd fought in that terrible war. It wouldn't be easy to change the future for them, either, if Daisy's reaction to Frank's offer to help was any indication.

We are not charity cases, she'd said. Good, because it wasn't charity Frank offered. It was the duty owed by his family to hers. Something Albert had earned with a lifetime of service. Frank intended to see that Albert, and the others who'd marched through hell on Walter's say-so, received everything they deserved.

But that was a fight for another day. Today, there was another issue at hand. One which needed to be addressed as soon as possible.

"Why didn't you tell me about the baby?" His voice was little more than a whisper. It hurt so much that she hadn't told him. Instead, she'd run from him, given him no chance to help her and, by so doing, had robbed him of his son's childhood. He would never have thought her so vindictive.

"I did tell you."

He glared at her. Another lie. Why on earth would she even try to claim such a thing?

"I did! Don't deny it. I sent you a letter. You sent it

straight to your father." She made a sound that was almost a laugh, but was bitter and totally devoid of humor. "I should have realized before then, of course. Silly little me. It never occurred to me why you were ignoring me, until then."

Frank stilled. Even his breathing slowed to an almost indiscernible level. What she said made no sense. Her accusations went against everything that he was. Everything she *knew* him to be. What was more, it was something he could call her out on.

"I never received any such letter from you, so how could I send it to Walter?"

Daisy didn't back down. She glanced at him, her eyes sparkling with anger. "How did he get it then?" She almost spat the question at him. "Because it was in his hand when he…" She broke off and turned away, not willing, or not able, to complete the sentence.

That wasn't going to fly. "When he what?"

A second ticked by. Two. Three. She didn't turn back to him. Made no effort to answer him.

"When he what, Daisy?"

Still, she did not turn to him.

"What did he do?"

Pieces of the conversation he'd had with Walter last night rattled through his brain.

"She demanded money from us…Saw an eye to the main chance, mercenary little baggage…Wanted recompense, if you please…We gave her six months of her father's wages…Your mother was terribly worried about her."

It hadn't made sense to Frank last night. The Daisy he knew would never have demanded money simply because her father had died. And Walter wouldn't have given it to her if she'd asked. But if she'd been pregnant, and Walter knew it...

"What did he do, Daisy?" he asked, again. "Did he throw you out? Send you packing and tell you never to darken his doorstep again?"

That was far more believable. Walter would never have paid her for Albert's loss. Especially when that loss hadn't actually happened. But if Walter thought Daisy carried Frank's child, if he thought she was a threat to his family's line and reputation, that he could rid himself of her and buy her silence...

That Walter could treat Daisy like that was not a surprise. Nor would it have garnered him much public disapproval. Many men would have reacted as Walter had done—turned her out, paid her off and left her to it. Some, a few, might have forced a marriage, made their son step up and do the right thing. But not Walter. His unshakable belief in the superiority of his family line meant he wouldn't even have considered that possibility.

"Your mother was terribly worried about her."

Did that mean his mother had known? She must have known. Daisy's pregnancy, the taint of an illegitimate child on the family name...that would have worried Mother. But that would mean she, too, had lied about it. In her letters to Frank at the time. In all the years since.

No wonder she'd been so affected yesterday, when he told her he'd seen Daisy.

Daisy, who now sat in his van, fuming at him, believing him as guilty as his parents.

His stomach roiled. His throat closed on hot bile, and the cold, hard lump that had lodged there. His fingers curled into fists. He wanted to hit something. The van's door. The window. Walter's over-privileged, smug face.

It took several deep breaths before the feeling abated, and sanity returned.

Retribution for past sins was not an urgent issue here. Walter could wait. Mother could wait. Even Albert could wait, come to that. Daisy was what mattered to Frank now. Daisy, and Bertie.

When Frank spoke, his voice shook. "I didn't know," he said. He swallowed, and said it again, more firmly this time. "I never received a letter from you." He frowned, and amended that. "I never received any letters from you at all. If I had, I would never have passed them to Walter."

She turned sharply and looked at him, her eyebrows low, face filled with confusion. "But he had it."

"Not from me." Which brought another question to mind. "How about you? Did you get any letters from me?"

Daisy shook her head.

"I sent you…I sent letters. Postcards. My photograph. The one you asked for."

She shook her head again. "I never got anything from you."

"And I never got anything from you." Although, how that could be was beyond him. The Postal Service was reliable. It had been impressively so in wartime. The odd letter or two might have gone astray, but every single one of them? That wasn't possible. Not by accident.

Why would someone intercept and steal every single letter from Frank to Daisy, and her to him? The only person who might have wanted to do such a thing was Walter, and he couldn't have done it. He didn't command the Post Office. So how could it have happened?

There must be a logical explanation, although what that might be was not apparent to him at this moment.

Frank ran a hand over his face. He was confused and bewildered, angry and sad. "I thought you'd changed your mind," he whispered. "That you didn't want me."

Daisy stared at him for several seconds, though he could not discern her feelings. He thought he saw her own anger, mixed with surprise and disbelief, but an instant later, it was as if a shutter had come down, hiding her from him. "It's old news, isn't it?" she said.

He shook his head. "No. It's not." He didn't want it dismissed, pushed away like that. He wanted to know exactly what had happened, and when, and why. He needed the truth.

"Just leave it, Frank," she said. "It's gone. Long gone. Past fixing." She stared out through the windscreen at the gathering gloom. It would be fully dark soon. Harry would wonder where he was. He'd be worried about him.

Frank would make amends with Harry later. He had a feeling his brother would understand.

"Your father had my letter to you," she continued. Her bottom lip quivered, but her voice was steady, the tone strong.

Frank could feel his temper rising. "He may have done, but I didn't give it to him!" He almost shouted the words. How could he say them more clearly? How could he make her believe him?

He took a deep breath and forced himself to calm down. "I didn't send him anything," he continued. "I didn't write to him at all. Not once, in all the time I was away. I had no contact with him." He pushed his hand through his hair, as if that might push the frustration behind him. "Lord above, Daisy. You know I don't get along with him. Never did. So why would I send him something so personal, that was between us, and nothing to do with him?"

She sighed, heavily, and put her hand on the door handle. His gaze dropped to it and willed her to stay. He needed her to stay. It was, suddenly, the most important thing in the world to him.

He reached out and touched her arm. She looked down at his fingers, calloused from his work for Harry. His driving gloves were in his jacket pocket. He should have put them on by now. He was glad he hadn't.

Daisy stilled. His fingers were curled around her forearm, yes, but his grip was not tight. If she didn't want him to hold on to her, she could easily shake him off.

She didn't. She didn't move at all, except for the tiny flutter of the pulse at the base of her neck, the soft parting of her lips, the rise and fall of her chest. Her eyes met his, wary, uncertain, and yet there was something in them, something he could not define.

He wasn't aware of moving along the bench. Wasn't aware that she had moved, either. But suddenly, there they were, just a few inches apart. So close, he could see the tiny freckles on her nose, the long, dark lashes ringing her eyes, the tiny wisps of hair that escaped her hat and curled against her flushed cheek. The air filled with the scent of her: clean and fresh, a mix of sugar soap and fresh air, and the sweet, never changing essence that would always be hers alone.

Frank leaned in toward her. Daisy leaned in toward him.

The kiss was like coming home. Her mouth was soft

and full, cushioning his. She tasted of tea and strawberry jam, a sign she had not eaten since they'd shared elevenses in the tea shop. He wrapped an arm around her shoulders, holding her close to him. Her arms came around his neck, her fingers tickling the ends of his hair where they met the collar of his shirt. Shivers ran through him as the tiniest moan escaped her.

His tongue touched her lips and she opened them, letting him in. The warmth of her mouth welcomed him, her tongue dancing alongside his, touching, withdrawing, touching again. His body hardened. His fingers stroked the silky skin of her neck, then moved upward, dislodging her hat, caressing her soft, warm hair. His other arm pulled her toward him, closer, closer...

Something hard and unyielding pressed against his thigh. She must have felt it too, because her kiss stopped, abruptly. She tensed and her eyes flew open, full of shock and horror as she pulled away. Her breaths were shallow, fast, repulsed.

What the hell had he just done?

They both lowered their gazes, his in shame, hers in...fear? Confusion? He couldn't say.

He looked down and saw the crank handle, pressing hard and insistent against his thigh. And hers. Inside, he groaned at his own crass nature. Taking liberties like this, in the cab of a van, on a public street, where any Jack and his Jill might see them! It might have been better if she had brained him with it. Knocked some sense into him, before he...

"I'll put it right," he blurted.

Put what right?

Not that he'd kissed her. He wouldn't apologize for

that. He shouldn't have done it, he knew, but he wasn't sorry.

Daisy's eyes narrowed. She looked…angry. At what? The kiss? Or his promise to put it right? Lord, he hoped…

"You'll put what right?" Her voice was quiet, even, dangerous. This was, he realized, momentous. If he said the wrong thing now…

He wasn't sorry for the kiss. He would not pretend to be. It wasn't the thing that needed putting right, and it wasn't what he'd meant when he'd said that.

"Everything," he answered her, and felt the truth of it deep in his bones. "I'll deal with Walter." And with Mother, if it came to that. "I'll find somewhere better for you to live. Somewhere that won't make your dad ill."

This time, she grabbed his arm, but her touch was not gentle. It was rough and hard and angry, just like the look in her eyes. "I told you, we're not charity cases."

Her words were forced between clenched teeth. They came at him with the rhythm and anger of bullets from a machine gun.

He ignored them.

"And then," he continued, decisively, "we'll marry."

Chapter Thirteen

Daisy stared at Frank, astounded. He would put it all right, and then they would marry? Who did he think he was? Clearly, Frank saw himself as some silver knight on a white charger, armor gleaming and feathers streaming as he galloped to the rescue of the damsel in distress. Which, apparently, was her.

Not if she had anything to say to it. If there was any rescuing to be done, Daisy would do it herself. She didn't need a knight in armor to see her through. Knights in armor weren't even real. They lived between the pages of fairy tales, not in the back streets of Tunbridge Wells. Besides, Frank was, to put it mildly, too late to try and save the day. Twelve years too late, to be precise.

He would put it all right! As if he could.

Even if his kiss had left her senses reeling and her wits scattered to the four winds.

She'd like to say he'd taken her by surprise, caught her with her guard down, but that would be a lie. He hadn't sprung on her like a tiger from ambush, taking down a deer. His moves had been slow, deliberate, giving her plenty of time to back away, to refuse him. And if she had, he would have let her. He would have held up his hands, retreated to his corner, and released her.

Daisy hadn't wanted him to release her. She'd wanted that kiss as much as he had. She had wanted—

needed—him to touch his warm lips to hers, savored the feel of his stubble, harsh and raspy against her cheek, his soft hair beneath her fingers, his tongue dancing with hers, a shadow of that night in the summerhouse, when…

No! That had been a different time, when she was a different woman. The whole world had changed since then.

Even if she was able to turn back the clock, it would be impossible to undo the damage and hurt of the last twelve years. It couldn't be done. Walter Pearson had decreed things should be as they were, and his will was not easily pushed aside.

Nor, for that matter, was Albert Redmond's. He didn't have Walter's reach, of course, nor his power. But he had as much pride as his former employer. He was not about to let Frank, or anyone else in the Pearson family, find somewhere better, that wouldn't make him ill. Albert would rather sleep under the bandstand in the Calverley Grounds than take a Pearson up on such an offer.

And as for dictating that she and Frank would marry…

"No." The word was strong and decisive, and left no room for doubt.

It clearly took Frank by surprise. He blinked. "No?"

"No," she repeated. "We will *not* marry."

He opened his mouth to speak, his objection clear on his face.

"If and when I ever marry," she continued, before he could say anything, "it will be because I choose to do so. Because I've met someone I want to spend my life with, someone who makes me happy. It certainly will not be because some bombastic idiot says so."

"I didn't…" He frowned. "I didn't mean it like that. It wasn't my intention."

She sniffed. "Seem to be a lot of things you don't intend."

He sighed. "I'm sorry if I sounded 'bombastic.' But you must see—"

"What I see," she said, turning to fully face him, "is a man who didn't want to marry me before—"

"I did!"

"And now," she ignored his outburst, "thinks he should do it to assuage his conscience. Well, I am nobody's Hail Mary."

"That isn't why…" Frank pressed his lips together. She could see his frustration in the tightness of his jaw and the tic of the muscle in his cheek. "What about the boy?"

Oh, no. He was not going to use Bertie to make her feel guilty. Daisy would not be manipulated like that. And anyway…the *boy*?

"Bertie," she said. "The *boy*'s name is Bertie."

"Bertie," he acknowledged. "I can provide for Bertie."

Daisy wished she could tell him to take a running jump. She wanted to say she didn't need him to provide for Bertie, that they'd do perfectly well without Frank, but she couldn't. Not only did she not have the wherewithal to refuse his help for their son, she didn't have the right. Bertie deserved the best life possible, and she could not provide that. Not on her own. No matter how much she gave up to make sure he had all he needed, there would always be some things that were beyond her. Frank could provide those things.

Even so, this was not a conversation she wanted to

have. Not now. She was raw from all that had happened this afternoon, and there was little fight left in her. She needed to regroup, to recover her nerve before she faced him in another skirmish.

"Do we have to talk about this now?" she asked. "I have a pounding headache, and I still have to cook supper for Dad and Bertie."

To say nothing of working out what I'll tell him. How do I make all this understandable to a boy of his age?

"I'd like to meet him," said Frank. "Properly, I mean."

"Frank—"

"He's my son, Daisy. I'd like to know him."

She nodded, unenthusiastically. "Give me time." When it looked as if he would argue, she added, "Monday. Come after school on Monday." By then, she would have worked things out with Albert, if nothing else.

Without waiting for his answer, she thrust open the van door, climbed down to the road, and hurried away. Behind her, she heard Frank's door open, heard him call her name. She didn't look back and, thankfully, he didn't follow her.

Albert and Bertie were sitting at the table when she got home. Bertie had his homework in front of him, and he made a show of concentrating on it. Albert played Patience. Silently, he moved a row of cards from one pile to another. Both worked too hard at not looking up when she came in.

"Dinner won't be long," she said. They didn't answer. She hung her coat and hat on the back of the door, then crossed to the kitchen. "The wind's getting up out there." Neither of them acknowledged her small talk. She put the kettle on the hob and checked the teapot. It still had the leaves Frank had spooned in earlier. "You can't beat a cuppa, can you?"

"Has he gone?" asked Albert. He stared at her, his eyes full of accusation.

She nodded.

"Was that my dad?" Bertie's question was quiet and flat, lacking in fanfare. Absurdly, Daisy thought there should have been fanfare. Such a big question deserved a dramatic entrance.

"Not in any way that matters," muttered Albert.

"Dad!" Daisy gave Albert a warning glare. He turned over the next three cards and slapped them onto the table. She smiled, too brightly, at Bertie. "How's your homework coming on?"

"You said you lost him in the war," scowled the boy.

Daisy sighed. Clearly, her son was not to be deterred. "I did."

It was the truth. She had lost Frank in the war. The boy he'd been, the promise he'd held, all they'd meant to one another, it was all buried in Flanders' Fields. Dead and gone, as surely as if he'd fallen to the German guns.

"I thought you meant he was dead," insisted Bertie.

"Just lost. Finish your homework."

"I don't like him."

"You don't know him. You can't *not like* someone you don't know."

Albert mumbled something Daisy didn't catch, but she could work it out. She gave him another of her annoyed looks. He made a show of studying his cards.

"You should have told me about him," said Bertie.

He was right, of course. Which did not make her feel

better.

"And I *don't* like him! I hate him!"

Daisy stared up at the ceiling, tracing with her eyes the outline of the discolored damp patch as she silently counted to ten to calm herself. At seven, she knew it wasn't working.

"I hate him!" Bertie yelled. "And I hate you!"

She closed her eyes against the pain of that. Before she could respond to it, Dad did.

"Oi!" He threw down his cards and stood up sharply, startling Bertie, who reared back in his chair. "You don't speak to your mother like that!"

"But she—"

"*She?*" Albert leaned on the table, his weight on his knuckles, his anger-reddened face closer to Bertie's. Bertie shrank into his seat. "*She? She* is the cat's mother, not yours! You do not speak to her like that. I won't have it!"

Bertie's bottom lip quivered. His eyes filled with tears. He raced to his room, and slammed the door.

Daisy lowered herself onto the seat he'd just left. She put her elbows on the table and covered her face with her hands.

Dad patted her shoulder, his anger gone, his touch now gentle and reassuring. "Ah, Daisy-Dais," he sighed. He patted her again. "I suppose it's up to me to make that pot of tea."

****

It was fully dark by the time Frank drove away from Camden Road, having thought through all that had happened, sorting it out in his head and pondering what to do for the best.

He had a son! It struck him with wonder and elation

and, at the same time, confusion. And fear. Fear that there was, in this world, a child he helped to create. Fear that, for the first time in his life, things truly mattered. What he did mattered. Because now, what he did affected somebody else.

His son! Bertie.

From what Frank had seen today, Bertie was a fine boy. In looks, he was a Pearson through and through, with his unruly dark hair, blue eyes, and even the set of his jaw when he was thinking. There was no denying the child's paternity.

Not that Frank wanted to deny it. He never would have done such a thing. No matter what Daisy seemed to believe, he would have acknowledged Bertie, claimed him, and cared for him. He'd been robbed of the chance to do that in the past, but now…now, he would do whatever Bertie needed him to do. Including marrying his mother.

Frank had wanted to marry Daisy twelve years ago, but it was doubly important now. Bertie needed married parents. Frank knew that marrying now would not make their illegitimate son legitimate, but that was only a point of law. In all other respects, having parents who were married to each other would ease Bertie's passage through life, considerably.

But Daisy didn't want to marry Frank. She'd turned him down, flat. No hesitation. No doubt. Then she'd run away before he could regroup, before he could begin to work out how to change her mind.

He *did* want to change her mind. The thought hit him like a thunderbolt. He *wanted* to marry her. Not simply for Bertie's sake. Not for convenience or expedience, either. No, Frank wanted to marry Daisy because…he loved her. Had always loved her.

Time and circumstance had not dulled his feelings. He still loved her. He wanted to marry her, to spend the rest of his life caring for her. So help him, he would do all he could to make her see that, to make her change her mind about him.

Monday, she'd said. He could see Bertie on Monday. Which gave him this weekend to plan how to not only get to know his son but woo the boy's mother.

On that thought, he finally drove away.

Harry and Reggie were gone when he got back to Ramslye. Frank had expected that. It was gone seven o'clock, well after business hours, and they trusted him to take care of things.

In a way, he was glad not to see them tonight. Harry wanted to talk to him about something that was clearly important and, at the moment, Frank didn't think he could give him the attention he deserved. It would keep. There were others with whom he needed to talk more urgently. The first thing he intended to do when he got home was to have a long chat, first with his mother, then with Walter. He would get behind the lies and half-truths and learn what had really happened while he was away. He'd refuse to stop until he knew everything. No ifs, no buts.

However, when he got home, his parents were not there. "They weren't here for dinner," said his sister, Margaret, with an eye roll. Almost twenty, his youngest sister was skeptical about Walter taking Mother out, unless there was a business deal in the mix. Other couples might go out purely to enjoy themselves. The Pearsons never did.

"When will they be back?" Frank suspected it would

be too late for him to confront them tonight. His questions would need to wait until tomorrow.

"After the weekend. He's taken her to London, if you please. They're staying with a friend." She guffawed in a very unladylike way. "Friend! Business prospect, more like." She sighed. "Poor Mother. She'll be bored to tears. Although Father said he'd take her to the theater—there's a Gershwin show on at the Prince of Wales, *Lady, Be Good*. I wouldn't have minded going to that myself. Fred and Adele Astaire are in it."

Frank had heard of the Gershwin brothers, though the actors' names meant nothing to him.

Margaret laughed. "You are such a heathen, Frank Pearson."

"I'm not into theater," he admitted.

"No, but Mother is. She'll enjoy it."

"And they won't be back until Monday?"

Margaret shook her head. "Why? Is it important?"

"It can wait." It would have to.

Frank left her and went to the kitchen, where he helped himself to a sandwich, using the cold beef left over from dinner. Monday looked set to be an eventful day. He would see his son again, and talk to Daisy. Plus, he would learn the truth from his parents. Whether they wanted him to or not. Meanwhile, he could do nothing.

It was going to be a long weekend.

Chapter Fourteen

Monday 10th May, 1926.

Frank spent the entire weekend on tenterhooks. He could do nothing until Monday, when he could talk to his parents, and then to Daisy, Bertie, and even Albert, if it was possible. He wasn't sure Albert would ever be amenable to it, considering his anger on Friday, but Frank would try. Until he could do that, though, nothing was certain.

The uncertainty made sleep difficult. Frank tossed and turned at night, tangling himself in blankets and dislodging the sheets so that, by morning, his bed looked like a war zone. His appetite was gone, too. He didn't join his family for dinner: what would be the point when he not only didn't want the food, he wasn't sure he could stomach it.

By Monday morning, he felt like death warmed over. His eyes were gritty and heavy, his muscles sluggish, his brain slower than usual. Even so, he had come to some decisions.

Firstly, he would provide for Bertie, whether Daisy wanted him to or not. Bertie was his son, and Frank would do right by him. To do that, he needed to find a paying job. That wouldn't be easy, since the employment situation was not good at the moment. But he had to do it.

Until he found a job, he would continue working for Harry, although he'd have to warn his brother he was going to leave. He would never leave Harry in the lurch. Then again, he knew Harry wanted to talk to him, so Frank's plans might be moot. With a huge drop in deliveries thanks to the strike, coupled with the fact that Harry had now completely recovered from the attack he'd suffered a couple of months ago, he may not need Frank anymore.

"I might be the first volunteer in history to be laid off." The thought made him chuckle. It was the first thing that had amused him for days. "Probably the only thing that will amuse me for some time to come." Until he knew exactly what had happened between Daisy and his parents back in 1914, and figured out what to do about it, there would be little to make him laugh.

The wait for information frustrated him beyond belief, but there was nothing he could do about it. He couldn't question his parents until they arrived home, which Margaret said would not be until after lunch today. That had surprised Frank. He would have expected them to return on Sunday night, so that Walter could be back at his desk on Monday morning. He'd already taken Friday off work to travel up to Town, which meant he was taking two full days away from the office. Three, if one counted Saturday, which was a busy day for the stores, although of late, Walter rarely went in on Saturdays, leaving that side of the business to Ray.

Even two days away was quite something for Walter. Frank had never known his father to take that much time before. Still, Margaret had said this was a business trip, so perhaps he hadn't taken it now, either.

Not that it mattered to Frank. He could not have

cared less about Walter's work ethic, business trips, and deals. All he cared about was confronting him, and Mother, and learning the truth. That *would* happen soon, whether they liked it or not.

Frank's last delivery job involved loading up milk churns from a farm outside Sevenoaks and delivering them to a dairy in Tonbridge. After he'd done that, he headed back toward Ramslye. It was only just after ten-thirty but, to his knowledge, he had nowhere else to go today. Perhaps Harry would be available for the talk they needed to have. Then, after that, he could go home and prepare himself for this afternoon, and his son.

His son! He didn't think he would ever grow tired of those words. *His son*. The boy he had created, with Daisy Redmond.

An image of Daisy came into his head. She was still slender, though she seemed curvier now than he remembered her being in 1914, and she had an assurance about her that she'd lacked then. He knew life couldn't have been easy for her in the intervening years, but one would never guess that by looking at her. Her face was still unlined and unblemished, her hair glossy and bright, her back straight, shoulders unbowed by the burdens she carried. To Frank, she was as beautiful today as she'd been that stormy evening in the summerhouse…

It did no good to chase his thoughts down that blind alley! Yes, Daisy was beautiful. He still desired her, still wanted her in his life, wanted to be part of her life. At the moment, though, that did not seem possible. It might never be possible, unless he could come up with a way to persuade her to give their relationship a second chance.

He was still trying to think of something when he

drove toward the Five Ways in the heart of Tunbridge Wells, and slowed to a crawl.

Something was wrong. Very wrong. People, most of them women, along with a few children and one or two elderly men, stood in shop doorways, staring along the road.

Actually, that was not correct. They weren't just standing in the doorways. They were huddled there, gathered like nervous sheep seeking safety in pens, unwilling to venture out. Some of the women clutched at each other's arms. Others held the children tightly. The children cried. Sobbed, inconsolably.

The town center was drenched in an atmosphere of terror.

Frank looked, confused, from the cowering crowds to the road ahead. Then he pulled up sharply, jumped out of his van, and stared in appalled disbelief. The stretch of pavement in front of the bus ticket office, and the Opera House next to it, was carnage. Pebbled glass from broken windows glittered. A quick glance at the buildings told him there was hardly a pane left intact. The ticket office door was broken, hanging haphazardly on its hinges. Special constables picked through the rubble, crushing glass under foot and looking every bit as shell-shocked as the pickets. Some of those pickets sat on the ground, their faces bloody, clothes disheveled and torn. Others crouched beside them, tending to injuries, cleaning away blood, applying salve onto small cuts, and bandaging larger ones.

John Harold, the butcher, handed out steaks to men with swelling, blackened eyes. Jerry Balcombe tended Matt Fuller, whose head was bleeding badly enough that Frank thought he would need stitching.

Around the perimeter stood a dozen men, including Charlie Taylor, who sported an impressive black eye himself. These men faced outward, makeshift coshes gripped, two handed, across their bodies, ready for further trouble. Not a single regular police officer was in sight.

Charlie saw Frank, said something to the man next to him and left his place in the defensive wall to come to the van. Glass crunched beneath his feet, shattering to spots of white dust. As he approached, Frank saw that, as well as the shiner, Charlie had a swollen jaw, and a thin line of dried blood under his nose. His jacket was dirty, with a clear imprint of a muddied boot sole on one side.

For an instant, Frank braced. Then he forced himself to relax. Charlie might look grim and keyed up from the fight he'd been in, but there was nothing threatening about the way he moved, and the cosh he carried was now held by his side rather than ready to strike.

"Well, they came," he said, when he was near enough to speak in a low, confidential voice.

Frank nodded once at the battleground. "R Company?"

"About a dozen of them. Armed to the teeth, and looking for trouble." Charlie glanced over his shoulder. "Could have been a lot worse. If you hadn't warned us, the women would have been here, too."

Daisy. Frank closed his eyes for a moment. The idea that she might have been here, in the thick of it, was enough to bring him to his knees. Pain flared in his chest, and he felt sick.

"They enjoyed it, Frank." Charlie shook his head, his eyes sparkling with his emotions. "Don't get me wrong, I enjoy a dust-up as much as anyone. You know I do. Bit of rough-and-tumble on a Saturday night, couple of bouts of fisticuffs. But this…this was… They were out to hurt people. I mean, *really* hurt people. Wear-it-for-life kind of hurt. If you hadn't warned us, we'd have been sitting ducks."

"Is there anything I can do?" Frank pointed his thumb over his shoulder at his van. "If anyone needs to go to hospital, I can take them."

Charlie glanced back at what had been the picket line, then ballooned his cheeks and exhaled, hard, before he shook his head. "Two lads got taken a few minutes ago, by some geezer with a car. A broken leg, I think, and a nasty-looking head wound. But the rest of us are all right."

"If you're sure."

"It'll be worse at your dad's place." Charlie tightened his jaw again, then winced as it pulled on the swelling there. He put his fingers to the bruise that was forming and massaged it, gently. "One of them said they were going to Pearson's delivery depot next. Going to crack some heads, he said. We did warn all the other pickets these thugs were coming, which might help, but, well, after us, and the fight we gave them, any resistance down there won't be so much of a surprise, will it?"

Frank ran his hand over his face, as if he could wipe away the horror of the morning.

"That thug said something else, too," Charlie continued. "Make of it what you will. I know what I think."

"What did he say?"

Did the thugs plan to do something worse than knock a few heads together? Now they were here, blood up and adrenaline crashing through them, anything could happen. He'd seen it in the war. After a battle, when one would think men just wanted to relax and catch their breath, that's when some of them were at their most dangerous, not only to their enemies, but to everyone. Some picked fights with each other, some squared up to their officers. And some attacked anyone and everyone who came near.

In the trenches, the victims had been other men who could, by and large, take care of themselves. Here, they might pick on anyone. Men. Women. Even children.

He thought of Daisy and Bertie. Although Bertie should be in school now, and thus relatively safe. But Daisy…Daisy might be in the wrong place at the wrong time. The Pearson's delivery depot, the place where the vans were stored and where the official picket line stood, was in High Brooms, a suburb of Tunbridge Wells. There were a couple of ways to get there from here, but the easiest, most direct route, was along Monson Street and Camden Road. Just where Daisy might be.

Frank wanted to drive there as fast as he could, and make sure she was all right.

But first, he needed to hear whatever else the R Company thugs had said. He had a feeling he wasn't going to like it.

"He told his mates," Charlie reported, "to remember, no property damage there. Just heads."

For a moment, Frank simply stood and stared, as if he had not understood what Charlie had said. He wished he didn't understand him. Not his words. Not his meaning. Unfortunately, both were all too clear.

Shame washed over him. Shame and disgust, so strong it threatened to unman him. He felt the prick of frustrated tears sting the back of his eyes. Nausea churned within him.

"I'm so sorry," he whispered.

"You've nothing to be sorry for." Charlie reached out and shook his hand. "You're nothing like your old man." That didn't make Frank feel better. "Best get back to my post."

Frank watched Charlie return to the defensive wall around the devastated picket line before he climbed back into his van and drove away, along Monson Street.

The roads between the town center and High Brooms were quiet. Calm. Along the way Frank saw women scrubbing doorsteps or standing in small groups, arms folded under ample bosoms as they chatted. Some pushed prams and pushchairs, others held toddlers by the hand. There was no sign of trouble here. No sign that the thugs had even passed this way. In fact, it was as if this was a different town to the one he'd just left. The people here didn't even seem aware that anything untoward had happened.

They would know soon, he thought as he drove by. There would be worry and upset and distress for them all, then.

He took a detour and drove past Daisy's home. This road was quiet, too. There was no reason it shouldn't be, he supposed. There were no pickets here, no strikers to beat. R Company had their orders, which clearly didn't involve quiet residential streets. So Frank turned around in the road and made his way to the Pearson's depot.

The damage there was not as immediately obvious as it had been at the ticket office. No windows were broken, no buildings or vehicles damaged. Here, the men on the picket line had taken the entire attack upon themselves. There were a number of nasty-looking injuries, and two ambulances were now being loaded with men on stretchers. Blood soaked into the ground in small patches. He could see men with makeshift splints, as well as bandages.

Frank did not get out to see what he could do here. He didn't even stop. These men would not want him, or his help. They wouldn't see him as an ally. To these men, Frank Pearson would be no more than Walter's son, and that meant his presence here was not only unwanted, it might even be dangerous. So he drove away, looped back around, and headed instead for Fieldhurst.

It was time to tell the bastard who'd sired him exactly what he thought.

Walter's Bentley stood in the driveway, which let Frank know his parents had returned. He parked next to the car, still seething from all he'd seen and heard. Walter had gone too far this time. Somebody might have been killed today. That nobody had been was little short of a miracle.

He marched down the corridor to Walter's study, guessing that was where he would most likely find his father. Walter would be conscious of having taken so much time off and would be eager to catch up.

Frank stopped outside the door for a moment. He pressed his lips together and fought the anger that had bubbled within him since he'd come across the scene outside the ticket office. In his mind's eye, he saw it all once more: the damage; the injuries; the shock on the men's faces.

What gave his father the right to order such an attack on people going about their lawful business? For Frank was in no doubt about it, Walter had ordered that attack.

If there had been any uncertainty over that, it had been wiped away by what Charlie had heard.

No property damage at Pearson's. Just heads.

The bully boys had followed their orders when they'd reached Pearson's depot. They hadn't broken a single pane of glass, or left a mark on any of the walls and doors there. They hadn't even scuffed their boots on the pavement.

But they had drawn blood. They'd broken bones. Ruined lives.

Frank didn't knock on the study door. He thrust it open, pushing it so hard it bounced off the credenza behind it with a thud and a bang. It swung back at him and he pushed it again, repeating the bang. Then he strode across the room to the desk where Walter sat, a thick old ledger open in front of him, his ink pen in his hand, poised, midair, above the page. To the side of the ledger was an ornate inkstand, the well open.

Walter looked up, surprised. Then, seeing who his visitor was, he allowed his expression to change to one of quiet disdain.

Frank leaned on the desk, both hands flat on its polished wood surface, his glare fixed on Walter. He took a moment to further calm his anger, and vowed he would not swear, or call the old man the names he badly wanted to hurl at him. He didn't raise his voice, either, though his disgust dripped from every soft-spoken word he aimed across the desk.

"What kind of monster are you? How could you do that?"

Walter sniffed, unfazed. "If I knew what *that* was," he said, coolly, "I might be able to answer you."

"You know very well what I mean."

206

Walter shrugged.

"I know what you did. You went up to London."

"I didn't realize it was against the law."

"I know why you went there."

If Frank had thought being caught out would discomfit Walter, he had another think coming. Walter just smiled, with his mouth but not his eyes. He reminded Frank of a shark—cold, unfeeling, and deadly.

"Oh. *That.* Your mother enjoyed the show. Not my cup of tea, but there you are."

"I'm not talking about the show!" Frank's temper strained at its leash at Walter's insouciance.

Walter turned his head, letting Frank know he didn't consider him worthy of his full attention. The older man looked through the window, then did a double-take before he narrowed his eyes and pursed his lips. "Get that abomination off the drive," he said, his voice venomously gravelly.

Frank glanced at the window himself, and realized the "abomination" was Harry's van. Frank wouldn't normally have driven here in that vehicle, but he'd been so incensed by all that he'd seen, he hadn't taken the time to go to Ramslye and swap it for his own car.

Not that it mattered. He would not allow Walter to steer the conversation, or change the subject.

"Abomination," he said, quietly, as if he was examining the sound of it. "That is an interesting word." His tone sharpened. "One that perfectly describes your new…'business associate' in London, wouldn't you say?"

Annoyance flared in Walter's eyes. "No. I would not say. How dare you insult a man you don't even know."

"I know enough." Frank pulled a face, as if he had

encountered a particularly awful smell. "I know he's a nasty piece of work. And I know about his army of thugs and hooligans."

Walter lifted his chin so that he seemed to look down his nose at Frank. It was astounding, really. Even sitting down, the man had a way of making others feel that he towered over them. "I do not mix with thugs and hooligans," he said, haughtily.

"You don't have to. Not when you've got people like Ralph Roberts to do it for you." Frank huffed. The sound conveyed his anger and disdain, mixed with disbelief that his own father could do this. "Was he expensive?"

That broke through Walter's cool facade. "Watch your tongue, boy! I'll not have my friends and colleagues spoken of like that. Roberts is an honorable man. He was a captain in His Majesty's army."

"I don't care if he was a bloody colonel!" Frank's voice rose. "He's a thug. He runs a gang of thugs. And they are a gang," he added when Walter opened his mouth to object again. "Calling them a company does not change the truth."

Walter's jaw worked. His face reddened and his lips thinned. Then he breathed in sharply through his nostrils, and Frank could see him determinedly regaining his control. "I'm busy," he said at last.

"You're busy? You're *busy*? After what you did, you think it can be business as usual?"

Walter looked down at his ledger as if, by ignoring Frank, he could make him go away. Well, not this time.

"You set those bully boys on your own workers. Men who've worked for you, given you their all, for years."

"Given their all?" Walter laughed, nastily. "To me? I doubt it." He fixed Frank with a sneer. "For your information, Francis Pearson, Captain Roberts sent his company to reason with—"

"Reason with?"

"Reason with," Walter talked over Frank, "a group of agitators and troublemakers. Any man caught up in it has only himself to blame. If he'd been at work, where he should have been, he would not have found himself being roughed up a little, would he?"

"They were not roughed up! They were *hurt*. Some of them were nearly killed."

Walter shrugged again, unbothered.

"And what of the people at the bus ticket office? What did they do to you? They don't work for you. Their actions don't affect you in the slightest, so why did you target them?"

Walter sighed, heavily. "I have work to do." He looked back at his ledger again.

Frank saw red. He snarled and swiped his hand across the desk. He intended to push the ledger over the edge and to the floor, because it was either attack the book or hit his father, and he knew he couldn't do that. That would make him as bad, if not worse, than Walter.

The side of his hand caught the edge of the inkstand, which toppled, spewing ink everywhere. It spattered the desk and half of it puddled on the open page of the ledger, while the rest landed on Walter, spotting his shirt and covering the lap of his grey trousers. He jumped to his feet, his attention on his ink-stained clothing.

"Hell's bells!" he yelled. "Look what you've done!" He pulled out his handkerchief and made to dab at his trousers, then changed his mind and began to pat at the book instead, frantically trying to mop up the spill. After a few moments, he threw the ruined handkerchief aside, pulled the blotting paper from its frame on his desk, and used that instead.

"You idiot!" he muttered. "Do you have any notion of the damage you've done?"

It's not as much damage as you did.

"This whole page will have to be rewritten. If I can even see the figures to rewrite them properly! I'll have to go back through the receipts and find the information all over again! It will take days to put this right."

Frank wanted to say it would take weeks for some of the pickets to be put right, but he would be wasting his breath. Walter would never see what he'd done was wrong. So instead, he simply said, "You sicken me." His voice was, once more, low and even.

The look Walter gave him was hate-filled. "Never stopped you enjoying my hospitality, though, did it?"

If Walter thought the veiled threat would make Frank back down, he was very much mistaken. Frank was not about to be blackmailed. "Not for much longer," he answered.

He had a small nest egg. It was a legacy from his godfather and, although it wasn't enough that he could call himself wealthy, it would cover the cost—or most of the cost—of a modest house. Nothing fancy, but it would be enough for his needs.

Enough to give Daisy and her family a home, too. If she would agree.

It was the perfect solution. Frank couldn't think why it hadn't occurred to him sooner. In his defense, he'd never touched the money, and had quite forgotten about it. But now, he realized, he could use it to make things right. He could buy a house, and move Daisy, Bertie, and Albert into it. He would certainly rest easier at night knowing they were in decent accommodation.

Then, after he persuaded her to marry him, they could set about repairing everything else. Build their lives together, the way he'd once thought they would. If only she would give them another chance, give *him* another chance…

"Feel free to leave here anytime you like," said Walter, bringing Frank back to the present conversation. His father pressed the now-soaked blotting paper onto his ledger once more, then tossed it aside and reached into a drawer for a fresh piece.

"Kicking me out?" Frank tried to sound nonchalant. It wasn't ideal, because he didn't know where he would live between now and when he bought a house of his own. Such things took weeks. Months, sometimes. It was a long time to be homeless. Still, he'd work something out. He would rather sleep on a park bench than beg his father for more time.

"I only wish I could," muttered Walter.

Which was, Frank thought, a strange thing to say, and not what he'd expected at all. He'd expected Walter to point to the door, give him ten minutes to get his stuff—if Frank was lucky—and make him leave, while shouting that he never wanted to see his son again.

Walter looked up. His eyes said he hadn't meant to voice that sentiment aloud. Quickly, he added, "It would upset your mother if I did. But I won't stop you from going, if you decide you want to do so."

Frank frowned. This conversation had taken a decidedly strange turn. He opened his mouth to say so, but stopped when he heard a gasp behind him.

"Oh, no!" said Mother.

Walter groaned and stopped his blotting. Frank turned to face her. She wasn't looking at either of them, though. Instead, her eyes were fixed on the ruined ledger. After a moment, she came forward and dabbed, ineffectually, at the ink Walter was already mopping. He pushed her hands away, testily.

"I'll call for the maid," she said, and she moved to the button that would summon her.

"Later," said Walter. "Leave it."

"But it will stain."

"I said, later!" Walter stopped pressing on the blotting paper. He stood straight and put his ink-blackened fingers on his hips, smudging more into his clothes. Mother took a step back and let her hands drop to her sides. She looked from her husband to her son.

Frank watched both of them. He needed to see each movement, each facial expression, if he was to make sense of anything. The tension within him stiffened his back and made his neck muscles tight.

Mother seemed to feel it too. She bit on a corner of her lower lip for a second before she asked, "What's happening?"

"Nothing," said Walter. His answer was quick. Too quick. His face was dark, his jaw clenched, eyes hard.

Mother swallowed and turned to Frank instead. "We don't usually see you at home at this time of day."

"No," Frank agreed. He glanced at his father, then back at her. "Did you enjoy your trip?"

Walter made a sound somewhere between a growl of anger and a huff of impatience.

"Yes, thank you." Mother smiled. "It was a good show."

Frank nodded. "And your host? Was he good company?"

She frowned, confused. "He seemed charming. Though of course, your father spent more time with him than I did." She looked from Frank to Walter and back. "Do you know him?"

"Of course he doesn't know him." Walter made it sound as if she'd asked the most stupid question he had ever heard. "Why would he know him? Francis doesn't run in the same circles as Captain Roberts."

"Thank goodness," murmured Frank.

"They were both in the army—"

"Along with a million other men," Walter pointed out. "Besides, Francis was only an enlisted man. Ralph Roberts was an officer. The two do not mix, socially."

She lowered her gaze and clasped her hands in front of her. "Oh," she said, quietly. "I see."

Frank felt sorry for her, but at the same time, her timidity frustrated him. He wished she would stand up for herself. Unfortunately, after almost forty years of marriage to Walter, he doubted anything would change now.

He also felt guilt, because he was about to add to her mistreatment with his planned interrogation of her. Not about Roberts and his men. He doubted she knew anything about the "business" aspect of their trip at all. Besides, that didn't matter as much as other issues that needed addressing. So he pushed away his guilt and watched her closely.

"I had an eventful weekend, as well," he said. "I saw Daisy again. To talk to, this time."

Mother's eyes widened. Her mouth formed a horrified O, and the color drained from her face.

Walter sprang to her defense. "How dare you?" he shouted. "I told you not to mention—"

"Because it upsets Mother?" Frank's eyes narrowed. "Because Albert died?"

Mother whimpered. She felt behind her with a trembling hand, latched onto the visitor's chair, and lowered herself onto it.

"Only he didn't die, did he?"

She took in a sharp breath and covered her mouth with her fingers. In the background, Walter shouted. Both Frank and Mother ignored him. They stared at each other. Her eyes were frightened and brimful of tears that had yet to spill.

"Did. He?" Frank pressed. He felt like the worst of bullies, but he couldn't stop now. He needed the answers, *all* the answers, if he was to move forward and make things right.

A few seconds passed. It felt like an eternity. Walter continued to rant in the background. Frank thought he said something about not in this house, and that Frank should leave.

Finally, Mother shook her head. "No," she whispered, and brought Frank's world crashing down. He realized, even as his heart cracked, that he had hoped she wouldn't know what he was talking about, that she would be dumbfounded by the truth, overjoyed, even, to hear that her former chauffeur had survived after all.

The truth hurt. Badly.

"Why did you lie?" Frank's voice cracked on the question.

Mother glanced at Walter. His face was a deep, dark red now, and a vein stood out on his forehead. Frank worried, fleetingly, that he would have an apoplexy.

Walter snarled, and moved from behind his desk. Mother flinched. Frank took a step forward and stood between them, but Walter didn't come near her. He went to the drinks cabinet in the corner of the room, and poured himself a generous measure of whisky. He drank it in one, then poured himself another. He didn't offer any to anyone else.

"This does not concern you, boy," he said, after taking a large sip of his second drink.

That made no sense. "Like hell it doesn't."

Walter pointed, angrily. "Watch your language! Your mother's in the room."

Mother gave another little sob.

"You said he was dead."

Tears spilled down Mother's face. Walter glared at her, as if her crying disgusted him. "If you must know," he told Frank, "I had to let him go."

Frank raised an eyebrow. Firing a man was a long way from declaring him dead.

"He was complicit in his daughter's behavior. The trust was gone. I cannot employ someone I don't trust."

In which case, Frank thought, Walter shouldn't employ anyone, because it wasn't in his nature to trust anybody. But then, something else occurred to him.

"He got no pension."

Mother looked up, shocked. "That's not true," she said. "Albert got his pension."

"Did he?" Frank waited for Walter to confirm that. Mother, too, stared at her husband, wanting to hear his answer.

Walter drained his drink and slammed the glass down so hard it was a wonder it didn't shatter. "I am not in the habit of discussing business matters with people who are not involved."

Mother stood, her eyes never leaving her husband's face. "Walter?"

"The man left my employ in 1919. I fail to see what relevance it has today."

Her gaze hardened. "Did you give him his pension?" she insisted.

"His *full* pension," Frank qualified.

There was a moment of silence. Then Walter growled. "Sacked employees forfeit their company pension," he said. "That's common practice." He turned to Mother, a strange desperation on his face. "For God's sake, Sarah! You know what they did! That gold-digging harpy had her eyes on our money! She thought she could get her talons into our son."

"That was not Albert's fault," Mother cried, at the same moment that Frank said, "I asked her to marry me before I left."

Both his parents stared at him. They were shocked, as if that was the last thing they'd expected him to say. Then Mother gave a distressed cry and ran from the room.

Walter rubbed his hand across his face. His inky fingers left a faint smudge on his cheek. "See what you've done?" he asked. "She'll lock herself in her room for the rest of the day now. For crying out loud, Francis. Just...go. Go on. Go. Before I say something we'll both regret."

Frank thought they were well past that point, but he didn't say so. Nor did he pursue the topic of Albert's pension. He sensed it would do no good to do so today. But, he resolved, he would find a way to get the man his money. Somehow.

Meanwhile, there were other questions to address. "Daisy said she wrote to me."

Walter gritted his teeth. "Haven't you done enough?"

"What happened to the letters?" It amazed Frank that his voice sounded so calm, when inside he was a mass of swirling, churning emotion.

"How the hell should I know?" Walter's eyes, though, gave the lie to his words. He chopped at the air with his hand. "This conversation is finished!" he said, and he stalked from the office and marched upstairs.

Frank watched him go. "Not finished," he murmured. "Postponed."

He ballooned his cheeks and blew out a harsh breath. He needed to see Daisy.

Chapter Fifteen

After a weekend of tension and silent animosity, Daisy and Albert were coldly civil on Monday morning. She made his breakfast and the pot of tea, and put them on the table at his place with exaggerated care, determined not to slam them down. He, in turn, said a polite and distant thank you, as if to a stranger. On the other side of the table, Bertie stirred his spoon through his porridge, pushing the oat-and-water mixture into the little moat of milk that rimmed his bowl.

"Eat up, Bertie," said Daisy, and she sat down. Bertie made a show of putting a spoonful into his mouth while he glared at her. She pretended not to notice. There was only so much argument one could have with a child before one began to sound like an unreasonable shrew.

"You seeing him today?" asked Albert, after the silence had stretched for a full minute. His tone was flat, with none of the anger from Friday, but it still managed to convey what he thought.

Daisy sighed and sipped her tea. "Come on, Bertie. You'll be late."

"You should send him packing," muttered Albert. "He's got no call coming round here where he's not wanted." Daisy rolled her eyes. He'd said the same thing many times since Friday.

She was torn. On the one hand, she knew how her father felt about the Pearsons, and being civil to one of them seemed, somehow, a betrayal of him. On the other hand, Bertie was Frank's son, and she owed it to both man and boy to allow them to meet.

"After the way he treated you," continued Albert. He bit into his bacon sandwich.

Obviously, ignoring him was not going to shut him up. So she tried a different tack. "I'm not sure he treated me like I thought he had," she said.

Albert's eyebrows rose and he stopped chewing, astounded.

"He didn't seem to know what had happened back then."

"So he said."

"I believe him."

"Bigger fool, you." Albert jabbed the table between them with his index finger, as if pressing his point into the wood. "He left you to Walter's tender mercies, don't forget."

Daisy had had the whole weekend to ponder that. The more she thought about it, the less happy she was to believe it until, now, she thought it might not be as simple as that.

The sticking point was, of course, the letters. She'd written several to Frank, which he swore he'd never received. He said he'd sent her a few as well, and she didn't receive a single one. Which meant something was very wrong. She had an inkling what that could be, and she also had a plan to discover the truth, although she didn't want to say anything to Albert until she knew for certain. That was because, if she *was* right, there was a lot more at stake than a couple of brokenhearted youngsters and a fatherless boy.

The idea had come to her during a long night of

sleepless tossing and turning. The bench she used as a bed was never comfortable at the best of times. It was narrow and hard, and the cushions did little to help. But the last three nights, her brain had worked eighteen-to-the-dozen, asking questions she couldn't answer, trying to square a circle so everything could make sense, even though that seemed impossible.

Last night had been the worst night of the weekend. No matter how she lay, her hip pressed into the wooden seat until it hurt, and her neck stiffened, giving her a headache. There was a dull pain in the small of her back and, this morning, her eyes were hot and puffy.

Just before dawn, she gave up trying to sleep and sat at the table, staring out of the window. Silhouettes of the houses opposite stood black against the slightly lighter sky, and a lone figure scurried along the road, on the way to an early shift, no doubt. In a while, she would light the stove, boil the kettle, and start the day. She had Bertie's porridge to make, and Dad's bacon to fry. There was just enough bread left to put the rashers into a sandwich for him, but she'd have to get another loaf today. More milk, too. It was all cost, cost, cost.

Frank said he wanted to provide for Bertie. It would be a huge relief if he did, although Dad had let her know he disagreed. He had far more pride than they could afford. She couldn't get him to see that Frank had a right, as well as a duty, to give Bertie a good start in life. He was driven by his hatred of the Pearsons, and was convinced he'd been sent to war to get rid of him, so Daisy would be alone and easier to deal with. Nothing she said would sway him from that belief.

Every argument throughout the weekend came back to that final letter. She'd sent it to Frank, who said he never received it. Yet, as Albert pointed out repeatedly, Walter had had it. How could he have got hold of it if Frank hadn't given it to him?

As the street lamps died and the sky changed from navy to pale grey, Daisy came up with a scenario that could, somehow, make sense of it.

She'd sent her letters to Frank through the post office at Fieldhurst. There was a postbox there, of course, but she'd never used it. Why would she, when she was going to the counter to buy the stamp? Each time, she stuck the stamp onto the envelope and gave it to Mr. Godson, who put it into the sack behind him.

Except, now she thought about it, he hadn't put her letters into the sack. He'd put them on the desk beside him. She'd made nothing of it at the time. She assumed he put them in after she'd gone.

But what if he hadn't? What if he separated her letters to Frank and made sure they weren't sent? She couldn't think why he would do that, of course, other than that he'd been instructed by Walter to do so. Which would mean that Walter *had* known Daisy was what Frank had called "his girl," and that they planned to marry. Which, in turn, gave credence to Albert's claim that he was deliberately sent to the frontline to get rid of him.

It also meant both Walter and Mr. Godson had committed a crime. Letters from home were considered vital to soldiers' morale, and although they were censored, they were encouraged. Anyone interfering with that would be guilty of a very serious offence.

It was this consideration that kept her quiet about her theory. She couldn't simply accuse men of a crime that could send them to prison. She needed proof. Until she had it, she couldn't say a word. Not even to Dad. *Especially* not to Dad.

She would take Bertie to school, then make her way to Fieldhurst. With luck, Mr. Godson would still be at the post office, or the people there would know where to find him, since he might be retired by now. He was the only person who could answer her questions. She only hoped he would be willing.

Fieldhurst was seven miles from Tunbridge Wells and, with no buses running, she'd have to walk. It would wear her out, and use most of the day, but if she discovered what had truly happened, it would be worth it.

From the corner of her eye, she saw Bertie swirl his spoon through his porridge again. He'd hardly eaten any of it, and time was knocking on. "Bertie," she said, more forcefully than before. "You're going to be late. Eat up!"

"Don't want it," murmured Bertie.

"You'll be hungry later."

He still didn't make any effort to eat.

"I'm not having you waste food," she continued. "So, unless you want it cold for your tea tonight, you'll eat it now. And hurry up. You'll be late for school."

"Don't want to go to school."

"Tough."

His eyes filled with angry tears. "Everyone's going to laugh at me."

She hadn't expected that. "Why would they laugh at you?"

"Because they'll all know, won't they? They'll know that chinless wonder is my dad."

"That's enough!" She fixed him with her sternest mother-glare. "We do not call people chinless wonders."

Especially when they're not any such thing.

"Grandad does. He says that's what all those toffee-nosed idiots are."

Daisy gave Albert a flat look. He suddenly found his sandwich very interesting.

"Them people that like to lord it over the rest of us," continued Bertie. "They think they're better than we are. And they're not. They wouldn't last five minutes in the real world."

"Those people," she corrected, automatically. "And your grandad and I will be having a long talk about bringing his politics home."

Albert glanced up then, his expression full of injured innocence. She narrowed her eyes at him. He took another bite of his sandwich.

Daisy sent Bertie to finish getting ready for school and waited till he was out of the room before she spoke again.

"What you and your mates discuss in the club is up to you. Keep it there."

"I didn't know he was listening."

"Then be more careful. He is a little boy. Leave him to be a little boy."

"But—"

"It's not up for discussion, Dad. He's my son, and I don't want him hearing it."

He looked disgruntled, but he didn't pursue the matter.

After a moment, she went on, "I shall be out most of the day. Once I've taken Bertie to school, I have an errand to run. I'll be home by four."

Albert scowled. "When *he'll* come around."

"Don't start."

He sniffed, contemptuously. "You know what I think."

"So you've no need to tell me."

"I will tell you this, though. You should think twice about walking Bertie to school. Your *little boy* won't want you doing that."

"Then he'll have to let want be his master, won't he? Frank said there were some nasties coming down from the Smoke. I don't want Bertie out on his own until I know they've gone."

"Frank said," sneered Dad. "Frank said. How would Frank know?"

"He heard a rumor. And he had the decency to come and warn us." She held up her hand. "Don't say a word. Just…be careful yourself."

Albert shrugged, nonchalantly. "Always am. You make sure you are, too." His words brought about a tentative truce.

Twenty minutes later, Daisy left Bertie at the school gates and walked along Camden Road, the first step on her long trek to Fieldhurst.

It was a warm day. The weather was sticky and close, and the air held the threat of a coming storm. The countryside had a strange quality, as if someone had polished it and made it clearer, every detail enhanced. Bees buzzed as they moved from flower to flower on the verges, and the birds in the hedgerows chirped loudly. Cows in the fields swished their tails furiously, as if they were more bothered by the flies than usual, and the horses beside them seemed skittish. Daisy blew out a heavy breath and hoped all of that didn't mean the storm was imminent. She'd like to make it home without getting wet, if she could.

She reached Fieldhurst just after ten thirty. She was hot and bothered. Her clothes stuck to her, her hat was heavy on her head, and she could feel the sheen of sweat on her face. Her feet hurt, her throat was dry, and she knew from the way her mouth felt that her breath smelled unpleasant.

Daisy couldn't go to the post office like this. She needed to freshen up and collect herself before she faced Mr. Godson. It was important that she was at her best when she met with him, especially considering what she intended to ask. So, although she couldn't really afford it, she made her first port of call the Fieldhurst Tea Shop.

The tea shop was an oasis of cool calm on the clammy day. The large windows that looked out onto the street gave enough light to make the place feel welcoming without being too bright. The walls were a dark blue-green, and the polished wood floor matched the tables and chairs, about half of which were occupied. The customers sipped tea from beautifully painted teacups that matched the teapots, milk jugs and sugar bowls, and the plates on which the cakes were served. Daisy chose a table in the corner.

"Daisy?" The voice sounded incredulous. "It *is* you, isn't it?"

She looked up and saw Sally Ann Ambrose, someone she'd known at school. Her hair was still the bright blonde it had been back when they were thirteen, although the roots were slightly darker now, a ginger-ash color that matched her eyebrows. Her eyes sparkled a deep blue, with only the faintest of lines around them. A chef's apron clung to her curvy figure.

Sally Ann's smile was wide and welcoming. "Daisy Redmond! What are you doing here?" She gestured at the woman behind the counter, and sat down. Almost instantly, the waitress brought over a tray with tea for two, including two slices of Victoria sponge. Mindful of what she had in her purse, Daisy tried to refuse the cake, but Sally Ann would not hear of it.

"My treat," she said. "What's the point of owning a tea shop if you can't offer your friends a piece of cake now and then?"

"You own this place?" Daisy's eyes widened. Sally Ann's family had not been wealthy. They certainly wouldn't have had the money to invest in a business like this, and as a woman, Sally Ann herself would have had difficulty financing it.

"Technically," she answered, her voice lowered, confidentially, "my brother does. Steven took out the loans to get me started. I work to clear them." She rolled her eyes. "I long for the day when I won't have to hide behind him, but I can't see it happening in our lifetime."

Daisy understood Sally Ann's frustration. She'd had problems herself, when she wanted a bank account. Although she was allowed to have one, as a woman, she wasn't legally entitled to it and several bank managers had turned her down. She'd been stuck until Hugh Burgess had agreed to help her. She had, of course, never applied for a loan. She didn't think even Hugh, sympathetic as he was, would countenance that.

"Now," said Sally as she poured two cups. "What have you been up to? I want to hear everything."

They spent more than an hour chatting before Daisy said her goodbyes and left the tea shop. She had enjoyed seeing Sally. They'd renewed their friendship and chatted as easily as if they'd seen each other last week, not more than twelve years ago. They swapped stories, not only of their own lives, but of others they'd known, and of Fieldhurst itself. It had been good to talk of happier, more carefree days. On top of which, Daisy had enjoyed being a lady of leisure for once, pretending she was the sort of woman who could idle away her time drinking tea and eating cake with a friend.

It occurred to her as she stepped out onto the High Street, that she'd been treated to tea twice within the past week. "How the other half live," she murmured, and she couldn't help the grin. For a moment, she *was* that other half. The thought straightened her shoulders and raised her head.

However, she was also conscious of the time. Unlike real ladies of leisure, she had responsibilities waiting for her, and she had to get back for them. It was noon now. The post office would be closed for lunch soon. If she had to wait for it to reopen, she wouldn't be back to collect Bertie from school. So it was now or never.

Fieldhurst High Street was a long straight road, wide and clean, and prosperous. Sally Ann's shop was at one end of the road, flanked by a women's wear shop to the left, and a greengrocer's to the right. Other businesses along the street included a men's wear shop, a grocer and a dairy, a cycle shop, a bootmaker, and a jewelry shop. There was a bookseller, a haberdasher, and a milliner, as well as two pubs, and two rival banks. There was also the Methodist book room, where those who wanted to improve their reading were encouraged to come. Further along the road was an ironmonger, a solicitor's office, a tobacconist, and a sweet shop. For a small town, it was busy; almost as busy as Tunbridge Wells itself.

That surprised Daisy. She'd always thought of Fieldhurst as a sleepy village. In the last twelve years, it seemed, it had grown beyond recognition.

The post office was at the far end of the street. A small building, it had three stone steps leading to a narrow door, which was painted red, presumably at the behest of the General Post Office, which owned it. The ground floor, she knew, was the shop, with a counter behind which the postmaster worked, and a space in front for customers. As well as stamps and postal orders, the post office sold stationery and newspapers. The first and second floors of the building provided accommodation for the postmaster and his family. Daisy remembered the Godsons had been a fairly small family. As well as Mr. Godson and his wife, there had been three children living here. Those children would all be adults now, of course, and probably had homes and families of their own.

But standing out here, staring at the door while she reminisced, was not going to help her at all. She'd come all this way, and she owed it to herself, and to Frank, to discover the truth.

Thinking of Frank conjured an image of him. She saw him clearly—not the shocked and angry way he'd looked when he first saw Bertie and realized he had a son, and not the frustrated, grim Frank who'd been confronted by Albert. No, the Frank she saw now was the man she'd met earlier on Friday, the man with whom she'd shared lunch in the Monson Street tea shop.

He'd smiled at her, then, and his eyes had held a friendly welcome. He'd touched her hand across the table. Even through her gloves she felt his warmth and his strength, a strength born of hard work and honest endeavor.

Whatever Bertie said, Frank was no chinless wonder. Far from it. Oh, there was a certain moneyed look about him. An air of privilege. It had nothing to do with the clothes he wore, although they were good quality, and more expensive than most men of her acquaintance could have afforded. No, what surrounded Frank was an essence, something that came through in the way he carried himself, the confidence that wrapped around him.

He'd once been a good-looking boy. He was now a handsome man. Handsome and dangerous because, after years of living away from him, telling herself he was a cad with a cold heart, it had taken just one glimpse of him for all her old feelings to come rushing back. If she was honest, she wanted him now every bit as much as she ever had. When they sat in his van last Friday evening, there'd been a magnetic *something,* pulling her in, drawing her closer. When he'd kissed her, she wanted it to go on forever. She had savored the touch of his lips on hers. He'd tasted faintly of tea and egg mayonnaise, mixed with fresh air. His cologne had filled her senses. He still used the same bergamot blend that he'd used before the war, its citrusy sweetness clean and enticing. His jawline was rough from the day's stubble. She'd felt it on her skin and loved it, even though it would leave a red rash that proclaimed to the world just what they'd been doing.

Then again, it was a wonder the world hadn't been watching what they'd been doing. They had been in a van, parked on Camden Road, in full view of anyone who might have happened by. Daisy should feel ashamed after such a display of wanton behavior. Strangely, shame was the last thing she felt.

And what did that make her? The trollop Walter had proclaimed her when he'd kicked her off his estate and out of his son's life? Back then, she'd given herself to Frank not because she was a trollop but because she wasn't. She was "his girl," the woman he planned to marry. So what if they'd anticipated the vows? They'd known the wedding would come, so it didn't matter.

Only, it hadn't come. It had been a pipe dream. A fairy tale. One Daisy would never believe in again. She knew now that girls like her didn't marry men like him. No matter how much she wished for it. No matter how much she loved him. Because, much to her consternation, she *did* love him, every bit as much as she ever had.

"Doesn't matter," she whispered. That time had passed. They had never been meant for each other, and that was that.

She would still let him into her life, of course. She had no choice. He was Bertie's father, and he wanted to know his son. She wanted him to know his son. She wanted him to love and care for Bertie, and stand by him. It was why he was coming this afternoon, so he could begin to get to know his son.

That might be easier said than done, though. Bertie had been so angry this morning, so resentful. She needed to be at their meeting today, to make sure the lad wasn't upset about it. And to see that he wasn't rude to Frank.

Bertie wasn't usually a rude child. He was, generally, well-mannered and polite. But he'd never been faced with the return of an absent father before. He was confused and scared, feeling as if the foundations of his life had been ripped away. It would take time and patience and understanding to get him to accept Frank. She hoped Frank possessed all three, because she had a feeling Bertie was going to need him in the coming weeks and months.

He'd been worried, this morning, about the other children at school, and how they'd react now they knew Frank was his father. With the innocence of childhood, Bertie thought they might laugh at him. If that was all he faced, Daisy would be relieved. There were worse things than your classmates being unimpressed with your dad. The children might not immediately realize the implications of what they'd seen at the school gates, but their parents would. Those parents would talk. There was no sin as unforgivable as being born on the wrong side of the blanket, and Bertie was likely to pay for that sin from now on.

Jean, bless her, hadn't changed toward either Daisy or Bertie. She'd still spoken to Daisy at the school gates, and she hadn't told Clive he couldn't play with Bertie. Others would not be so tolerant.

Daisy hadn't yet worked out all that might mean. Would Bertie have to change schools? Would his life become miserable? Would they have to move, go somewhere they weren't known, and begin again?

That would be difficult to do. She'd lived in those rooms since November 1914, when Walter Pearson found them for her. Over the years, they'd become her home, the only home Bertie had ever known. And while she agreed with Frank that there were better places to live, those places were well beyond her budget. There was little to be had when your entire income was a clippie's wage and a veteran's war pension.

So, yes, Bertie was likely going to need Frank now.

And Daisy needed to know the truth about what had happened. It was the only way they could all move on, the only way any of this might turn out as it should. So she took a deep breath, stiffened her spine, and pushed open the post office door. The little bell at the top of its frame tinkled.

Behind the counter sat Cecil Godson, the eldest son of Mr. Godson, the postmaster she had known. In 1914, Cecil had been an under-gardener on Walter Pearson's estate. He'd been an athletic young man, a promising footballer who'd had hopes of playing professionally. Now, she saw, he was missing his right arm, and his empty sleeve was pinned to the side of his shirt. He wore an eye patch, which did nothing to hide the long, white scar that ran down the right side of his face from his forehead to his chin.

He looked up, recognized her, and his face lit. "Daisy Redmond! How are you? How's your dad?" They spoke for a few minutes, exchanging snippets of news, before he asked what he could do for her.

"Actually, I hoped to see your dad," she said. She bit her lip, nervously. "I had some questions for him. Is he still here?" She meant was the elder Mr. Godson still living on the premises, but Cecil clearly thought she meant something else.

"Still alive and kicking. He'll outlive us all, I shouldn't wonder." She opened her mouth to put him right, to say she hadn't meant to imply he was dead, but Cecil didn't give her a chance. "He'll be in the kitchen now. Why don't you go on up? He'll be pleased to see you."

She had her doubts about that.

"Tell Mum to put the kettle on. I'm about to close up for lunch."

Too late to change her mind now. With some trepidation, Daisy walked up the steep narrow stairs to the Godsons' private quarters.

Chapter Sixteen

The Godsons' kitchen was small, no bigger than Daisy's main living room. Unlike her home, though, this was a proper family kitchen. There was a gas stove with six hobs on one side of it, and two ovens, one over the other, on the other side. Under the window was a proper wooden sink and draining board and, in one corner, a small pantry. A Welsh dresser stood against the wall, its shelves taken up with plates and cups. There was even what looked like a cold box in one corner, big enough to hold a joint of meat as well as cheese, butter, and milk. In the middle of the room was a wooden table, its top scarred with stories of many a happy family meal.

There were six chairs around the table. Mr. Godson sat in one of those chairs, reading a newspaper by the light from the window. Mrs. Godson chopped vegetables on the draining board, then tipped them into a large saucepan.

Mr. Godson looked up at the sound of Daisy's footsteps on the last few stairs, and his face wrinkled with his huge smile. "Mother," he cried, "get the kettle on. Come in. Come in, sweetheart. Don't stand on the stairs." He stood up, a little more stiffly than he'd moved twelve years ago. "You're a sight for sore eyes, and no mistake."

Mrs. Godson rushed over to give Daisy a warm, tight hug. Daisy, unused to such physical displays of affection, stiffened for an instant, but then relaxed into the embrace, and put her arms around Mrs. Godson's wide back.

"Don't suffocate the girl," said Mr. Godson. "Let her sit down." As thin as his wife was stout, Mr. Godson's back was stooped, and he'd lost most of his hair, but his eyes shone bright, and the lines around them gave testimony to the fact he smiled a lot.

Daisy sat. The kettle boiled while she talked with her hosts, catching up with the events of the last few years. She repeated much of what she'd told Sally Ann in the tea shop, and heard again many of the stories her friend had already told her. Mrs. Godson filled the large brown teapot, then let the brew steep for a few minutes before she poured four cups. Cecil joined them then, taking a seat across the table from his father.

"Now then," said Mr. Godson when he'd sipped his tea and let out a loud sigh of satisfaction. "To what do we owe the pleasure of this visit? Because, after twelve years without sight nor sound of you, I get the feeling there's a definite reason for you coming today."

Daisy felt her cheeks burn, and her mouth dried. Suddenly, she didn't want to do this. Didn't want to ask her questions. These people had made her welcome, and she was about to accuse one of them of a serious crime. Worse, it seemed she would have to accuse him in front of his family, shaming him even further. For two pins, she would flee from here, make her way back to Tunbridge Wells, and forget the whole thing.

She had wanted to know what had happened. Wanted to know if her suspicions were correct. But, after twelve years, did it truly matter? What good could knowing do? Yes, she and Frank could put their animosity behind them if they knew, rebuild a friendship untainted by lies. But, to an extent, they could do that anyway. The rest of it, the blossoming of friendship into romance that she'd once thought possible, the dreams of a lifelong love, of marriage and everything else she wanted at eighteen? That was gone. They had grown up now, and they faced the real world. No revelations would change that.

"Oh, my word," whispered Mrs. Godson. She sat down heavily beside her husband. The color drained from her cheeks and she bit her bottom lip, frightened. Her eyes filled with tears. "It's about the letters, isn't it?"

"What letters?" asked Cecil.

"I always knew someone would come, one day." Mr. Godson looked grim. "He said they wouldn't, but I knew they would. There's no such thing as a forever secret. Everything comes out in the end."

"What secret?" asked Cecil, anxiously. "What letters?"

"It's true, then." Daisy spoke quietly. She had hoped, prayed, even, that this would not be the answer. She'd trusted this man. His betrayal chipped at her heart.

Mrs. Godson sniffed. Tears trickled down her cheeks. Mr. Godson didn't comfort her. He looked as if he needed comfort himself. He lowered his eyes and nodded.

"What happened to them?" asked Daisy. Her voice was almost too low to be heard now.

For a moment, she didn't think he would answer her. Then he sighed, heavily, and said, "I gave them to Walter Pearson."

So Walter *had* known. She had been convinced he hadn't, but she'd been wrong. He'd known from the first that she and Frank were romantically involved, and he'd known about her pregnancy. He'd read her letters, seen the declarations of love and affection she'd poured out, her hopes for the future, her fears for her man.

More than that, he'd made sure Frank did *not* know. His theft involved far more than small pieces of paper inside envelopes. When he took those letters, he stole Frank's chance to be a proper father to Bertie. He robbed Daisy of the life she might have known, with the man she loved. And, reading between the lines, he'd taken her father from her, too, forced him to the front line where, thank God, Albert had not died.

He hadn't died, but she'd still lost him. The Albert who went away to war was a good-humored man with a ready smile, a joke on his lips, and an optimistic outlook. The man who returned was embittered and cynical and filled with hate.

Walter had done that to him. To them. And he'd done it with the help of this man.

"What letters?" insisted Cecil. Daisy didn't answer him. She didn't feel it was her place. It was his father's crime and, she thought, his father should tell him of it.

But Mr. Godson could not meet his son's eyes. Nor could he look at Daisy, for that matter. He kept his gaze down, though his shame was still plain to see.

In the end, it was Mrs. Godson who spoke. She answered Cecil's questions, though she looked squarely at Daisy as she explained, her voice clear, steady, and strong. A woman defending her man, no matter what he had done.

"Walter Pearson come in the shop just after Frank went off to training," she said. "Says if anyone who wasn't family wrote to Frank, we should keep back the letters until he'd seen them. Said he'd decide which ones to pass on. Give us some cock-and-bull story about how people were bothering Frank and he could…weed those ones out."

"You agreed to this?" Cecil was horrified.

"I had to be…" Mr. Godson's voice trailed off as his excuse died.

"He didn't agree at first," his wife said. "Told him no, straight out. We couldn't do that. It's against the law."

"I'll say it's against the law!" Cecil paced the kitchen now, his face pale with agitation. "You can get hard labor for that!"

"That's what I told him," said Mr. Godson. "but he…he said, if I didn't do it, he'd find me guilty of something else. Mother too. And then, there was you, working in his gardens, and your sister was a maid in his house, and your other sister, working in his shop."

"He threatened to turn us off?" Cecil looked dumbfounded. "Do you think we'd have cared? There's other jobs. And both our Violet and our Maud got married. They don't work for anyone anymore."

"They wouldn't have got married if they'd been inside, would they?" argued Mrs. Godson. "He said he'd see them in Holloway, and you in the Scrubs," she went on, referring to two large prisons in London, one of them for women. "I believed him."

Daisy would have believed him, too. She was beginning to think Walter Pearson was the devil incarnate. It seemed not to matter to him who he hurt as long as he got his way.

"In the event, the only letters sent to Frank come from his mum, his sisters, and you." Mr. Godson glanced at Daisy. "When I sorted the incoming mail, I put all Frank's letters to go to Jacobs Manor." The Pearson family home.

"The Post Office Act is very clear about officials stealing letters, Dad," said Cecil. He was appalled. Daisy felt sorry for him. He'd clearly believed in his parents, in their integrity, and he must be devastated to learn what they had done.

"It's a felony," he continued. "You can get anything from two years to life. With hard labor," he repeated. He rubbed his hands across his head, making his hair stand on end, and pressed his lips tightly together. "Of course, Walter Pearson, not being a post office official himself, would probably get away with a fine." He turned to Daisy. Fear creased his forehead and paled his cheeks. "What happens now?" he asked.

Daisy looked from Cecil, to his parents, and back. She felt sick. The tea she'd drunk today lay heavy in her stomach, and her chest ached with the weight of all the truths she had learned.

Frank *had* written to her. He hadn't lied. He hadn't abandoned her to her fate and callously turned his back on his son. She owed him a huge apology for believing those lies. No matter how plausible they'd seemed, no matter how much the evidence pointed to his guilt, she should have known better. Realized the man she knew and loved would never have done those things. Instead, she'd… She owed him an apology.

It wasn't only Frank she owed. She needed to say "sorry" to Albert, too. And to Bertie. Most of all, to Bertie.

Because she had believed the worst of Frank, Bertie had never met his father—not until last Friday. He'd had no chance to know his dad, to love him and be loved by him. Worst of all, he was—and always would be—illegitimate, his life blighted before it began. Chances would be denied to him, opportunities refused. Everything would be that little bit harder for him. All because of Daisy's decisions. Daisy's actions. Taken because she'd fallen for the lies of Walter Pearson. Aided and abetted by this man, who now sat here, watching her, terrified.

Part of her thought he should be terrified. He should pay, and pay dearly, for what he'd done. Considering the misery he'd caused, he deserved everything he got. But then again…

Mr. Godson was an old man now. Yes, he had broken the law twelve years ago, but it was probably the only time in his entire life that he'd done such a thing; he wasn't a rule breaker by nature. What would it serve to make him pay for it now? Daisy would have a modicum of revenge, that was true. But in the grand scheme of things, her revenge would right no wrongs. Her life, Frank's life, Bertie's…none of them would be altered because this man was convicted.

Not only that, he wouldn't be the only one to suffer. Mrs. Godson had also known what was happening. Under British law, she was as guilty as her husband. But Cecil had known nothing. He'd done nothing wrong. Daisy suspected that Violet and Maud were just as innocent. Yet all three would be touched by their father's disgrace. Cecil would, almost certainly, lose his position, and with it, his home. Violet and Maud would be shamed, gossiped about, sneered at. Their husbands might lose their jobs, their children would be bullied.

Meanwhile, Walter Pearson, the truly guilty one,

would sit in his big house, presiding over his business empire, clicking his tongue over the perfidy of the working classes, and remain untouched by it all.

That was not what Daisy wanted.

All three Godsons watched her, carefully, as they awaited her decision. The air in the room grew taut, difficult to breathe. There was no sound. Even the slow tick of the grandmother clock faded to nothing. Daisy looked from one to the other of them.

Finally, she nodded, and said, "Nothing. Nothing will happen. I'm not going to tell anyone."

Her answer didn't seem to relieve them. Cecil narrowed his eyes, suspicious. His father watched her, warily.

Mrs. Godson voiced their concerns. "We haven't got a lot," she said. "And we won't steal. Not again. Never again. No matter what the consequences."

It took Daisy a moment to realize what she meant. When she did, her jaw dropped and her eyes widened. They thought she planned to blackmail them!

How could they think that? Of her! She glared at them, letting the daggers in her stare convey her opinion of them. "I don't want you to steal," she hissed. "I don't want anything from you. I said I wouldn't say anything, and I won't. Not because I think I'll profit from it, or… I am not Walter-bloody-Pearson!"

She took a deep breath that made her nostrils flare. Her heart raced, and she knew her color was high. "I won't say anything because there's no point. No good to be had from it. For crying out loud! It was twelve years ago! What good would it do to…to…" She growled, frustrated. "I don't want you to go to prison. I just…I just wanted to know the truth. To know what happened.

That's all." She swallowed, hard. "Well, now I know. Which means that now I can put it behind me."

Her voice broke on the last words and tears burned her eyes. She cursed them. She did not want to break down and cry in front of these people. She didn't want to cry over this at all. It wasn't worth her tears. If she kept telling herself that, perhaps those tears would not come.

"I'll be going now." She stood, her shoulders straight, head held high.

"I'm sorry," said Mrs. Godson. "We didn't mean…please. Stay. Drink your tea."

Daisy's bottom lip trembled. It took a moment to overcome it. She shook her head. "I have to get back," she said. "I need to be in Tunbridge Wells before m-my son c-comes out of school."

"Cecil will give you a lift in the van, won't you, Cec?" insisted Mrs. Godson. Cecil nodded, and his mother gave Daisy an imploring look. "Please. It's the least we can do."

Perhaps she was right. Daisy certainly wasn't looking forward to the long, hot trek home. To refuse the lift would be the very definition of cutting off her nose to spite her face.

"All right," she said, and she sat down again.

An hour later, Cecil stopped the Post Office van on the corner of Monson Street and Mount Pleasant Road. It was three thirty, and she had enough time to get to the school before the bell rang to release the children without leaving herself breathless and flushed. The sky was dark with the threat of rain, the air buzzing with electricity, the breeze nonexistent.

"Thank you," she said to Cecil.

"No, thank *you*," he replied. "I'm sorry for…well.

Thank you. If you ever need anything—"

"I have what I need." She opened the van door, gave him a last, uncomfortable smile, and climbed out, then watched him turn around in the junction and head back toward Fieldhurst.

Automatically, Daisy looked up the road to the picket line. It was empty of people, which made her frown. It was too early for the pickets to have gone home yet. There should be somebody there for at least another two hours.

Intrigued, she took a few steps closer. She saw the newly swept area, cleaner than the pavement either side of it, the dust and grit of everyday life gone. The ticket office door and windows, and the Opera House windows, were covered in wooden boards that looked as if they'd been tacked into place in a hurry.

It took less than a second to figure out what had happened here. R Company had arrived. They had come to Tunbridge Wells and attacked the strikers, just as Frank had said they would. Daisy prayed nobody had been hurt, or at least, not badly, because the fading and dried splotches on the pavement indicated some injuries had occurred.

She looked up the road. There were a few shoppers around, but most shops had closed, their awnings retracted, windows in darkness. Those with shutters had pulled them down, though again it was hours too early.

Near the Five Ways, she saw two men she didn't recognize. They wore what looked like some kind of uniform, a dark shirt and trousers, and berets. They walked with a certain swaggering pride, as if the world was theirs. One held a thick stick, like a policeman's truncheon, which he patted in rhythmic threat against the palm of his other hand. She could see the other man had a truncheon too, though his was in a kind of holster on his belt. They looked around, taking in every detail of their surroundings, seeking out…trouble?

Daisy had no intention of giving them any. All she wanted to do now was go to the school, pick up Bertie and get him safely home, then wait for Frank to come and see him.

A frisson of fear passed through her, for Frank. Out and about, making his way to her home, through this. Then she made herself relax. Frank would be all right, even with those bully boys around. He wasn't a striker. He wasn't their target.

Although, what guarantee of safety that brought was debatable. Thugs were thugs. They may have come here to break the strikes, but if non-strikers got in their way, she didn't think they would care much about hurting them, too. They would happily cause damage to anyone. Whoever they were. Frank. Daisy. Even…

Oh, Lord! Bertie. She wouldn't put it past those men to attack a little boy, if he crossed their paths. She needed to get to him. Now. She turned tail and fled along Monson Street.

Daisy didn't slow down until she reached the school gates. She was hot and out of breath, sticky and flushed, but she felt the panic drain from her as the playground came into sight. Safe. She was safe. Bertie was safe.

There were a lot more mothers waiting than there'd been on Friday. The women looked grim, faces pinched and tight, pale and worried. Some saw Daisy approach, and threw her venomous glances before whispering to others, who glanced at her while they listened.

Jean came to Daisy, stopping her a few yards from

the main crowd. "Go home. I can bring Bertie," she said, her voice low.

Daisy sighed. "Are they calling me a trollop?" She swallowed. "And Bertie? Are they saying—?"

"No." Jean shook her head. "That'd be people living in glass houses and throwing stones."

"Then, what?" Daisy could think of no other reason for their animosity toward her.

"Pearson's depot was attacked. Bus pickets, too. And the train station. People were hurt."

Daisy closed her eyes in despair. She'd seen the bloodstains on the pavement. She had known. Until this moment, though, she had not allowed herself to believe how bad it might be.

Jean gestured with her thumb at the other women. "Some of them are married to men who are on strike. Some of their husbands got hurt."

"What's that got to do with me?" It was terrible, yes, but Daisy wasn't responsible.

Jean's eyes flicked toward the school. "Bertie's dad. They know who he is."

"He's…" Walter Pearson's son. Daisy sighed, seeing the situation as others would see it. Frank was a Pearson. One of *them*, against the *us.* Guilty by blood. "He didn't have anything to do with it," she said. She would shout it, if it would help.

"They don't care. Go home, Daisy. Give it a few days. Let it die down."

Daisy shook her head, emphatically. "I can't. I can't leave Bertie to face that lot."

"I'll look after him. Bring him to you."

That wouldn't work. Never in a million years would Daisy turn tail and flee, saving herself and leaving Bertie to face the haters without her. "Would you leave Clive?" she asked, and Jean grimaced. Daisy pressed on. "Precisely. I won't leave Bertie."

A moment later, the point was moot because the school bell rang and the children came out. In ones and twos and threes they reunited with parents who ushered them away. The crowd thinned, until only Jean and Daisy were left.

"Where are they?" she muttered, just as Clive appeared. He dragged his feet across the playground, as if he didn't want to come home. That was certainly not normal. And where was Bertie? Daisy hoped he hadn't been given a detention. Not today.

Did they give detentions to be served on the same day? Bertie had never received one before, so she was unsure, but she'd always thought they gave a twenty-four-hour notice, so parents knew why their child was late home. She could be wrong, though.

Clearly, the teacher wasn't going to enlighten her, because she headed back into the classroom as Clive finally reached the school gate.

"Where's Bertie?" Daisy asked, although she was afraid of the answer. Which was absurd. What was there to be afraid of? Bertie was in school. He would show himself at any moment.

Clive looked away. His guilt could not have been plainer if he had worn a placard around his neck to proclaim it.

Jean narrowed her eyes at her son. "Clive," she warned. "Where. Is. Bertie?"

The boy swallowed. Mumbled something. His mother pressed him to repeat it. His eyes flicked up at Daisy, then he looked away again. Finally, he said, "He bunked off."

Bertie had played truant? Daisy was horrified. To her knowledge, Bertie had never done such a thing before. But he had been sullen and angry, and anything was possible.

"What do you mean, 'he bunked off'?" asked Jean. "He was here this morning. We watched you both go in, together."

"Yes," agreed Clive. "Then he sneaked out again. He said he couldn't come to school today because he had something more important to do."

The world stopped turning. The sky grew more dark. Daisy's pulse beat, loud and fast and erratic in her ear. A thousand dreadful scenarios flashed through her head— all the places he might be, all he might have seen and done and been caught up in. Bile burned her throat.

Clive spoke again. It sounded as if he shouted the words at her down a long, narrow tunnel. "He said his granddad's sick. That means Bertie's the man of the house now."

Those last words echoed through her, taunting her. *Man of the house now…Man of the house…Man now…*

Her breath shallowed. She couldn't swallow. Every muscle quivered. Every nerve stretched.

"He's got to look after his mum," said Clive.

Look after his mum…look after his mum…his mum…

Oh, God! Her son was out there, somewhere, in the middle of all the trouble and violence.

Daisy turned and ran back toward the town.

Chapter Seventeen

Frank left his parents' home without trying to see his mother. Even if he could get her to talk to him—and that was doubtful since she had taken to her room—he wouldn't get any information from her. She always left such unpleasantries to Walter and simply rose above them. On the rare occasion when that didn't work, she became upset. More than upset. Put upon. Victimized. If he tried to talk to her, Frank would simply end up feeling like a bully, and for no real reason. He knew what he needed to know.

He had to get out. To quit living under his father's roof as soon as he could. Which meant he needed a paying job. Which meant, in turn, giving notice to Harry that he'd be leaving his brother's firm. Frank had to take the van back; he could tell Harry at the same time.

Harry's car was parked next to Frank's Bentley behind the barn they used as a depot. That meant Harry was here, since he couldn't walk far. Time to get this sorted, then. Frank pulled the van into the shed and went to see his brother.

Reggie was in the office with Harry. He could hear them arguing good-naturedly. Harry, apparently, wished to knock out the partitioning wall between their two offices, making them into one big space. Reggie said that if they were in the same room, they wouldn't get any work done. Considering the laughing and murmuring,

Frank agreed with her.

He needed to let them know he was here before his accidental eavesdropping embarrassed them all, so he rapped his knuckles on the door, then pushed it open in time to see the pair jump apart as if they'd been given electric shocks. Reggie's face was scarlet. Harry cleared his throat.

Frank grinned. "Am I interrupting something? Should I come back later?"

"No, come in," said Harry. He smiled, though his stiff posture gave the lie to his attempt to seem carefree. He cleared his throat again. "I've wanted to speak to you for days. You're a hard man to find. I was beginning to think you were a figment of my imagination."

Reggie moved toward the door, saying something about inventory to check. She smiled at Frank as she passed, then slipped out of the room, leaving the brothers to talk. Frank wasn't sure if her swift departure was a good omen or a bad one.

Harry pulled himself from his chair and stood upright. He hesitated for a moment, gripping the edge of his desk for balance while his legs adjusted to his weight, then grabbed one of his sticks, moved awkwardly to the filing cabinet, and took a file from the top drawer. The file was marked with Frank's name.

Inside, he groaned. It looked as if Harry had prepared the paperwork to end Frank's employment here. Frank didn't want to be fired. Even though he knew he'd be leaving anyway, it was a matter of semantics. There was a huge difference between choosing to leave and being asked to do so.

Quickly, before Harry could say the fateful words, Frank made his announcement. "Before you say anything else, I have something to tell you. I can't work for you anymore."

Harry froze, his eyes wide with shock. He stared at Frank for a long moment, then looked down at the file in his hand.

Frank felt guilty. He didn't want Harry to think he would leave him in the lurch. "That is, I can. For the time being. If you've got the work for me. But only until I find a proper job."

His brother's shock turned to puzzlement. "This isn't a proper job?"

"A paying one. I need to earn money, Harry. I have to make a living. I've got…well, you might as well sit down and listen to the whole story. I'd rather you hear it from me, because you're bound to get your ears pinned back from our father about it." He grimaced. "I have a son." Frank stiffened, ready to defend his last statement.

Harry raised an eyebrow. "Like you say, I should sit. This sounds like it will take longer than I'm able to stand." He sank into his chair.

Frank perched on the corner of the desk and tried to seem relaxed, although every nerve within him was on edge. He knew Harry would listen, but he had no idea how he would react. Harry wasn't judgmental in the way Walter was, but he had a business to run and a reputation to maintain. Would he feel Frank risked those things for him?

"Go on," encouraged Harry.

Frank took a deep breath, blew it out, drew another, then launched into his tale. He told Harry everything. Daisy's disappearance twelve years ago, and finding her again now. Discovering Albert had survived. Learning of Bertie, and what Walter had done.

Harry sniffed. "Might have known he'd have something to do with it."

"The upshot of it is," Frank replied, on a weary sigh, "I have a family, and I need to provide for them. Plus, I need somewhere to live, pretty sharpish. Walter's going to kick me out of his house soon. I'm surprised he hasn't done so already."

"I'm not." Harry grinned. "He can't. He doesn't have the power." Frank frowned, and Harry went on, "It's not Walter's house."

For a moment, Frank was lost for words.

"It's never been his house," Harry continued. "It belonged to Mother's father. I don't remember Grandfather Jacobs well, but I believe he didn't like Walter much."

An understatement, if Frank had ever heard one. "He didn't like him at all." Though he'd only been a child, Frank remembered the frosty atmosphere whenever the two men met.

"Which explains why Grandfather Jacobs left the house to Mother, with the stipulation that it would never be owned by Walter, could not be bought by him and, should it be sold, he can't take a penny of the proceeds. If Mother dies before him, he can't inherit it. And…" Harry grinned. "*She* alone has the power to ask people to leave. In fact, she has the power to evict *him*."

Frank was astounded. "That's in the will?"

"Apparently. My understanding is, Walter was furious. Took legal advice. The will's airtight. Watertight, even. Now, you know, and I know, Mother won't stand up to Walter about much. But owning that house gives her a little power. Power she will use to protect her children, and he knows it. He tried to kick Joe out a few years back, before I joined up," Harry referred to one of their other brothers. "Mother intervened. She said she wouldn't see one of her children homeless, regardless of what he'd done to upset Walter. Made it clear, if it came to it, Joe would stay and Walter could leave. Before you ask, I don't know what Joe's crime was. It doesn't really matter, does it? What matters is, Walter can't kick you out. So you may as well stay there until you're ready to leave."

That didn't seem like a situation Walter would have tolerated. "He doesn't own it, has no power over it, yet he stays there? Why didn't he buy somewhere else?"

"He couldn't buy anything as impressive as Jacobs Manor, and appearance is everything. He needs somewhere he can entertain his business contacts and have them believe he's wildly successful. Jacobs Manor fits that bill. And since Mother never tells anyone it isn't his…"

"Nobody thinks he's a kept man." Frank thought for a moment. "In that case, I'll stay until I find something else. But I will still be leaving in the long run."

"Meanwhile, oh, brother mine," Harry opened Frank's file, satisfaction filling his smile. "You don't need to leave here. Reggie and I have gone through things and, we're proud to say, we're doing well. Even with the strike, which will affect us if it goes on too long, we're hitting our targets far quicker than we thought we would. Which means we can pay you for what you do. That's why I wanted to see you. We had a contract of employment drawn up for you." He took a sheet of paper from the file and handed it to Frank. "Fair's fair. You do the work, you deserve the pay."

Frank took the paper and skimmed over it. He could

scarcely believe this. It was all he could have asked for, and more. "You can…pay me?"

"Same rate we'd give to any other driver. Are you in?"

"Oh, yes." Relieved, Frank shook Harry's hand. They agreed his paid employment would start tomorrow, and he signed the contract.

It felt as if a burden had been lifted from him. He had a job with a steady income, he wasn't homeless, he could afford to support his family. Plus, he had the money his godfather had left him. It was enough to buy a house where they could live, if not in luxury, then certainly in greater comfort than the boarding house offered. Now, if he could just persuade Daisy to marry him, his world would be completely set to rights.

Reggie smiled as he passed her on his way out. He kissed her cheek, then thanked her.

"You're welcome," she said. "You're worth your weight in gold to us." He inclined his head at the compliment. "By the way, did you know who that boy was?"

Frank frowned. "What boy?"

"I don't know. Young lad, about ten. Looked enough like you and Harry to be family, though Harry didn't know of any cousins or such of that age. He said he'd ask you, see if you knew, especially since it was you he was looking for. I expect he forgot."

Everything within Frank stilled. "He was looking for me?"

"Hm-hm." She nodded. "Asked me nicely if Mr. Frank Pearson was available. He wouldn't leave a message, or his name or…Frank? Are you all right?"

"What? Yes. Yes, I'm fine." A lie. Frank knew the

color had drained from his face, because he could feel it. He felt the lightheadedness, too, and the overwhelming, sick fear for his son. Bertie should have been in school, not wandering the countryside looking for Frank. He'd put himself in danger, what with the R Company thugs roaming the town, looking for trouble. The thought that Bertie might have crossed paths with those monsters turned Frank's legs to jelly, and filled his stomach with ice.

And why was he here, looking for Frank? What could he want that couldn't wait until later, when Frank was due to call?

Was something the matter with Daisy? Had she sent the boy because she needed him to come? To help her?

"Are you sure you're all right?" Reggie studied him, concerned.

"Yes, honestly. I'm fine. Which way did the boy go?"

She shrugged. "He headed back into Tunbridge Wells, but I only watched him until he left the farm track. I didn't follow him."

"I—I've got to go." *I've got to make sure my son is safe.*

Frank raced for his car and drove toward Tunbridge Wells as if the devil himself were on his tail.

The center of Tunbridge Wells was quiet as Frank drove up the hill toward Monson Street. The few people walking on the lower part of Mount Pleasant Road had a grim, grey air about them, as if the joy of life had been sucked from them. The train station looked much as the ticket office up the road had done: broken windows, damaged trim and door panels. Across the road, people were mopping up outside the kinema and the Bridge

Hotel.

Frank shook his head. Why had the London thugs targeted those places? Their employees weren't part of the strike, and there would have been no pickets there. It seemed to be destruction for its own sake.

A man stood outside the hotel, two pieces of broken wood held loosely in his hands. He scowled at Frank as he drove by. Frank couldn't blame him. His father had a lot to be sorry for, and as his son, Frank was certain to take some of the blame, and the anger. Nothing he could say would prevent that. He'd just have to weather it.

He approached the turn to Monson Street and slowed down. Outside the ticket office, Charlie, Matt, Jerry, and a couple of other men were maneuvering a new door into position. The debris of the morning had been cleared away.

Further up the road a man with a walking cane hobbled along the pavement. His steps were slow and labored, his back stooped, but there was something familiar about him. A moment later, the man stopped at the mouth of an alley and Frank saw it was Albert. The older man stiffened, called out something and hurried into the alley, out of Frank's sight.

Frank frowned. Why on earth would Albert go in there? To Frank's knowledge, there was nothing in the alley except the backs of shops, and probably a few trash receptacles. It wasn't a cut-through, either, since it was a dead end. But Albert had gone in, purposefully, and he'd looked angry, braced for a fight.

Albert had no business fighting. He walked with a stick, for goodness' sake! Although his legs were stronger and less damaged than Harry's, nobody would call Albert nimble. Then there was his breathing problem. An argument with Frank had left him fighting for every lungful of air. He couldn't take on anybody who might truly wish to hurt him.

Three men sauntered toward the alley. Frank recognized them immediately from their clothes. They wore black tunics, similar in style to the khaki Frank had worn as a soldier. Black trousers and heavy, military-style boots. Their berets sported a red badge. He couldn't see it in clear detail from here, but he was willing to bet it showed some sort of insignia.

Alarms rang in Frank's head. Whatever was in that alley had attracted trouble, and Albert Redmond was in the thick of it. Frank abandoned the turn and drove his Bentley further up the road instead, stopping just before the alley mouth. For a second, he thought about alerting the men fixing the ticket office door, then decided not to. This might turn out to be a storm in a teacup, something easily defused, and the presence of pickets in a small space with members of R Company would only escalate the trouble.

As he climbed from his car, a strong gust of wind blew along the street, whipping up dust and grit and chilling the air, although it was still warmer than usual, and there was a heaviness about it that oppressed. His scalp itched, and his shirt felt sticky against his back. The sooner the coming storm arrived, the better.

The wind died again. Voices sounded from the alley. Albert's, angry and belligerent, mixed with the voices of at least two other men. One sounded low, gravelly. The other had a smoother tone. Frank couldn't hear the individual words, but he could tell they were not good.

Then things went from bad to worse when a child's voice rang out, clear and loud. "It's none of your business!"

Oh, hell.

Frank hurried to the mouth of the alley and his heart missed a beat. The three louts stood just inside the alley, blocking anyone who might want to exit. Ahead of them was Albert. He was red-faced and fighting for breath, but his back was as stiff and straight as it could be. Albert's gaze darted back and forth between the three men in the alley mouth, and a fourth one, also in R Company uniform. This man stood between Albert and Bertie, whose face was set in aggressive defiance, his fists clenched. In fact, it looked as if the only thing that had stopped him attacking the nearest man already was his mother's firm grip on his shoulders.

Frank swore under his breath and stepped into the alley.

Chapter Eighteen

Daisy had rushed from the school, hardly able to think straight for fear that her son was on the streets. She'd seen the damage on the drive from Fieldhurst. At both rail stations, and at the bus ticket office, as well as various other places, there was evidence of vandalism and violence. Windows were smashed, buildings defaced. Wooden boards were nailed in place to replace glass, and some of those clearing up sported bandages, and even slings. This was not a day for a boy to skip school and be out on his own.

She'd heard Jean call after her that she'd get the men searching for Bertie, and if he turned up, she would keep him with her. Daisy nodded her thanks, and hurried on.

At the corner where Monson Street met Mount Pleasant Road, she hesitated, uncertain which way to go. Then common sense kicked in. Since she'd come up the hill in Cecil's van a short while ago, she reasoned, she would have seen Bertie, had he gone that way. Therefore, she headed into the town center, hoping to find him lollygagging in the shops.

Of course, he might already have gone home, hoping to get there before she discovered his truancy. Part of her wanted to go back and check, but if she did that and he *wasn't* there, she would have wasted precious time. Time when he might face any number of dangers.

Two bus men stood outside the ticket office,

smoking cigarettes and looking around, warily. Further along the road, women were being harassed by three men in some kind of uniform. They reached for shopping baskets and checked the contents, waving off protests.

"Bullies and thugs," she whispered, her anxiety for Bertie growing by the minute. "Please let him be all right," she prayed.

She was about to ask the two bus men if they'd seen him when she spotted him herself. He sidled past the impromptu checkpoint the three men had set up, and started toward the Opera House. As he did so, a fourth man in a black tunic stepped out of the tobacconist on the other side of the ticket office. The man stopped to light his cigarette. Bertie saw him and ducked into an alley. The man who, Daisy thought, had to be from R Company, flicked his spent match carelessly to the pavement, and walked toward his comrades. As he passed the mouth of the alley, Daisy's heart leapt to her throat and stopped her breath. If he turned his head, he would, surely, see Bertie. What would he do then? Would he pick on a small boy?

Hide, Bertie. In her head, Daisy screamed the words. In reality, she didn't dare so much as whisper them.

The man passed without even glancing into the alley. Daisy's breath left her on a huge whoosh and she ran forward. The sooner she got Bertie out of there and home, the better.

At first, she didn't see him. The alley was narrow and dark, the sunlight blocked by buildings on either side of it. Most of them were three or more stories high, shops topped by storerooms and flats where shop workers and others lived. The shop fronts were on the other sides of the buildings, on the clean, respectable roads. Here, there were dingy rear entrances—doors where ancient paint peeled and grimy windows were covered, on the ground floor at least, by steel bars. The walls were grey with age and smoke, and although there were bins all along the alley, rubbish gathered where building met street. There was a faint smell of rotting vegetation and old urine. It made the tip of her nose twitch and turned her stomach.

At the far end, the alley branched to right and left in a tiny T-junction. More shop backs lined that part of the road, sealing it, so the only way in or out was the way she had come. The cross bar of the T was where Bertie must have hidden. It was where Daisy headed.

She was almost there when Bertie walked around the corner and into view. He looked like any boy at the end of the day: his school jumper tied around his waist, his socks wrinkled around his ankles. His shoes were scuffed and his hair tousled, his face grubby with sweat and who-knew-what-else. He saw Daisy and stopped. For a moment, guilt showed on his face. Then he pushed it away and glared at her instead.

A hundred things raced through her mind. She wanted to hug him and savor the fact that he was safe and in one piece. She wanted to turn him over and spank him until he couldn't sit down. To scold him until his ears bled, and tell him how worried she'd been.

The only thing she could actually think of to say was, "What are you up to? Where have you been?" The words came out on a harsh, angry note.

His chin jutted defiantly. "Looking for *him*," he said. The word "*him*" was delivered like a curse word.

Daisy closed her eyes. There could be only one *"him"* that her son would be looking for. "You won't find him down here," she answered.

"Why did he have to come back?" he demanded. His bottom lip stuck out, petulantly. "We don't need him. He should have stayed lost."

"Bertie—"

"Tell him to get lost again! We don't want him."

"Why don't we go home and talk about this—"

"Is there a problem here?" The question was delivered in a deep, gravelly voice that carried a strong South London accent.

A quick glance confirmed her fear. This was the man from the tobacconist. Instinct told her he meant them no good. A shiver ran down her spine and threatened to turn her legs to water, while the hairs on her neck stood to attention. Her heartbeat raced painfully, and her stomach flipped over on itself.

The man was a head taller than Daisy, his shoulders broad, his hands as big as coal shovels. She could see, even through the black serge of his uniform, that his arms and legs were thick and muscular. His eyes were hard, and a cruel smile played on his lips.

Hoping against hope that she could somehow smooth their way past him, she smiled and said, "Thank you for your concern, sir. It's just a family matter." *Please go away. Leave us alone.*

"Family matter, eh?" The man sniffed. He stood with his legs apart, those huge hands on his hips. He glanced at Bertie, then back at Daisy, and he licked his lips, appreciatively.

Oh, Lord. How would she get them out of this?

"What kind of family matter?" He took a step toward her.

Then everything happened all at once, quickly, yet at the same time, in a strange slow motion, as if the air had turned to aspic and everybody struggled to wade through it.

Behind the thug, Dad hobbled toward them, his cane clicking angrily against the concrete. His face was red with both the exertion and his fury, and his shoulders moved up and down heavily as he fought for his breath.

"You leave my daughter and my grandson alone," he commanded the man, who glanced back, saw Dad, and chuckled, nastily. Dad's eyes widened and his nostrils flared as the insult hit home. Daisy shook her head, watching the catastrophe unfold and helpless to stop it. It was no use telling him to go, to fetch help, even though that was the best thing he could do. Dad would no more leave her and Bertie than he would…sit down for a drink with Walter Pearson.

A moment later, three more uniformed men appeared in the alley's mouth, blocking off any and all escape. Their faces told Daisy their mood was no more reasonable than that of the first man.

Still, she had to try. If she could stop this before it became too ugly, maybe nobody would be hurt. She opened her mouth to try to reason with them.

Before she could utter a word, though, everything went to hell in a handbasket. Bertie stepped forward, his face set, fists clenched, body stiff. He glared at the man nearest to him. Daisy caught his shoulders and held him, so he couldn't launch himself at the man, but she couldn't stop his voice. It rang, clear and loud, and challenging.

"It's none of your business," he said.

For maybe two seconds, the boy's bravado shocked the thugs into stunned silence. Then the one nearest to them narrowed his eyes at Bertie. "Your family should have taught you better manners than that, boy."

He moved with astounding speed for such a thickset man and grabbed Bertie from Daisy's grasp. Bertie yelled, more in surprise than pain. Dad roared and lumbered forward, cane raised like a mace. Daisy thought she might have screamed, but it could have been in her head.

She reached for Bertie. The thug pushed her and said he'd deal with her next. The shove sent her reeling, and she slammed into the back door of a shop. Her shoulder jarred and her head cracked against the aged wood so hard she saw stars.

Dizzy, vision clouded, she watched Dad bring his cane handle in a vicious arc. It should have hit the man square on the head, but the thug must have seen it, because he jerked aside at the last instant, and it hit his shoulder instead. It didn't knock him down, but it still did damage. He shouted his pain, and let go of Bertie, who stumbled a few steps but managed to stay upright.

"Run, Bertie!" yelled Dad, and he raised his cane to hit the man again. He didn't get the chance. The big man's fist shot out and caught Dad squarely in the face. The older man staggered back and would have fallen, but two of the other bullies grabbed his arms and held him upright. The first man hit Dad again, in the solar plexus this time, putting all his force behind the blow.

"Get off my grandad!" Bertie grabbed the first man around one of his massive thighs and tried to hold him back. He had as much influence over the thug's movements as a butterfly would have had.

"Bertie, get out of here!" cried Daisy. Nobody took any notice of her.

The fourth man grabbed at Bertie, who clung on to

the first man's leg for all he was worth, and a desperate tug of war began. Daisy took a step forward to join the fray, though what she might achieve against strong and seasoned street brawlers, she didn't know.

An animalistic roar sounded and suddenly Frank was there. He pulled the fourth man back, spun him round, and slammed him into the wall opposite her before hitting him with a one-two movement, first driving a fist deep into his stomach before delivering an uppercut to the man's jaw. The man dropped like a stone.

The two holding Dad's arms let go and ran to tackle Frank, clearly seeing him as the bigger threat. The first man hit Dad again, this time knocking him to the ground, then struggled to free himself from Bertie's tight grasp. Bertie bit the man's leg. The man howled and swung a meaty fist, putting everything he could behind the blow, and knocking Bertie a clear four feet away. Daisy screamed as Bertie landed in a heap beside his grandad. The big man aimed a last, vicious kick at Dad's ribs, then raced to join his mates in attacking Frank. Dad curled into a ball, clutching his middle and groaning. Bertie scrambled to his knees and leaned over him.

Daisy pulled herself upright, fighting the nauseous headache behind her eyes. For an instant, she thought she should go to help Bertie and Dad, then decided it was more important to help Frank first. If those three bested him—and they would, if someone didn't help him—they'd come for her family next.

Frank was holding his own. For now. But it was only a matter of time. Three on one would never end well. If Daisy could jump onto the back of one of the men, perhaps she could choke him, or gouge at him, or…she didn't know what. Daisy had never been in a fight in her life, but she was going to give this one her all.

There was a blur of movement. The number of bodies in the melee doubled. She heard grunts and groans, and the sound of flesh hitting flesh. Bins clattered as they overturned, scattering their contents across the alley. Glass shattered and old food squelched, cardboard thwacked dully against the ground. Paper rattled and rustled and skittered away, as if trying to escape the chaos. Men slammed into walls and doors with bone-jarring thuds.

A shrill whistle overlaid all the other sounds. Daisy's vision finally cleared as half a dozen police officers ran into the alley and peeled men away from the fight.

And then, it was over. Almost. Jerry Balcombe still held Frank tightly, pinning his arms to his sides, while Frank struggled against him and glared murderously at the man who had hit both Dad and Bertie.

"Calm down, Frank," said Jerry. "It's over. They're beaten. Calm down, mate."

An angry red swelling tightened the skin on Frank's cheek. His eye was already closing. His lip was split, and his coat torn. Beside him, Charlie, Matt, and the two other bus men stood, panting heavily. Charlie's gloves were torn, displaying grazed knuckles, and he, too, sported a black eye and a split lip, but he looked satisfied, as if his bruises were a price worth paying for the chance to put these thugs down.

The bullies sat on the ground, their hands cuffed. Police officers stood over them. Regular officers, not the specials who'd guarded the picket lines. Daisy was relieved by that. The specials were good at what they did, and willing to do the job, but the regulars were better trained and better equipped.

"You lot all right?" asked one police officer.

"Never better," answered Charlie. He grinned, then winced as it pulled on his cut lip.

"You can't arrest us!" declared one of the thugs. He looked appalled that anybody would even try.

"We just did," growled the officer. He turned to the pickets. "We were confined to stations earlier. Told not to come out, under any circumstances." He sighed. "Someone will say the order was a mistake, I've no doubt, and there's no way to know who gave it. All I can say is, 'Sorry.' "

Jerry nodded. "Not your fault."

The others murmured. Daisy couldn't tell if they agreed with Jerry or not.

The officer turned back to the protesting thug and leaned in, so his face was close to the prisoner's. His eyes were narrowed and his jaw clenched, which made his words come out on a menacing hiss. "You're resisting arrest. Keep it up. Please."

"You'll be sorry," said the thug. He sounded a little too sure of himself. Daisy hoped that didn't bode ill for the officers or the men who had rescued her.

"Not as sorry as *you're* going to be," said a second police officer. He, too, sounded confident, and he smirked as he turned to Frank. "Are you all right, Mr. Pearson?" Was it her imagination, or had the officer emphasized Frank's name?

"I'm fine," whispered Frank. He touched his tongue to his split lip. "They went after my family." He looked around, anxiously. "Are they all right?"

He shook off Jerry and came to her. "Daisy?" he whispered. He pulled her into a hug. He was strong and warm, a protective cocoon and, for the first time since she left the school gates, Daisy felt everything would be all right.

"Did they hurt you?" he asked.

"I'll be fine, but my dad—"

Her words were cut off by one of the thugs. "Pearson?" he asked. His attitude had changed from arrogant smugness to fear.

"Yeah," sneered Charlie. "Pearson. He's Walter Pearson's son. And you just attacked him and his family. Still think *we'll* be sorry?"

The thug groaned.

Daisy didn't hear any more of the conversation, because Bertie sobbed, "Grandad?"

She pulled out of Frank's arms and they both turned to their son. He knelt beside Dad, who was slumped against the wall, wheezing loudly, and sporadically coughing.

"Dad!" Daisy fell to her knees beside him. Every breath he took was an effort. Bertie held his hand, his young cheeks shiny with tears. He looked up at Daisy as if he expected her to fix it. She didn't know if she could.

Frank crouched on the other side of Dad. He looked from him to her, then to the police officers. "Get an ambulance," he said.

Daisy gasped, though she knew he was right. Dad needed medical attention, far more than she could give him. For all she knew, those villains had cracked his ribs, perhaps even punctured a lung. Bertie sobbed. Dad clutched at Frank's arm.

"No," he said. "No…amb…ulance. Can't…"

"Don't worry." Frank patted Dad's shoulder.

"No…char…charity," wheezed Dad.

"No charity," agreed Frank. He leaned in and whispered to Dad, so quietly that Daisy barely heard him. "It's part of your pension. I'll make sure Walter pays." He glanced over his shoulder where the officers waited for the Black Maria that would take their prisoners and the ambulance to take Dad. The bus men stood nearby, slowly coming down from the state of high alert the fight had left them in. "This is his fault, after all," reasoned Frank.

Dad smiled at that. "You're…all right," he said. Then he passed out.

Bertie sobbed again. "He won't die, will he?"

Frank and Daisy both said, "No, of course not," while at the same time one of the officers muttered, "If he does, it'll be murder. And these swine'll swing for it."

"I didn't touch him," insisted the fourth man.

"All for one," answered Charlie, referring to the law that said if one person committed a murder while carrying out another crime, all his accomplices were also guilty of murder. The fourth man began to cry, protesting his innocence.

"We thought they were communists," said the big man who had started it all.

Frank gave him a contemptuous glare, then turned to Bertie, whose face was white with terror. "Your grandad's going to be all right, Bertie," he said, gently.

Daisy prayed he was right.

****

Two hours later, Frank, Daisy and Bertie sat in a long, green-and-white corridor in Pembury hospital, waiting for news of Albert. They had followed the ambulance in Frank's car, Bertie sitting on Daisy's lap in the two-seater Bentley. Frank knew he would have to trade it in for something more practical now. One could not have a family and a bachelor's car.

The door to the ward swished open and they looked up expectantly, but it wasn't someone for them. A nurse carried an enamel pan covered with a white cloth. She disappeared into another room farther along the corridor, and all was still again.

They'd glimpsed Albert briefly, before the ward sister shooed them away and told them there would be no access to him tonight, although they were welcome to wait and see if his doctor had anything to tell them. It seemed visiting hours were strictly adhered to, and she wouldn't budge on it. Frank didn't think King George himself could have made his way past this particular dragon.

They had seen enough to know that Albert was in an oxygen tent, receiving the care and attention he needed. Frank had already spoken with a hospital official, telling them to give whatever treatment Albert needed, and that he, Frank, would foot the bill.

In an ideal world, of course, Walter would pay, just as Frank had said he would. Alas, this was not an ideal world. Walter would no more pay for Albert's treatment than he would jump from the roof and try to fly. The man had neither the compassion to do something solely for the benefit of another human being nor the shame to help put right the wrongs he'd set in motion.

Daisy sat beside Frank. Bertie was on her other side, his hand held in hers. The aftermath of the fight had drained her of energy, and she rested her head against the wall. Frank half expected someone to come out and scold her for that, although so far nobody had. He longed to put his arm around her, to draw her close and let her rest against him, but he didn't dare. She wasn't exactly enamored of him as it was. Now that her father lay in a hospital bed, thanks to decisions taken by *his* father, Frank dreaded to think what she'd say, should he try to take such a liberty.

Bertie leaned forward and looked across his mother at Frank. He'd done that several times now, his face scrunched in thought while he studied Frank as if he were a bug in a science laboratory. Frank didn't say anything. He pretended not to notice. He didn't want to upset the boy.

This time, Bertie spoke. "You helped my grandad." There was an uncertainty in his voice, as if the idea confused him.

Frank looked him squarely in the eye. "I'll always help him," he vowed. "And you. And your mum."

"But Grandad hates you." A matter-of-fact statement. The truth of it cut Frank to his core.

"Grandad doesn't hate him," whispered Daisy. "He was angry with somebody else. You know what he's like. He shouts at the next person he sees, whether they're to blame or not. This time, that was…" She hesitated, sat up straighter, and glanced at Frank. "That was your dad."

Frank's heart soared at her words. He felt as if all his Christmases and birthdays had come together. All he needed to make his life complete would be for Bertie to call him Dad, too. And for Daisy to agree to marry him, but that was a different argument, for a different time.

"I'm sorry I caused so much trouble," said Bertie. Frank watched Daisy squeeze the lad's hand, but it didn't reassure Bertie. "If I hadn't bunked off…"

"We'll talk about it tomorrow," Daisy told him.

Frank had a feeling the punishment wouldn't be too onerous. He suspected the boy had well and truly learned his lesson.

"It was…" Bertie bit his lip. His eyes flickered as he looked at Frank, then looked away again. "I didn't want…I didn't want you to come and…" His voice choked and a tear slid down cheeks that were already chafed from his earlier crying.

Frank felt a burn behind his own eyes. He longed to hold this boy, to be a part of his life, to build the kind of relationship with him that a father should have with his son. But he couldn't force the lad to want him. He couldn't command his love.

"Tell you what," he said, his voice thick. "You tell me when I can come and see you, and that's when I'll come. I won't force you till you're ready. How does that sound?"

With her free hand, Daisy pulled a handkerchief from her pocket and dabbed her eye.

"But," continued Frank, needing to make everything crystal clear. "That doesn't mean I don't want to see you. I do. But I want you to be happy, so I'll wait until you say."

Daisy gave a sniff, then blinked rapidly. It was as if she didn't want her emotions to intrude and attract their attention.

There was no chance of her succeeding there. Everything about her attracted Frank's attention. Always had. Always would. Even when they'd been apart, she'd always been there, in the back of his mind, a memory he couldn't rid himself of, even if he'd wanted to. And, he acknowledged now, he'd never really wanted to.

Bertie's face creased in thought. Then he stood,

moved two paces to be in front of Frank, and said solemnly, "You can come tomorrow, if you like."

Frank's bottom lip trembled. He swallowed, then nodded. "I would like that very much."

His son held out his left hand. Frank shook it. A deal sealed between two gentlemen. The light in the corridor seemed to grow brighter, and a pressure Frank hadn't even known he was under lifted from his chest, making his breathing easier.

Footsteps clicked rhythmically against the tiled floor. He looked up to see a man, a woman, and a boy. Frank recognized the woman and the boy from the school gates. Bertie's friend—Clive?—and his mother. The man looked enough like the boy to be his father.

The thought went through Frank's head that, perhaps one day, that could be him and Daisy and Bertie, walking together. Belonging together.

"We came as soon as we could," said the woman—Jean, he recalled now. Daisy stood and the two women embraced. "Are you all right?" asked Jean.

Daisy assured her they were.

"They said your dad's a hero," Clive told Bertie, his eyes wide with awe.

Frank wouldn't go that far.

"He duffed up a dozen villains, all on his own!" continued the boy.

Bertie looked bewildered. He had clearly never before been on the receiving end of the Chinese whispers the gossips churned out.

"There were four, and I had help," said Frank. He didn't know why he bothered. By tomorrow, he would likely learn he'd taken on the whole of R Company, run them out of town, then fixed all the damage, single-handedly.

Clive's dad shook his hand and gave him a sympathetic look as Clive continued the embellished tale of Frank's exploits, as if he'd never been contradicted.

"The town's buzzing with it," said Jean. "The police are throwing the book at those men. Mr. Pearson, your dad, that is, is demanding they get hard labor. Said they've got to be made an example of."

Frank and Daisy exchanged a look that told him she thought the same as he did about that. Then he pushed it aside, refusing to give it any of his attention. Walter wasn't worth it.

"They said they're part of some company or other," continued Jean.

"R Company," supplied Frank.

"That's it. But the man in charge said they're not his men. He said his men would never attack innocent people and cause trouble. Says he's law-abiding and respectable. Appalled at what happened here."

Perhaps Roberts *had* been an officer in the war, after all. He was certainly quick enough to throw his men into the line of fire to protect himself.

"As long as they've gone now," said Daisy. "And they don't come back."

"But that's by the bye," said Jean. "We came to see if you wanted us to have Bertie overnight. He can share Clive's bed, and I'll take them both to school in the morning."

The boys, of course, thought that was a capital idea and, less than ten minutes later, they left with Clive's parents.

Daisy watched them go. "I hope they're strict. Otherwise, they won't get a wink of sleep."

Another hour went past before Albert's doctor came to talk to them. Mr. Redmond was going to be fine, he assured them. His ribs were bruised but not fractured, but because of his underlying breathing difficulties, they wanted to keep him in the ward for another day or so.

"I think we can make things better for him," the doctor said. "Get it under control. There are treatments that can alleviate the symptoms. Meantime, you should go home. It won't help if you come tomorrow looking exhausted and worrying him."

Daisy nodded. She turned as if to go.

"One other thing," the doctor continued, and he turned to Frank. "He gave me a message for you, Mr. Pearson. He said he expects you to look after his girl and to do the right thing."

Frank opened his mouth to thank the doctor, but he didn't get the chance.

"Did he, indeed?" huffed Daisy. "He can keep his messages and his expectations. And you, Frank Pearson, you'd better stay quiet, too. I don't need looking after, thank you very much!"

She took off down the corridor, leaving Frank and the doctor behind. The poor doctor looked astounded. Frank, on the other hand, was not in the least surprised. This was the Daisy he'd grown up with. The woman he'd fallen in love with. He only hoped Albert's clumsy message hadn't scuppered his chances with her.

Daisy was almost at the end of the corridor when a senior nurse appeared. "No running in the hospital," barked the nurse. Daisy slowed to a quick walk, though she was still moving fast.

Frank couldn't dally. Not if he wished to catch her up this side of Tunbridge Wells. "Thank you, Doctor," he said, and he hurried after her, taking care not to break into an actual run himself, although that's what he truly wanted to do, with every fiber of his being.

Daisy was halfway to the hospital gates before Frank managed to catch up with her. He called her name but she pretended not to hear him.

The sky was a deep, dark black now. At past nine o'clock, full night had settled in, but added to that was the cover of thick, low cloud which obscured the moon and stars, and even seemed to dim the street lamps. There was a wetness in the air, too, the sort of sticky hot wetness that promised rain was near, and made a body look forward to its arrival. In the distance, thunder rumbled softly. It sounded like the warning growl of a dog that wasn't quite ready to attack but soon would be.

"Daisy, wait!" he called again. His longer legs finally outpaced her speed and he cut across her path. She pulled up and reared back, as if terrified she might plough into him.

"Get out of my way." Anger and hurt pulsated in every word.

"Where are you going?"

"Home."

Her home was more than two miles away. Probably nearer three. "On foot?"

She threw him a look of disdain. "No," she said. "I thought I'd walk there on my hands."

He decided it would be prudent to ignore the sarcasm. "I'll give you a lift."

Her lips puckered as if she had just sucked a lemon. "No, thank you." She sidestepped him, her head held high, back ramrod straight.

"Daisy…" She couldn't walk back to her home from

here. Not at this time of night. There were several pubs between here and there, and even though there was still more than an hour till last orders, there would inevitably be some who'd left the bar and were now on the streets, looking for trouble. The mood Daisy was in, she'd give it to them.

"I can walk," she insisted. "No reason why not. It's not a bad journey. And it's a fine evening."

That had to be the most absurd thing anyone had said all day. A fine evening? With heavy cloud pressing down, low thunder, and strobes of lightning on the far horizon?

As if it had been waiting for its cue, the weather delivered the punchline when a full, fat teardrop of rain landed with a plop onto the brim of her hat. It teetered on the very edge for a second, then fell again, and hit her nose.

Daisy wiped it away. Frank bit the end of his tongue to stop the threatening laughter.

A second raindrop hit her cheek. It made her blink. It ran down toward her jaw and she swiped at it. More drops spotted the pavement, big and thick and round, coming faster with every second. Frank looked up. It looked like they were in for quite a downpour.

"Fine," said Daisy, "you can give me a lift." She walked briskly back to his car.

By the time they reached the Bentley, they were both wet. Her hat sagged and she shivered as water ran, unimpeded, inside the collar of her coat and down her back.

Frank's light wool jacket was no match for the deluge, either, and his shirt stuck, cold and uncomfortable, to his spine. He sat her in the car and cranked the engine as quickly as he could, but by the time he got into the driver's seat, he was dripping.

He drove toward Tunbridge Wells. Silence stretched between them, long and thick and unbearable, until he broke it with what he hoped she would recognize as logic. "I didn't ask him to send me that message, Daisy."

Daisy looked out of the side window.

After a moment, he tried again. "I wasn't expecting it."

She glanced at him, sighed, and looked away again. "I know." She turned and studied him more fully, her eyes narrowed. "You're not going to take any notice of him, are you?"

How was he supposed to answer that? Whatever he said had the potential to be the wrong thing. Frank felt as if he stood in the middle of no-man's-land, barbed wire stretched all around him and the artillery trained on him. He went for the only answer that wasn't likely to get him shot. "He just wants what's best for you."

Daisy folded her arms. "He doesn't know what's best for me. *I'm* the one who knows what's best for me."

"Must be hard," he said. "As a parent, I mean. Hard to let go and… I've only been a father since last Friday, and I know already I'd do anything to protect Bertie. Your dad's only feeling the same way about you."

"Except I am not ten years old."

"Perhaps you are to him."

She turned squarely forward again, her face as thunderous as the sky.

Frank frowned, thoughtfully. "Is this what it's like?" he asked. "Forever?"

Daisy eyed him, suspiciously. "What do you mean?"

"Being a parent. The way you feel… I wanted to kill

that man. When I saw him knock Bertie flying, I…I frightened myself! I didn't know I could feel like that. I've never wanted to kill anyone before. Not even the Hun. Oh, I shot at them. I might even have hit one or two of them. But I didn't actually *want* to kill them. But today, when that bloke hit Bertie…"

"Yes." She repeated it, louder. "Yes. That's being a parent. It makes all the difference."

Frank swallowed, hard. She would either accept what he said next, or she wouldn't. All he could do was say the words and hope. "I don't think it's just being a parent, though. Because, well, I felt the same way when he hurt you."

A flash of lightning flickered in the sky. The rain lashed the windscreen and bounced off the Bentley's roof. The windscreen wipers swished and the tires shushed over the slick road surface. The headlights picked out oily rainbows on dark puddles.

Daisy turned her attention back to the passenger's side window.

Frank took a deep, fortifying breath. "I spoke to Walter," he said. He tried on a smile for size. It felt tight across his face, so he discarded it. "More accurately, I shouted at him."

"I looked into things, too. I know you didn't get my letters. I know it wasn't your fault."

There was no way he could take the absolution she offered. Frank didn't deserve it. "I think it was. It was my fault because I didn't try harder. When I got home and you weren't there, I should have tried harder. Looked harder."

"Doesn't matter."

But it did matter. It always would.

They reached the boarding house. The rain no longer lashed at them now, but came down in a steady pour. Frank heard it in the gutter drains, gurgling and singing along with the thunder, which was still some miles off. He hunched his shoulders inside his jacket and raced around to open her door for her, then hurried to escort her inside her home. By the time they were through the front door, they were soaked. Tiny puddles formed on the hall floor around them.

"Well," he said, more brightly than he felt. "here we are."

"Here we are."

They stared at each other, neither saying anything for several moments. If only he could speak. Find the words he wanted. But the power of speech seemed to have deserted him, at the very moment he needed it most. Not a single coherent sentence came to him.

He would just have to go home, regroup, and try again tomorrow. All would be well tomorrow. He took a step back, and half turned to the front door.

"You can't drive back to Fieldhurst like that," she whispered. "In those wet clothes, I mean. You'll catch your death."

Frank turned and looked at her. Was she saying what he thought she was saying?

A moment later, he realized that, yes, she was.

"You'd best come in for a few minutes," she continued. "I'll light a fire. Enough to dry your things a bit while you have a cup of tea."

He followed her up the stairs.

Chapter Nineteen

Daisy could not believe her own audacity. She had
invited Frank Pearson into her home! He had been
leaving and she had called him back. What did she think
she was about?

The truth was, she hadn't wanted him to go. It had
nothing to do with the soaking he'd received. There was
no way her meager fire would be enough to dry his jacket
in the time it took to make and drink a cup of tea. If
anything, he'd be more comfortable, more quickly, if he
drove home, soaked in a hot bath, and then put on clean,
dry clothes. She should let him go.

Instead, she unlocked her room. He followed her in
and quietly closed the door. He didn't move, didn't come
farther into the room, and yet he seemed to fill it. His
presence flustered her, left her uncertain what to say,
how she should feel.

She turned away from him to light the stove and put
the kettle to boil. When she turned back, it was to see
Frank, kneeling at the fireplace, where he'd piled
kindling around balled-up newspaper. A match flared.
The newspaper caught and the flame took hold, but it
would be some minutes before the fire gave off any
warmth.

He stood, shrugged off his wet jacket, and draped it
over the back of one of the dining chairs, which he put
close to the fire. "Do you mind?" he asked.

She shook her head. She couldn't have answered with words if she tried. Her mouth was too dry, her heart too full, and her brain too empty. His shirt, almost as wet as his jacket, pressed against his skin, showing every contour of his broad shoulders, his powerful chest, and washboard stomach. The cotton was as translucent as a veil; below it she saw the light tan of his skin, and the darker hue of his round, flat nipples. A dusting of hair shaded his chest.

Daisy swallowed. "You should…" She swallowed again. "Get out of that wet shirt. Before you c-catch your death." With an effort, she pulled her gaze from him and concentrated on the fireplace, where the flames now licked at the kindling.

"Do you have a blanket?" he asked.

She pointed to her bedding, under the bench. He unbuttoned his shirt and turned away as he peeled it from his body. The muscles in his back flexed as he bent to pick up her blanket. He wrapped it around himself, then busied himself hanging his shirt over the back of a second chair.

He glanced at her, then looked into the fire, as if the flames fascinated him. "You should change, too. Before you get pneumonia."

Daisy nodded, then retreated to the room Albert shared with Bertie. She closed the door and leaned against it, her heart beating fit to burst from her chest. At eighteen years old, she'd thought Frank Pearson a fine figure of a man. Tall and lean, he'd certainly looked good then, but he'd been a boy. Now…the person in her living room was no boy. The difference between the Frank she'd known then and the one she saw now was…the difference between that ambushing tiger she'd likened him to, last Friday, and her landlady's tabby cat.

Lightning flashed outside the window. It made her jump and brought her back to the present. This had been a mistake. She should never have invited him in. He was too big, too manly, too…Daisy, whose one and only experience with the male body had been that adolescent coupling in the summerhouse, was so far out of her depth now she was drowning. He had to go. He couldn't stay. As soon as she'd dried and dressed, she would tell him that.

Although…how could he leave? His clothes were so wet. He couldn't put them back on. And she could hardly make him go home in her blanket!

He could borrow Dad's shirt. As soon as she thought that, she dismissed it. Dad was a lot smaller than Frank. His shirt wouldn't even go over Frank's arms, let alone cover the rest of him.

She should stay in here, in this room, until his clothes were dry enough that he could leave. Not that she could do that. She'd invited him in; she could hardly ignore him now. It was her own fault. She tugged off her dress and dried herself, while trying to banish the image of the half-naked man next door. The image which did more to warm her than any fire could ever have done.

When she returned to the living room, Frank was crouched before the fire, using the poker to encourage the flames. On the stove, the lid of the kettle rattled, and steam rose from the spout as it boiled. Daisy busied herself pouring the water into the teapot.

Frank cleared his throat. Daisy glanced over her shoulder. He stood near the fire, where the two chairs stood, temporary clotheshorses. Draped across them, his clothes had begun to steam.

"I—erm—I'm going to buy a house," he said, quietly.

His words made the hairs on the back of her neck stand up. Why was he telling her this? Was he trying to make her aware of the difference between them, between their capabilities? If so, he was wasting his time. She was all too well aware of those differences. Why would he draw attention to them?

Her first panicked thought was that he intended to take Bertie from her. Could he do that? Daisy wasn't sure where they stood, legally. Frank wasn't named on Bertie's birth certificate. Her unmarried status and Frank's absence at the baby's registration meant she'd been forbidden, by law, to use his name. But even without documentary proof, nobody seeing Frank and Bertie together would ever doubt that one was the other's son. And with the Pearson money and connections behind him…

"I'd like you to help me choose the right one," he continued.

Daisy's eyes widened. He wanted to buy a home for Bertie, and he wanted her to help him?

"Can you not decide on your own?" she asked, her voice taut.

Frank shrugged. "I can. Of course I can." He sat down on the edge of the bench where she slept. "But since I'm hoping you'll live there, I thought you'd like a say."

She would live there? What did that mean? Was he saying…?

"Thing is, Dais," he went on, "you—all of you—need somewhere to live."

The bubble burst, dispelling the dream of a moment

ago. This was nothing more than his misguided notion of honor. His need to provide for his son. To use Pearson money to make charity cases of her and her family. Well, not if she could help it.

"We have somewhere to live." She stirred the tea in the pot, more so she didn't have to turn to him than because it needed doing.

"Somewhere with a bedroom for you. With a proper bed in it."

She couldn't deny that was a tempting proposition. Who wouldn't welcome such a thing? But not at the expense of her pride. Not at the cost of her heart.

"And a proper kitchen."

The words "if only" flashed through her head. She pushed them away. Wonderful as it sounded, she had to be able to live with herself afterward.

"Plus, it's damp in here." He looked up at the ceiling.

She knew it was covered with mold spores. It didn't matter how often she cleaned them off, they grew back, bringing with them the musty smell she could never get rid of.

"Your father needs somewhere drier."

That was not fair. How could she turn down the chance to make Dad's life easier?

But living in Frank's house? That was, quite simply, wrong. Daisy would be a kept woman. Even though she wasn't Frank's mistress, she'd be seen as such. Her reputation would be destroyed. No comfort was worth so much.

The lightning flashed again, its strobe more prolonged now, indicating it was closer than before. A few seconds went by, then thunder rolled over them, loud and long and low. She judged its epicenter was over Fieldhurst.

The thought of the village where she'd grown up brought to mind the man who believed he owned it. She was grateful for that—thinking of Walter was the perfect antidote to any temptation Frank offered.

"Your father found this place for us," she said. "It was good enough for us in his eyes."

In fairness, when he'd rented the rooms, Walter had meant them for Daisy and her baby. She'd had a bedroom then. It was only when Dad came home that she'd moved to the bench.

"My father should be ashamed of himself." The rain beat an angry tattoo at the window, as if it reinforced his words. "I'm ashamed for him. You deserved better."

Discomfited, Daisy turned away and poured two cups of tea.

"You can't argue with that, Daisy. Because you *do* deserve better."

She looked over her shoulder at him again. He sat on the bench, the blanket over his shoulders. She could see the strong column of his neck, and the muscles in his upper chest. A thousand wanton thoughts flitted through her. Her mouth dried. A strange craving hollowed her chest and built an ache between her thighs. It took all she had within her to raise her eyes to his face.

He watched her, his own gaze soft, yearning. He knew. He knew where her eyes had strayed. What she was thinking. Feeling. Wanting.

Daisy felt the blush heat her cheeks. She picked up her cup and brought it to her lips, trying to distract herself from his stare. Shaken, she had to use both hands to hold it steady.

"I want to ask you something." His voice was low, a gentle caress, yet it sounded clear above the sound of the rain on the window, and the boom of her heartbeat in her ears. He stood.

Nervously, she licked her lips with the tiniest tip of her tongue.

He moved closer. Her heart beat faster. Her breaths shallowed. Hardly surprising, since he'd taken all the air in the room. Then, he lowered himself onto one knee and looked up at her, his eyes earnest, searching, pleading.

"Daisy Redmond." His voice was caught on gravel. He cleared his throat and started again. "Daisy Redmond, would you do me the inestimable honor of becoming my wife?"

She stared, wide-eyed with shock. Her brain wouldn't work, thoughts wouldn't form, words would not come. He stayed still, his skin painted orange-red by the firelight. His eyes were fixed on her. His Adam's apple bobbed up and down. Once. Twice.

Eternity passed. Or maybe it was merely seconds.

Frank had asked her to marry him. Down on one knee, romantic words, the whole shebang.

And oh! how she wanted to say yes. To fold herself into his arms and lose herself in his kiss. To spend forever with this man, shower him with all the love she felt for him, and feel his love for her...

Did he love her? He hadn't said he did. He'd asked her to marry him, called it an inestimable honor. But never, not once, had he said he loved her.

Then again, why else would he get down on one knee and propose? Unfortunately, the answer to that came all too readily. Bertie. Frank had a son. He wanted that son to know him, and to carry his name. Which meant marrying Daisy.

It wasn't the right thing to do. Not for those reasons. If Daisy said yes for those reasons, she would consign them both to a lifetime of misery. She'd been right to refuse him the other day, and she'd be right to do so again. Even though refusing him was the hardest thing she would ever do.

Her heart cracked. She ignored the pain, lifted her chin and gave him her most determined look. "I already said no."

The light in his eyes dimmed. He swallowed again. "You did. But that time, I didn't exactly ask, did I?"

That was true. He hadn't asked. "You decreed it," she agreed.

"I'm not decreeing it now. I'm asking. Begging, even." He scrubbed his face with one hand. She fancied she heard the rasp of his stubble over the calloused skin of his fingers. "I know you don't want me," he said. "Not like I want you."

How wrong could a man be? Had she hidden her feelings so successfully? Fooled him so well? Because the truth was, she did want him. She'd always wanted him.

Lightning flashed again, filling the room with blue light. Thunder sounded almost immediately, a loud and angry roar right over their heads. But it was only a roar. It was not an explosion of hot temper. There were no loud cracks and sudden bangs.

Frank smiled sadly, and stood. "I won't force you into a corner. The house is for you, whether you say yes or no."

Tears pooled in her eyes, blurring her vision. Rain pushed at the window and the fire crackled over the wood. Her heart pounded, blood rushing past her ears in a raging flood.

"I wanted us to live there together," he said. "A family. But if that's not what… I can live somewhere else. I'll visit Bertie. Get to know him. But I wish…" He shook his head. "I will take care of you. I won't take no for an answer on that. I will take care of my family." His Adam's apple bobbed again and his eyes glittered with his emotion. "Even if I'm not there."

There was a silence. They stared at each other. Neither moved. They didn't blink. They didn't breathe. The fire didn't crackle. Even the rain stopped drumming on the window.

Frank shook off the blanket and put his wet shirt on. It stuck to his skin and he had to tug it into place. He began to button it, from the bottom up. Each button fought his fingers.

This was not what Daisy wanted. She knew, instinctively, that if he left now, she would regret it. And while she knew they shouldn't marry, not without love, that didn't mean they should walk away completely.

It was now or never. She either spoke or she lost everything.

He pushed the third button into its too-tight buttonhole. Daisy put her hand over his, stilling his fingers. A slight frown creased his forehead, myriad questions in his eyes.

"What if I want you to be there?" she whispered.

A slow grin curved his mouth. It softened his beautiful face, and chased away her doubt. Daisy put her arms around him. His shirt was damp, but the skin below it was warm and inviting. He smelled of rain, and night air, and the smoke from the fire. His head lowered.

She closed her eyes as his lips met hers. His arms held her close. The wet of his shirt damped the front of her dress.

He picked her up as if she weighed nothing. She wrapped her legs around his waist, felt his hard warmth pressing against her. Her breasts were heavy, her nipples erect, her stomach swooping and her core throbbing, and all that mattered was now. Here. This man.

She wasn't aware that they'd moved into the bedroom until he laid her down on the soft mattress. She felt the silky coolness of an eiderdown, the starchy cotton of a pillowcase. Daisy wrapped her arms around him, and he followed her down onto the bed.

Somehow, his shirt disappeared and she touched bare flesh. His shoulders flexed beneath her touch and his fingers made short work of the buttons on her bodice, then slipped inside, brushing over her. She arched her back, pushing her breasts further into his hands. A soft moan escaped her. His mouth came down on hers, swallowing the sound. He pushed her dress off her shoulders, exposing her upper body to his worshipful gaze.

"Beautiful," he whispered, and lowered his head to her breast, taking her into his mouth. His stubble abraded the sensitive skin. She didn't want this to end. Ever.

His mouth moved from one breast to the other, then down, over her stomach, pushing her dress further and further as he worked his way lower. The cold air of the room touched where his kisses lay wet upon her skin. A delicious ache built within her belly, then spread between her thighs. She craved…more. She needed…more. The ache for more built and built inside her, threatening to explode. Her hips bucked, pressing her core into his hand. He found the tiny nub of nerves at her center and rolled it between the tips of his finger and thumb. She almost flew off the bed. He anchored her with his own body. His mouth covered hers, his tongue playing with her tongue, mimicking what she wanted him to do, down *there*.

She gasped as he slipped one finger inside her. Her muscles tightened around it, responding to it, wanting…more. He added a second finger. The tightness within her loosened.

Her hands roved over his shoulders, his back, his buttocks. She caressed his stomach. His muscles flinched at her touch. Clumsy with haste, she fumbled with the buttons on his trousers.

Frank moved away. She growled her displeasure, then smiled as he discarded his boots and socks and peeled off his trousers and everything else. He threw the clothes aside, and Daisy finally saw him, in all his impressive glory.

Her mouth dried. Her gaze softened. She ached to touch him. And more.

"Where were we?" He grinned and kissed her again, his magic hands bringing her back to the boil, until every nerve within her stretched to breaking point, and every muscle trembled with the force building, growing, overwhelming her.

The room lit. Daisy could not say if it was the lightning outside, or stars exploding within her. Thunder cracked. She flew over the edge, and everything within her fell apart.

Frank covered her with his body. She felt his naked skin, the springy hairs on his chest against her smooth breasts, his rough legs between her thighs. He nudged against her center, then pushed forward, filling her with tantalizing gentleness until she wanted to scream at him to go harder, faster, stronger. His mouth played with hers. His hands caressed her skin.

When she could take no more, she thrust her hips up to his and he entered her fully. Triumph swelled within her. Then he moved, pulling out and pushing in, slowly at first, then faster, more frantic. Sweat slicked his skin. His breaths kept time with the thrusting of his hips. His hands were on her, warming her, claiming her.

The want within her rose again, higher and harder than before. Warm flames spread through her, consuming her until, once more, she broke apart. Frank shouted her name, then followed her.

The last thing she heard after he took his release was his desperate, breathless whisper. "God, Daisy. I love you so much."

****

Daisy slept. She didn't mean to, but it came on her and pulled her under. She half woke in the night, and felt Frank beside her, his warm arms around her, his front against her back. Somehow, he'd maneuvered them so the quilt covered them, warming them in the cold, early hours. He snored softly, his deep, even breaths reassuring. She smiled, closed her eyes, and reveled in the moment.

The next time she woke, dawn peeked through the window, making everything a dull grey. Raindrops raced each other down the glass, but the fury had gone from the downpour. The thunder and lightning had moved on.

Frank lay beside her, warm and solid. She could tell he was awake by the way he held himself—relaxed, but not in the slackness of sleep. She turned her head and saw him gazing at her, a smile playing on his lips and crinkling his eyes.

"Good morning," he murmured.

"Good morning." She wanted to lie here like this forever, every muscle heavy and relaxed, every limb boneless. At the same time, she wanted to stretch like a contented cat, then reach out for him once more.

He kissed her shoulder. "You are beautiful in the morning," he said. "Is it any wonder that I love you?"

A memory pushed its way through her half-awake haze and filled her with hope. "You said that last night."

"What?" He propped himself up on his elbow. "I love you?"

She nodded.

"I do. I'm sorry if you don't want to hear it, but it's true. I love you, Daisy Redmond. I've always loved you. Though I didn't always know it."

Daisy swallowed, hard. "You love me?" She turned the words over, tasting them, feeling them. Enjoying them.

"With all that I am. Always have. Always will."

He loved her? He loved her! That changed everything.

But she needed to be sure. "Not just for Bertie?"

Frank frowned, confused, then shook his head. "Bertie's important. Of course he is. But he's the icing. You, Daisy Redmond, are the actual cake. The cream tea. Hell, you're the whole bloody table. I love *you*, Dais. I love Bertie, too. But I'd still love you, even if he wasn't there."

She chewed her bottom lip as she contemplated his words. He reached up and stroked his finger over the tiny marks left by her teeth.

"What about your dad?" she asked. "What will he say about it?"

Frank sniffed. "Don't know. Don't care." He gathered her into his arms. "I know it won't be easy at first, my love. Not because of Walter. He doesn't matter. But your dad won't be happy, either. What he said last night notwithstanding, he's bound to have doubts about me. And I dare say Bertie won't always be…welcoming."

She shook her head, dismissing all of that. "They'll be fine. Once they know you're the man I love, they'll accept you."

A small smile spread over his face. "You love me?"

"Didn't I tell you that?" Surely she'd told him that.

Frank's grin spread. "Not since 1914, no."

"Well, I do. I do love you, Frank Pearson."

"Enough to marry me?" His grin faded. He looked uncertain. Endearingly so.

Daisy put him out of his misery. "More than enough to marry you."

He gave a triumphant whoop and gathered her in his arms.

Neither of them said anything else for some time.

A word about the author…

Caitlyn Callery lives in Sussex, southern England. She is passionate about writing and suffers withdrawal symptoms when she takes a few days away from her work.

Before becoming a full-time writer, she worked in banking, as a waitress, in the motor repair industry, in a call centre, and for a charity. As part of this last job, she helped build a school in Kenya, and drove a vanload of wheelchairs from the UK to Morocco.

She also loves reading, knitting, walking by the sea, the theatre and spending time with her family.

You can see more about her and her work at:
CaitlynCallery.com